Copyright © 2022 by Melody Tyden

Cover design by: amy4designs

Palace illustration by: Yanuar Laudy

PRINCESS IN HIDING

MELODY TYDEN

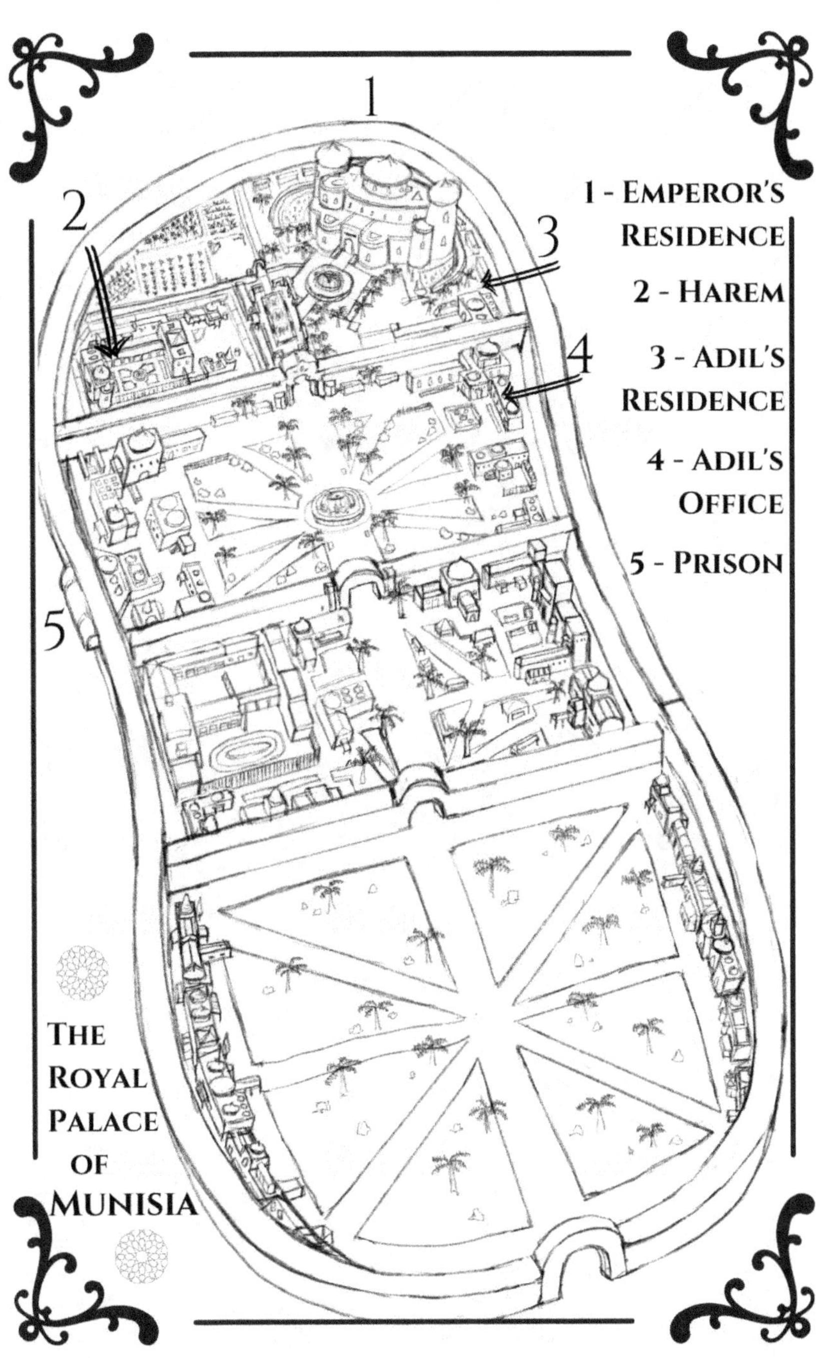

1 - EMPEROR'S RESIDENCE
2 - HAREM
3 - ADIL'S RESIDENCE
4 - ADIL'S OFFICE
5 - PRISON
THE ROYAL PALACE OF MUNISIA

In Case You Missed It...

This is the third book in the Lady in Waiting series.

For the full story, please make sure you've read the previous two books before diving in here.

Welcome back!

CHAPTER ONE

Spending the night alone in the inn felt like torture.

On the other side of the wall, in the room next door but as out of reach as if we were separated by an ocean, slept Zara, the woman who had captured my attention from the very first moment we met. A foreigner in our kingdom, her dark skin made her stand out in every crowd, and though it had been the reason I first noticed her, by no means could it be considered the most extraordinary thing about her.

Zara actually came into my life because one of my enemies hired her to get close to me in order to steal from me and ultimately kill me. Luckily for us both, she hadn't followed through with what he asked of her. Instead, we found a way to work together to find the information she needed about her family and to stop the man determined to take my throne. Along the way, we began to form a close friendship.

More than friendship, to be truthful. The feel of her hand on my cock the other night at the castle surged back to the front of my memory, and the more I thought about it, the harder I became, making me even more frustrated by the distance between us. Guards were positioned outside my door and hers, keeping watch for our safety, but also meaning we had no way to visit each other without attracting attention.

If they caught me going into her room, they might get the wrong idea, even if, in this case, it actually was the right idea. I wanted to be alone with Zara, to do intimate things with her as she'd promised me we could, but no one could know about it. The secrecy wasn't for my sake; if it were up to me, I would happily tell the world that this amazing, exotic woman had enchanted me, but she had told me flat out that she didn't want my men to think of her as simply the crown prince's whore.

The word made me wince, even though she said it with no emotion. Technically, that described what she had been in the past, trading her body for food or money or security when she found herself alone in a foreign land with no other means of supporting herself. But the word implied something more than that strict definition: it implied that the person who bore that title wasn't worthy of respect, or somehow mattered less than other women, and I didn't want anyone to see her that way either.

Therefore, we agreed that we would keep our feelings, and any physical closeness we decided to engage in, between ourselves.

I had a plan for how we would do that on the ship, but here in the inn where we spent our last night on Lassarian soil before our sea voyage began, I couldn't see any way around it. She must sleep in her room and me in mine, and it made for a long and fitful night's sleep.

At last, the new day dawned, bright and clear, a perfect day to set sail. Zara stood ready and waiting when I knocked on her door, as eager to get going as I felt, and after a quick breakfast at the inn with the last fresh food we would see for a while, we headed down to the port to board the ship.

Eric, a prince from the neighbouring kingdom of Silatria, would be travelling with us and he had already boarded, waiting to greet us as we stepped onto the deck. "I'm eager to know as much about the Munisian empire as you remember," he told Zara. "The customs, manners, the proper forms of address, everything."

"It's a long trip, Eric," I pointed out, rather amused by this sudden studiousness on his part. We had spent the better part of the last month together tracking down our common enemy, and he had been far less concerned with politics than with keeping his bed warm. Now, it seemed our roles were reversed. "We don't need to go over it all this minute, there will be plenty of time to discuss everything on the journey. For now, I'm going to show Zara to her cabin."

Unable to argue with that, he grunted his assent and I led Zara below decks to our accommodation for the next few weeks. First, we went to her room, a mid-sized cabin neither luxurious nor spartan, consisting of a single bed, a cabinet, and a small table. Her clothes had already been brought aboard and unpacked for her, the few things she had of her own and a few more dresses that I had managed to procure for her for the journey.

"I'm afraid the only privy is the communal one at the head of the ship," I apologized. "But let me know whenever you need to use it and I will come with you and stand guard."

She gave a throaty laugh. "I'm not going to call on the crown prince of Lassaria to accompany me if I need to relieve myself in the middle of the night. I've been taking care of myself for a long time, Your Highness. I don't need you to do it for me now."

I knew full well that she didn't need to be looked after, but I wanted to do it anyway. After all she had been through, she deserved to be spoiled and pampered, at least a little. "You're not starting with my title again, are you? I thought we were past that."

"We are," she confirmed. "When you don't act like such a prince. Just be a regular man, Arthur, and I'll treat you like one."

"I only know how to be what I am," I told her truthfully, and her expression softened with real affection.

"I know, and I don't want you to change. I'm only teasing. So, where is your room? Will I see you on the voyage, or will you be busy being all princely?"

This time, I recognized her teasing, but I ignored it to focus on showing her the provision I'd made for us. "My room is through here."

Instead of returning through the door we'd entered by, I led her to the wall next to her cabinet, where a small door concealed an opening, the wood panelling on the door matching the wall almost exactly. Opening it, I invited Zara to step through, and her eyes widened in surprise as she did.

The room beyond was twice the size of hers, the largest one on the ship with the biggest bed. I would happily trade it for hers, but it would raise too many questions, and she wouldn't allow it anyway. In the end, it made no difference since I hoped she would be spending most of her time in here with me anyway.

"We can visit each other without anyone knowing," I explained, though I felt certain she had already guessed my intention. Zara didn't miss much. "We can lock our main doors and no one will be any the wiser."

A smile played at her lips as she looked at the large bed and back at me. "Are you trying to seduce me, Arthur?"

My cheeks immediately began to grow warm at the thought of it. "I just meant, if you wanted to talk, or have some company, or..."

She cut me off by placing her lips gently on mine, setting my heart racing once again. "Or," she repeated mischievously. "I think I might like the 'or'. But for now, we should return above decks before anyone gets suspicious."

Unfortunately, she had a point, so we returned back to her room and exited out that door, just in case anyone had noticed us going in and might find it odd that we came out of mine instead.

Needing to hide and keep things secret might be exciting for a little while, but in truth, I would much rather be open about it. I adored this woman more with each minute we spent together, and though I hadn't said a word to her about it yet, I truly hoped that once she had reunited with her family and assured them of her safety, she might agree to return to Lassaria with me permanently.

I had the rest of this trip to convince her that her future lay in the land we were about to leave, and I would do everything in my power to make it happen.

~Zara~

As we finally cast off and set sail towards my homeland, I should have felt only excitement and satisfaction. For years, this had been all I wanted: to find my father and find my way home again, after being forcibly separated from him on a diplomatic trip as a young woman. Now, thanks to Arthur and his father, the King of Lassaria, I knew that my father had gone home many years ago. Finding him would no longer be necessary; I only needed to get home too, and Arthur had very kindly offered to not only provide my passage, but to take me there himself.

Being a prince had its advantages.

Arthur had never been just a prince to me, though. He was the sweetest, kindest man I had ever met, a type of man I didn't believe existed in these cold, northern countries until I met him. He asked nothing of me but loyalty and friendship, and though I could give him those things, I wanted to give him more too.

And so, the thought of him returning to this land without me, the thought of being separated from him forever, lay behind my melancholy as we watched the shores of Lassaria disappearing in the distance.

Arthur stood beside me on the deck of the ship at a respectful distance, though I knew if I gave him the slightest encouragement, he would move closer and put his arms around me to shield me from the chilly wind that whipped my dress around my body. Though I ached for his touch, I kept my distance too. There were too many people around and he had an image to maintain. The Queen, Arthur's mother, had pulled me aside just before we left the castle to make sure I understood that fact.

"You will never be more than a novelty to him."

Her words were so bitter and unexpected that I took a step back in surprise. "Pardon me, Your Majesty?"

Her tone remained hard. "I know my son is intrigued with you. You've sparked his curiosity, but if you think there is any chance he will ever marry you, you're deluding yourself. Arthur will marry a daughter of one of our noble families, or a princess. Those are the only possibilities. The best you could ever be to him is a mistress, shoved into the background while his wife and queen raises their children, and I suspect you are too proud for that."

She said it as if the very idea of me having pride was absurd, as though I had nothing to be proud about.

I did my best to remain dignified, though it would have been easy for me to bring her to her knees in one measured movement. "I don't know what you believe, Your Majesty, but I have no designs on your son. He is returning me to my home, and I am grateful for it. He will return to you afterwards."

Although I said the words she wanted to hear, she still appeared unsatisfied. "Don't think that you can get a child off him on this trip and use that to worm your way into his life. Any half-breed children he has with you will never be recognized."

My patience had nearly reached its limit. "Arthur is well aware of the problems that bastard children create. Look at what happened with your own husband's bastard."

That barb hit its mark, as I expected it to, and her face turned a very interesting shade of red. "At least my husband only messed around with another noblewoman. If he had been with someone like you, I would have refused to marry him. If you care about Arthur's future as you claim to, you'll ensure that there is not the slightest hint of impropriety between you which could hurt his future prospects."

With that, she turned on her heel and left, her head held high, secure in her ignorance. How had such a vile woman managed to raise people as kind and warm as Cordelia and Arthur?

When she spoke about 'someone like me', I didn't know if she meant my station in life or my skin colour, but both were offensive. Her words implied that I would be making him unclean by association, that if his cock had been inside me, no other woman would want it in her. If I were a more vindictive woman and had a little more time on my hands, I would be tempted to seduce her husband, the king, simply for the pleasure of her discovering I had.

I wouldn't have time to do it, though, nor did I really want to. The thought simply flitted across my mind, gone as quickly as it came. I only had eyes for one man right now, the very one she had warned me to stay away from, and the one who had arranged for us to be housed in adjoining rooms on this journey.

My sweet, virgin prince.

Arthur spent the day showing me around the ship, the two of us watching the sailors at work while he explained to me what they were doing. His knowledge on the subject impressed me, and I told him so.

"A prince is expected to be well-versed in many things," he explained with a casual shrug of his shoulders. "I could bore you equally well about swordsmanship or agriculture."

"I'm not bored," I assured him. "Though I am, perhaps, a little sleepy. I could use an early night tonight."

He knew exactly what I meant by that and his neck turned red at the thought of it, making me smile. Teasing him was too easy, thanks to his innocence.

We ate dinner with Eric and the captain and then, one after the other, we both pleaded fatigue, retiring to our rooms separately, all the while knowing we would soon be reunited on the other side of the wall. Once alone in my room, I removed my outer dress, leaving only the white linen shift worn by women in this climate to keep warm, and, without knocking, I let myself through the secret door Arthur had shown me earlier.

I found him in the middle of changing his clothes, the discarded ones lying on the bed where he'd tossed them. His bare chest revealed the defined muscles of a man who worked hard physically, and his breeches were short enough that I could see his firm calf muscles. It couldn't be clearer that he had never been the soft kind of prince who sat around on a throne all day, indulging himself. This was a man of action.

"Zara?" My sudden appearance caught him by surprise and he instinctively picked up his discarded shirt to cover his midsection, even though I had already seen him a few days earlier, at his father's castle when I made him come with my hand.

"You said I could visit you, right?" I reminded him, making my way over to his bed and taking a seat on the edge. His eyes followed me as he swallowed nervously.

"Yes, of course, I just... I wanted to change," he explained meekly, gesturing down at his half-naked body.

"I think you look wonderful as you are. Will you sit with me?"

My lack of nerves seemed to help calm him as he swept the remaining clothes off the bed and placed them all in the trunk against the wall. Wearing only his breeches, he came to sit on the bed beside me, and I immediately leaned into him, as I had wanted to do all day. With a sigh of satisfaction, he wrapped his arm around me.

"You look wonderful too," he assured me. "Just as you did on the night we met."

I had almost forgotten about that. I had purposefully let him walk in on me half-naked, hoping to distract and seduce him, but he had been so startled and naive, he simply apologized and left.

Tonight, I actually wore more clothes than I had then, which I reminded him of now. "I think that night went more like this."

Without giving him a chance to protest, I removed my shift, lifting it up over my head so that I sat naked beside him. Arthur's mouth dropped open as he looked down at me, then away, and then back again, unsure where to focus his gaze.

"You can look," I encouraged him. "And more than that, if you'd like."

Picking up his other hand, I brought it to my chest and placed it against my breast. He exhaled in pleasure at almost the same moment I did. With tentative movements, growing bolder by the second, he ran his hand across me, his fingers flicking across my hard nipple and drawing a further sigh of desire from my lips.

"Zara." His voice sounded tight as he said my name. "You told me the other day that there were things I could do to give you pleasure, as you did to me, things that wouldn't involve the risk of pregnancy."

I had said that, and I nodded now to confirm it. "Yes."

"Will you show me?" He made it sound like I would be doing him a favour rather than the other way around.

"I can tell you what I know from other women," I explained to him. "The truth is that, although men have done these things to me, it has never been all that pleasurable. I think it might be different with you, though."

It already felt different, to be honest. Although I had slept with many men, I had rarely enjoyed it. Most of the time, I simply endured it. But tonight, my body already ached for Arthur's touch, the steady pulse between my legs begging for him as I spread them apart and led his hand to my centre.

"This is where your cock would go, if we were to make love," I told him as his fingers slipped through my wetness. "But your fingers can take its place, just as I used my hand on you instead."

Understanding dawned on his face and he pressed his fingers against me more firmly until he found the entrance he sought. "Right here?"

I nodded, my breath catching as he teased me without even meaning to. "Right there. Push them in, as far as you can. You won't hurt me, I promise."

His eyes widened in wonder as he obeyed, pressing deeper inside me. Curiously, he moved his fingers around, brushing against my most sensitive spot as my hips bucked against his hand.

"Did that hurt?" he asked in worry as he noted my reaction.

"Only in the best way," I tried to explain. "It feels wonderful, Arthur. Keep going, move them in and out."

His brow lined in concentration, he did as I asked, his fingers beginning to pump into me, slowly at first, and then faster as he became more used to the sensation. When his confidence grew and he could pay less attention, I leaned over and kissed him, his tongue tangling with mine as his fingers continued their plundering. My hips moved against him naturally, craving even more, and when his thumb grazed against me, I moaned in sheer pleasure.

"You like that?" he asked, and I nodded once more. It felt amazing, actually. I had never felt anything that good before.

He did his best to repeat the motion, and as he found the sensitive spot again, I couldn't stop myself from calling out his name. "Arthur!"

Pride shone in his eyes before he kissed me again, his fingers thrusting faster and harder as his thumb played havoc with my senses, and soon, my whole world exploded around me.

That had only happened to me a handful of times before, and when it had, it had been completely by accident on my partner's part. This, however, was no accident. Arthur had wanted to bring me pleasure, and he did.

He withdrew his fingers from me, coated with the evidence of my enjoyment, and looked at them in fascination. "That means you liked it?"

I rested my head against his strong, warm chest. "I did. That felt incredible, Arthur. Just as good as what I did for you."

I reached for his cock again, seeing for myself just how hard it had grown beneath the fabric of his breeches, but he gently pushed my hand away. "We have time for that later," he promised. "Tonight, I want to focus on you."

By the time we finally fell asleep, wrapped up together in his large bed, he had brought me to those same heights of pleasure twice more, in between conversation and laughter. Just before I drifted off to sleep, the queen's warning sounded once more in my head, but this time, I realized where the danger truly lay.

The problem had never been that he might leave me with child at the end of the journey. The real danger was that he might take my heart with him when he left, and I would never be whole again.

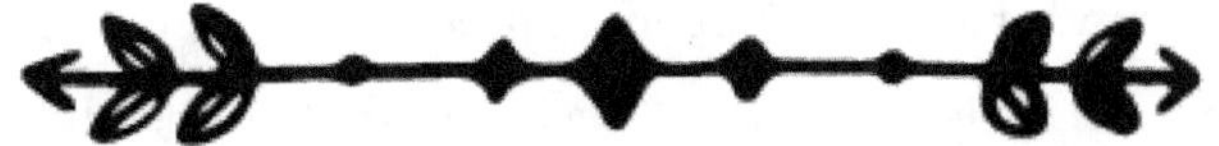

~Eric~

Arthur and Zara may have thought they were being discreet, but the situation couldn't be more obvious to me. They hardly ever left each other's sides, only parting to go to their rooms, which were right next door to each other. I would bet the whole of my homeland of Silatria on the fact that some kind of hidden passage existed between those rooms, giving my fellow prince access to *her* hidden passage whenever he felt like it.

I didn't begrudge them the fun they were having. I'd done enough of it in my time to know exactly how much fun it could be, but lately, my interest had waned considerably. Ever since I met Elodie, in fact, I hadn't slept with another woman. Just a few weeks ago, the idea of being confined to a ship for weeks where the only woman aboard had already been spoken for would have sent me into a sweaty panic, but now, it barely bothered me. I had other things to worry about, and I tried to address those concerns whenever Arthur and Zara came up for air.

"How do we make a good impression on the Munisian emperor?" I asked Zara one afternoon as the three of us sat in the small dining room together. She knew her homeland better than anyone else aboard, and I hoped to score some diplomatic and economic victories for Silatria during our visit. "What would offend him?"

"I only spent a little bit of time at court growing up," she warned me. "Don't take my word as the final one, but I can tell you what I know. My father made sure I understood the protocols for whenever I did visit."

"And they were?" I prompted, eager to get to the point.

She began to tick the items off on her fingers. "You should remain completely silent unless the emperor calls upon you to speak. The audience room is always quiet, and the emperor's attendants communicate mostly using their hands."

Arthur looked as intrigued as I felt. "Their hands? How does that work?"

"I'm not really sure," she admitted with a shrug. "There are special gestures that they all understand. They could be talking about you right in front of you and you wouldn't know it."

That could definitely come in handy, although it seemed like quite a lot of trouble to go to when whispering worked almost as well.

"You should keep your eyes on the ground until you are asked to raise them," Zara added, tapping on her second finger. "Maybe it is a little less strict for a foreign prince, but that rule applied to me. And should you happen to see any members of the emperor's harem, look away immediately. It is forbidden to look upon them."

"Harem?" I recognized the word, but I had never been to a place where one existed.

Zara's explanation confirmed what I thought it meant. "The emperor's wives and concubines are considered his property, and to touch any of them would mean death."

"How many does he have?" I wondered.

Zara gave me a wry smile. "Wives or concubines?"

Arthur and I exchanged curious glances. "Both," we responded together, making Zara laugh.

"It may have changed since I left, but usually four or five wives, in decreasing order of seniority. Concubines, it depends, but around two dozen, I suppose."

Arthur nearly choked in surprise. "Two dozen? What does he do with that many?"

This time, Zara and I were the ones who gave each other amused looks. "The same thing he does with one," she responded to the Lassarian prince sarcastically before her expression softened. "He does not bed them all regularly. He will have his favourites, but having a relative in the harem is considered a great honour by many families. They will campaign to have their daughters chosen for a place there. If a woman particularly pleases the emperor, her family is rewarded."

In some ways, it resembled the way marriages were arranged for princes in our two kingdoms. The only real difference was the number of partners.

"And they can't ever find husbands of their own?" Arthur wondered. "What if they fall in love?"

"They can't fall in love so long as they are in the harem," Zara explained. "The only men they are allowed to interact with are the eunuchs who serve them."

At the mention of the word 'eunuch', my legs immediately closed a little tighter, as did Arthur's. Again, I knew of such things, but luckily, it had never been a practice Silatria participated in. The intentional castration of young men to protect the honour of the emperor's harem did make sense from a practical point of view, but it seemed unnecessarily harsh to me. Those poor bastards. What was the point of living if you couldn't have a good lay every now and then?

"You said 'as long as they're in the harem'," I pointed out. "Do they leave at some point?"

Zara nodded once more. "When the emperor tires of them, or their family loses influence, or they pass their childbearing years, then they can 'retire' if the emperor allows it. It is completely at his discretion, though, it is not up to the woman at all."

It certainly sounded like they had very little choice in the entire matter.

All of this interested me, but we had strayed quite far from the original topic of conversation, and I tried to steer us back there now. "So, besides keeping our eyes down, not looking at the harem members, and not speaking until we're spoken to, what else do we need to know?"

Zara gave another elegant shrug. "I'm afraid I don't know much more than that. As I said, I only visited the court a few times as a child, but the emperor will send people to meet you beforehand and give you full instructions before you are introduced. They will not want you to make mistakes any more than you want to make them."

"What do you remember of your own visits?" Arthur asked curiously, simply reminiscing now rather than looking for information that could help us.

"The emperor is very intimidating," Zara recalled. "My father presented me to him once. He must have been about the same age as my father, but he seemed much older since he didn't smile. After looking me over, he asked my father a few questions about my education and my temperament, and my audience ended there. He never said a word to me directly."

"So, if he's your father's age, then he would be about the same age as the Lassarian king and queen?" I guessed.

"I think so. His eldest son is a few years older than me. I met him when we were at the palace too."

A shiver ran through Zara, which might have just been from the general temperature on the ship, but Arthur thought it had another cause. "What is he like? He's the emperor's heir?"

Zara nodded. "Yes, he's the son of the emperor's first wife, so he is next in line. He was only 12 or 13 when we met, but already spoiled and selfish. When he saw me, he dropped a book he'd been carrying, on purpose, and ordered me to pick it up. I refused, to my father's dismay."

"What did he do?" Arthur asked, and I listened curiously as well, eager to learn as much about these royals as I could.

"He told my father to pick it up instead, which of course he did, and then he told me that he hoped my insolence would be beaten out of me. My father pulled me away before I could fight him."

We both smiled at that idea, not entirely sure if she meant that literally, but her personal stories didn't interest me as much as the overall court structure did. "Does the prince keep his own harem?"

Zara pursed her lips in uncertainty. "Because of his youth, he didn't have one before I left, but I imagine he does now. He will want to have his own children to be his heirs in case he is killed before he can take the throne himself. He has at least 40 brothers, all of whom would be eager to take his place."

Forty brothers? I honestly couldn't imagine. Having one had caused me enough headaches.

"It sounds fascinating," Arthur concluded. "But I have to say that I much prefer our system of one queen to each king."

He gave Zara a tender smile, so intimate that it left no doubt clear where things were heading between them this afternoon. I excused myself to go back to my own room, while they no doubt would sneak back to theirs.

The conversation had yielded some interesting facts, but I supposed in the end, I could only do so much to prepare. For the rest of it, I would just have to wait and see what awaited us upon our arrival in this unfamiliar empire.

CHAPTER TWO

As soon as Zara and I were alone again in the privacy of my room, I pulled her close to me. Even though I had her right beside me, it almost felt like she had begun to slip away. "Are you sure you really want to go back to this place?"

After what she just told me and Eric about how the women of the imperial harem were treated, I couldn't understand what would entice any woman to return there voluntarily.

She understood my concerns immediately as she nestled against my chest, answering my question fully even though I had barely articulated it. "That is only the way of things in the palace. For the rest of us, things are much less restricted. I'm not going back to *that* life. I want to go back because my family is there. My people are there. It is my home, Arthur."

I wanted to argue that her home could be wherever she wanted it to be, wherever she felt valued, but I understand her feelings too. For so long, she had been a foreigner and treated as one, always judged by her appearance and frequently discounted as less worthy because of it. To be back among her own people would give her a level of anonymity she had not known in a long time, and which she could never have with me.

"Tell me more about your life, then," I requested, leading her to the bed so we could lay down together and be more comfortable as we continued our conversation. "What will it be like when you return?"

Her head rested lightly against my shoulder as her words built pictures in my mind. "My father worked for the king, but his appointment came through his own merits, not because he came from a noble family. Actually, he had no family at all, and as an orphan, his rise to his position in the emperor's court was a great achievement. He married into a wealthy family too, so that helped. We had a very comfortable life in a house in the outermost circle of the palace grounds, far from the emperor's own family. The palace is much bigger than your castle. It is almost a city within the city, with everything you could need within its walls."

"So, your family wouldn't be among those appointed to the emperor's harem?" I realized I kept returning to this point, but I wanted her to assure me before we arrived that I would not be delivering her to this fate if she chose to stay there rather than returning home with me as I hoped.

Zara shook her head firmly. "We are not nearly important enough. On very rare occasions, the emperor may add a woman to his harem simply because he is interested in her, but that is only in exceptional circumstances. The noble families don't like it, and the emperor needs the support of those families lest they conspire to replace him with one of his many sons."

It sounded almost impossible to try to keep track of all the competing agendas. My father's court seemed treacherous enough at times, but compared to this, it all sounded rather tame. How would you ever know who to trust?

"What awaits you there as a grown woman?" Zara still had not answered that part of my question.

Her hand trailed lightly across my chest, over my shirt. "I hope I can work with my father. I have learned many things in my travels that would be useful to him. And when the time comes, he will find me a husband, I suppose, one who will accept that I am not a virgin."

"That is important to the men there?" It certainly seemed that way, with the talk of eunuchs in the harem.

Zara nodded. "There are women who are hired to 'test' the women once a marriage contract has been made. They will stick their own fingers in her to see if she is still intact. If she is not, she and her family are disgraced."

She caught sight of the look of dismay on my face before I could hide it, and she laughed warmly, with a teasing tone.

"It is not so different from your own customs, Arthur. Don't your princess' maids check the bedsheets to see if the new bride has bled?"

She had a point there, and in Silatria, Dee told me they even had witnesses to attend the initial copulation. Perhaps no one tradition could be considered worse than the others, they were simply different.

"Therefore, it will do me no good to claim to be a virgin," Zara continued. "I will simply have to be honest and hope that there is a decent man who will want me anyway."

My arms tightened around her instinctively, trying to let her know that *I* wanted her. Her past made no difference to me; her indomitable heart mattered far more.

"Speaking of virgins..." The mischievous edge that crept into her tone let me know that she intended to change the subject. "There are more things that I haven't shown you yet, Your Highness."

With those few words, my cock immediately twitched in anticipation. We had been pleasing each other with our hands, as she'd shown me, for the last few nights, and although I had enjoyed it immensely, I couldn't deny my curiosity about what else she might have in mind.

"Other things that won't lead to pregnancy?" I clarified, since I knew she didn't want a child right now any more than I did. If I were to marry her, as I wanted to, it would be better if she weren't pregnant first. It would cast a shadow over the birth of our child which would not be fair to her or to them.

Zara nodded, still with that same gleam in her eye. "Shall I show you?" she whispered into my ear, her hand trailing down from my chest, making my cock jump again as she drew nearer to it.

My throat tightened and my mouth dried out as I managed to breathe out one word: "Please."

Quickly untying my breeches, Zara freed my cock, and I exhaled with the pleasure that always accompanied her touch. But this time, instead of taking me in her hand, she sat up, shifting her position before lowering her head directly over top of me.

As her lips connected with the sensitive head of my cock, I hissed in surprise and enjoyment. Nothing could have prepared me for how amazing it felt when she drew her lips down along my shaft, her tongue teasing me too. While spending time with my men, I had overheard them joking about women's mouths, but I never understood until this moment exactly what it meant and just how good it would feel.

Just when I thought I had it figured out, she took me into her mouth completely.

The warmth and wetness surrounding me felt blissful even before she began to move, her tongue pressing firmly against me as she slid her mouth over me, adding to the assault on my senses. This must be almost what it felt like inside her, I supposed, at least based on what it felt like with my fingers inside her.

Although her mouth did most of the work, it had some help. Her hands joined in too, pumping me and teasing me as her head continued to bob over me. Watching my cock disappearing between her lips, my control broke remarkably fast.

"Zara, I'm going to…"

I tried to warn her, but not in time. My pleasure broke, releasing into her mouth, but to my surprise, she didn't seem to mind at all. In fact, she simply swallowed it all before kissing me again, softer, all the way down my shaft as she laid my cock back down.

"What did you think of that?" she teased as she returned to her spot at my side, nestling against me once again.

I thought there were not many virginal princesses in the world who would know how to do what she just did, and I would much rather be here, being taught by her, than fumbling around with one of them.

However, I kept those thoughts to myself. "Amazing," I murmured instead. "Can I do something like that to you as well?"

She grinned up at me. "You can certainly try, Arthur. We have plenty of time to figure it out."

~Zara~

The journey could not be called short, but when we glimpsed the great, glittering Munisian capital city in the distance, it felt like it had flown by. For almost three weeks, nothing existed outside of me and Arthur and the time we spent together. He had no kingdom to help run, no king and queen to please, and there were no people who would whisper when they saw us together. We made a stop halfway along the journey at a sunny, multicultural trading port to stock up on fresh food and supplies, and Arthur and I were able to spend the day together off the ship, losing ourselves in the sights and sounds and smells of the market stalls and unfamiliar streets. People passed us with his skin colour and with mine, and every shade in between, all minding their own business. No one knew or cared that we were ill-matched, a prince and a woman on the run. We were simply two people enjoying each other's company and it felt like something out of a dream.

A dream that must now come to an end.

Arthur and Eric stood beside me on the deck, watching the harbour and the city coming into view. The palace stood on top of a hill in the distance, high walls surrounding the buildings that made up the complex. It all looked familiar to me and yet it felt like I saw it with new eyes too. Since I left, I had spent more than a third of my life away from this place, and as the sailors tied the ship up in the great dock, I had to wonder just how much had changed while I'd been away.

Two officials from the port boarded the ship to log our arrival and determine the purpose of our visit. Arthur and Eric both had the seals of their kingdoms, as well as a letter of introduction from the King of Lassaria, and the officials treated them with due deference.

"You would like to meet the emperor?" one of them asked Arthur, and he nodded.

"Yes, but our first order of business is to track down one of his advisors. His daughter was separated from him many years ago and it is our pleasure to accompany her to their reunion."

He glanced over at me tenderly, and the two men turned to follow his gaze, taking me in fully for the first time since they came on board.

The first man, the one who had spoken, had no strong reaction to me either way, but the eyes of the man next to him widened in surprise as he addressed me in our native tongue. "Zara? It can't be."

His recognition caught everyone by surprise, most of all me. This man looked completely unfamiliar to me, so how did he know me?

"Zara?" the first man repeated, looking at his colleague in disbelief. "You don't mean the chief minister's missing daughter?"

"What's going on?" Arthur asked me, not happy about the fact that the men had switched into a language he couldn't understand.

Although it had been many years since I had spoken it myself, I could understand them well enough, but I replied to Arthur in his own tongue. "They seem to be confused. They are saying my father is the chief minister, but he's not. He is simply one of the emperor's diplomats."

The two Munisian men exchanged glances before the second one spoke again, this time so Arthur could understand as well. "That may have been true some years ago, my lady, but after the plunder of the Actilian kingdom, he received a promotion."

Those words meant nothing to me but Arthur's eyebrows raised in a way that suggested he knew better than I did what they were talking about.

The Actilians, whoever they were, were of no interest to me anyway. I still wanted to know how they could be talking about my father. "The chief minister is the most important man in the empire after the emperor. You must be mistaken."

He didn't seem to think so. "I don't believe that I am, but if you would accompany us now, we will take you to the palace so we can find out for sure."

The men whispered something to each other in their native tongue once more, and I could have sworn I heard one of them say something about a reward while Arthur came over to me. "Are you ready to go now?"

We had come all this way for this exact reason, hadn't we? "I'm ready. Will you come with me?"

"Of course," he answered in a way that made it clear he had never expected to do otherwise.

Horses awaited us on the street once we exited the harbour. Along with me and Arthur, Eric came with us, as well as a small contingent of four of Arthur's men to provide an extra degree of protection. The officials led the way on horses of their own, glancing back regularly to ensure we were still behind them, but I had my attention focused entirely on the streets of the city around us.

Everything looked just as I remembered it: the low buildings with the circular, shuttered windows, the women with their heads covered and the men in their colourful, loose robes. Spiced aromas drifted to us from inside the buildings we passed: cinnamon, cumin and cardamom, so different from the thyme and rosemary scents of Lassaria. Children stopped and stared at the pale men who accompanied me, just as children in Lassaria always stopped and stared at me.

The horses climbed the steep streets with sure, steady feet until we reached the first of the palace gates. The palace had many layers, leading visitors closer and closer to the centre, and this marked only the first barrier. The men we were with showed their credentials and told the guards they were bringing guests to see the chief minister. After the guards gave us all a cursory glance, we were allowed in and we continued on horseback further up the hill until we reached the second gate. Here, the weapons of Arthur's men needed to be surrendered, and I assured Arthur and Eric that this all formed part of the expected protocol for visiting the administrative part of the palace. Everything would be carefully logged and returned to them on their departure.

When we approached the third gate, the men instructed us all to dismount and leave our horses in the stables outside the gate. Only the emperor himself would be allowed to go on horseback past the third gate.

A fourth gate further ahead led to the royal family's home and the emperor's audience chamber, but we were not heading that way. Instead, the men led us into what almost seemed like a separate town: the area which made up the administrative heart of the empire. Through every open door, we could see men at work, tallying the taxes, trades, crops, weapons and more that made up the running of a vast empire.

Ahead of us stood a large two-storey building, the main office of the emperor's advisers, and as we stepped into the courtyard with its fountain in the centre, a sense of déjà vu hit me, or perhaps just a very strong memory. I had been in this place before, I felt certain of it, and somehow, I had always known I would be here again.

Not slowing their pace, the men from the port continued straight ahead to the main administrative office. "We need to see the chief minister," one of them informed the clerk. "Immediately. It is of great importance."

"The minister is very busy," the clerk replied with the air of a man who had more authority than common sense. "You may take a seat but it will be a few hours until he can see you."

The man refused to back down. "Immediately," he repeated firmly. "Or you can explain to him why you kept his daughter waiting."

The man's eyes widened in surprise before coming to rest on me, when they grew even wider. "C-come with me," he stuttered out.

After all of this, I hoped for their sake that they had the right man, though I still thought it unlikely. The chief minister had always been a close relative of the emperor. He might employ men like my father to support him, but the title and the prestige went to someone of royal blood.

We were led down a wide corridor until we reached the end of the hall where a wooden door inlaid with coloured marble announced the presence of someone important just behind it.

The clerk knocked on the door before opening it, bowing his head reverently. "Please, minister, forgive the interruption. I would not disturb you if it were not very important."

Several men sat around a large wooden table, none of them looking pleased with the interruption, but my attention was drawn to the man at the far end, the one obviously in charge, and as his deep brown eyes found mine, so familiar that I would have known them anywhere in the world, I could see the same disbelief and awe in them as I felt inside.

"Zara?"

~Eric~

As we made our way through the emperor's palace, I paid close attention to everything and everyone around me. Westley Eastam, Arthur's half-brother who I had briefly teamed up with in an ill-advised attempt to get Princess Cordelia as my bride, may have been an ass in most things, but one thing he did know was how to get people to do what he wanted, and he gave me a few pointers during some of the conversations we'd had together.

People will give plenty of clues about how they expect to be treated, he told me. If someone approaches you with their eyes cast downwards, they know you are better than them. If they hold their head high, looking you straight in the eye, they think they are your equal or your better. How you treat them in return will determine how they respond to you. If you treat the man who thinks he's worse than you as your equal, you will earn his gratitude. If you flatter the man who thinks he's above you, he will feel gratified.

At the time, I hadn't paid all that much attention because I figured that, as a prince, people would treat me with respect no matter what. Only after I realized just how much Westley had played *me* did I realize he had actually been talking about me as well. He had seen in my response to him exactly how he could earn my trust and he used it to his own advantage.

Now, I would try to be more cautious, to pay attention and to really see people in the way he had explained. I had done it on the ship, mostly since I had nothing better to do, and it quickly became apparent to me which of the sailors had earned the respect of the other men and which they only tolerated. It actually amazed me how much I could see when I stopped thinking only about myself.

And here in the Munisian palace, the power dynamics were even more interesting. Zara's father had obviously become a man of importance, made clear from the way the other men spoke about him and the grandeur of his office. But when his eyes fell upon his daughter, his expression conveyed unbridled delight and joy, and he didn't care who saw it.

"Baba?" Zara whispered the word from her spot between me and Arthur as her father got to his feet and came towards us, ignoring everyone else in the room, his eyes fixed only on her. In the next moment, they had thrown their arms around each other, both of them speaking at once in their strange language, tears of happiness in both their eyes as the older man checked Zara over to ensure she'd returned safe and sound.

No one dared to interrupt, but eventually, he glanced at the rest of our group, and Zara seemed to remember we were there as well. She switched back to our own language as she made the introductions. "Baba, these are the men who have helped me return. This is Prince Eric of Silatria. Eric, my father, Adil."

I bowed my head to the chief minister politely. He may not be the emperor, but he had his ear, and it wouldn't hurt me to show him respect.

"And this," Zara added, her voice softening in blatantly obvious affection, "is Prince Arthur of Lassaria."

Arthur also lowered his head, but to the surprise of everyone, especially Arthur and Zara, her father pulled Arthur into a tight embrace, kissing him on each cheek. "I have your father to thank for my own safe return," he told Arthur, his speech more accented than Zara's but still fluent. "And now, you have brought my daughter home to me as well. You will be my honoured guest for your stay here in Munisia. Anything you require, you have only to ask."

That all sounded well and good for Arthur, but it left me feeling second-best, as usual.

Arthur looked rather overwhelmed by the warm reception but he quickly called upon his own training to respond in kind. "I only wished to see Zara safely reunited with her family. It has been my honour to be able to accompany her."

If he truly asked for nothing else, he would be throwing away a golden opportunity. I tried to catch my fellow prince's eye to remind him of the other goals we had in mind for our visit here, but he was too busy beaming at the woman in front of him.

Thankfully, Zara managed to keep a cool head even if Arthur didn't. "Baba, the princes would like to meet with the emperor. They hope to discuss how their kingdoms might cooperate with Munisia for their mutual benefit."

Adil threw me a far shrewder look than the one he had previously given me, and I could see his ministerial side taking over as he mentally calculated what I might have to offer. "Of course. That can certainly be arranged, but tonight, we will celebrate. You must all be tired after your long journey. I will send word to your mother and rooms will be made ready for you all. I'm afraid I must stay and conclude my work for the day, but I will see you all tonight and we can catch up then."

Those final words were addressed to Zara, his tone softening as he said them, and she gave him one more tight hug, whispering something to him in their own language. When they separated, Adil nodded again at both me and Arthur before turning to the clerk who had led us here, issuing rapid instructions in the Munisian tongue, words that I had to assume were to do with our accommodation.

Zara confirmed as much to me and Arthur, addressing us both in a whisper. "He is making arrangements for you to stay in his house. They have moved to a new dwelling, apparently."

That made sense when her father had obviously had a promotion since she left.

The men who had accompanied us here from the port then stepped forward to address Zara's father, and there followed what appeared to be a rather heated argument, though no one else in the room seemed concerned about the raised voices.

"What's happening?" I asked Zara in a whisper.

Her brow furrowed as she listened to the men arguing. "Apparently, a reward has been offered for my safe return. These men want it, but my father says it should go to you and Arthur instead, as you were the ones who brought me here."

I liked the sound of the reward, and also found myself both impressed and annoyed at the audacity of the port officials in trying to claim it for themselves when all they had done was lead us from the harbour to the palace, which we certainly could have found on our own.

At last, they seemed to reach an agreement, and we were all dismissed. The men from the port left empty-handed while the clerk led our small party back out of the building and through the maze of streets within the palace walls. When we approached yet another guarded gate, Zara's eyes widened in surprise.

"This is the royal gate," she said to everyone and to no one in particular.

The clerk turned back to her, his attitude far more subservient now that her identity had been made clear. "The minister's home is inside, my lady."

That surprised me too, in a good way. The closer we got to the seat of power, the better.

The clerk spoke to the guards at the gate and, after they double checked that we had no weapons, we were admitted. Once through the gate, which the guards closed tightly behind us, we found ourselves in a large, sunny courtyard with a beautiful reflecting pool in the centre of it. The peaceful space far exceeded anything we had in the Silatrian castle where I grew up, I had to admit.

And sitting on the far edge of it was perhaps the most beautiful woman I had ever seen.

Her hand trailed through the water absentmindedly, rippling through the reflection as if she did not want to see what the water showed her, though why she shouldn't, I couldn't guess. I certainly wanted to see it. Soft brown hair curled over her slender shoulders. Neither as dark as Zara nor as pale as Arthur and me, her skin appeared lightly bronzed, as if it had been kissed by the sun. Unlike all the women we had seen out in the street, her head was uncovered, along with most of her body. A triangular piece of fabric covered her chest, but her shoulders and stomach were bare, while a long, flowing skirt covered her lower half.

A flash of recognition went through me, though of course, that would be impossible. Perhaps it came simply from the fact that she looked so out of place here, and so melancholy as her fingers dipped into the water's clear surface, that I had to wonder if I had only imagined her. She looked too perfect to be real.

"Do not look!" the clerk with us admonished me, and when I glanced over at the others, Zara shook her head at me. They must be seeing her too, which meant I hadn't conjured her from my imagination, but their warnings confused me.

Zara quickly cleared up my confusion as the clerk led us down another hall, away from the water and the beautiful woman there. "She is a member of the harem," she whispered to me. "You can tell by the clothes she is wearing."

Disappointment sank in my stomach as I remembered everything she had told us about the harem on the journey here. "So, I cannot speak to her?"

Zara shook her head emphatically. "You must not even look. It is forbidden, and they will not accept ignorance as an excuse."

That could be a problem, since I didn't know how I would be able to rest until I found out who the woman was and how, exactly, she had ended up in a place like this.

~Fatima~

"There you are!"

The harsh voice jolted me from my daydreams, making me realize that I'd lost track of time while I sat by the reflecting pool in the courtyard. This had always been one of the few places I could go to be alone, since most of the other women disliked the public nature of it, at least by the standards of the rest of our quarters in the palace.

This courtyard sat at the very edge of the area where members of the harem were permitted. On the other side of the pool, corridors led to the emperor's private rooms and those of his son, as well as the chief minister and his family. On occasion, someone might enter the courtyard aside from the usual faces that I saw day in and day out, and that gave me another reason to sit here. Those brief glimpses of other people were my only reminder that life outside these walls still went on.

Today, however, I'd been so wrapped up in my own thoughts, visions of the past dancing before my eyes in the ripples my hand made in the still waters of the pool, that even if someone had gone by, I wouldn't have noticed them.

Now, an impatient-looking woman stood over me, her hands on her hips and a sneer on her lips. The child growing within her stomach made her appear swollen, nearly as wide as she was tall. "Minsa has been looking for you. You mustn't keep her waiting!"

Malek's first wife, Minsa, was the head of his harem. Dalia, the woman who stood before me now, was the third wife, the least important of his three wives, but she still considered herself superior to those of us who were merely concubines. Those of us who had no official position but were still bound to serve the whims of the emperor's eldest son.

The emperor had his own harem, but its numbers had dwindled over the years and we were not encouraged to mingle with them. Most of the women in Malek's harem didn't want to anyway. The emperor's wives were middle-aged while Malek's taste veered towards the much younger. Some of my fellow concubines were not much more than children, though Malek himself had recently turned twenty-five. The young girls would prefer not to be supervised by the older women of the emperor's harem, so by mutual agreement, the two sets of women kept mostly separate.

There were alliances among the women and rivalries and petty squabbles between them, as would be bound to happen when you cooped any number of people together in the same space, day after day. As the one who had never fit in anywhere, staying outside of any drama as much as I could, I had always been an exception, and I couldn't imagine what I had done to earn Minsa's summons now. Usually, she liked to pretend I didn't exist, and I happily went along with that pretense.

However, now that she *had* summoned me, there would be hell to pay if I disobeyed, so I reluctantly got to my feet, shaking the water droplets off my hand as I followed Dalia back to the main hall where Minsa liked to hold court during the day, confident in her position and sure of her own importance.

"I found her, my lady," Dalia announced, bowing her head to the older woman who sat in a large chair, being fanned by two of the eunuchs who kept watch over us. One of them, a young man my own age named Khalid, gave me a subtle wink as I approached. He had always been one of the few people here who treated me like an actual person, a feeling I might have forgotten by now if it weren't for him. I let my lips curl in greeting to him for just a second before bowing my head to the first wife, as she expected me to.

Along with being first in order of seniority, Minsa was the oldest among Malek's harem. Actually, she was even older than him but still stunningly beautiful. As usual, her dark skin had been highlighted with charcoal-coloured makeup and her long hair elaborately braided and arranged. She spent longer on her beauty routine each day than most women did in a month, but no one could argue with the results. As the daughter of the ruler of one of the empire's most important allies, her marriage to Malek had been an entirely political affair, and yet, she had fallen hard for him anyway. Even now, with so many rivals for his attention, she still went out of her way to try to please him, whereas I felt only gratitude every single day his eye fell on someone other than me.

There were many differences between us, but that, perhaps, was the most significant one.

"You asked to see me?" I kept my eyes on the floor as I spoke to her, knowing she would take it as an insult if I met her gaze. I had learned the Munisian language out of necessity when I arrived here, but even now, I spoke with a heavy accent which the other women mocked behind my back, and sometimes to my face.

Minsa waved the men with the fans away, leaning forward in her chair to speak directly to me. "I have just been informed that the minister's daughter has returned, safe and sound."

Before I could stop myself, my eyes darted upwards, looking to her face to try to determine the truthfulness of her words. I had spent so many days wishing for that news, but as the weeks, and months, and then years passed, eventually, I gave up hope. It seemed that Zara had been lost, the same as I had been to the world I had known. We had that much in common, me and this woman I had never met, but whose life intertwined with mine.

"Are you certain, my lady?" I managed to murmur, looking back down at the floor before she could chastise me for looking at her so directly.

"Are you saying my information is inaccurate?" she challenged, always eager for a chance to put me in my place. "My sources are never wrong."

I believed that. Gossip flew around the palace even faster than the seabirds who roosted in the eaves above the open courtyards.

"Does this mean..." I started to ask, but I couldn't force the words out. By speaking them out loud, by giving voice to my hopes, it felt like tempting fate. In the end, I didn't need to speak them anyway; Minsa knew exactly what I wanted to know.

"You were brought here as payment for the loss the minister suffered, in retribution for the crimes committed against him. If she has returned, your debt should be considered paid. I will speak to Malek about it tonight."

Hope swelled within me, even as I tried not to let it. Though I had no real idea what freedom would mean for me now, with my family dead and my greatest prize, my virginity, already lost, surely any kind of freedom would be better than captivity here.

Perhaps, after all this time, my life could finally begin.

CHAPTER THREE

My heart felt full to overflowing as we were led through the corridors of the royal quarters. Even though Arthur told me the Lassarian king had sent my father home, part of me still feared the worst. Perhaps his ship had been intercepted or blown off course or lost at sea. Maybe he had succumbed to illness. So many years had passed since we last saw each other, it seemed almost impossible that we could finally be reunited after all this time. I still made the trip, because any chance at all would be better than none, but inside, I tried not to get my hopes up in case something had gone wrong and he would not be waiting for me.

Now, all those fears had vanished, evaporated into thin air like the smoke rising from the incense burners outside the emperor's private temple that we passed on the way to my family's new home.

Not only was my father still alive, he had risen to heights I never could have dreamed of. To be the emperor's chief minister, to live within the royal quarters, these were things that simply did not happen to people of his background. Obviously, something significant had changed since I'd been away, but for now, in the bliss of my ignorance, I could simply bask in the warm glow of our reunion.

"Zara." He breathed my name almost reverently as he embraced me in his office, ignoring everyone else there. "How did you survive? How did you get here? I thought I would never see you again."

"I thought the same, Baba," I answered him with tears of joy in my eyes. "I escaped and went looking for you. I'm sorry it took so long, but I only found out a month ago that you had come home."

He shook his head in disbelief. "You should have come straight home when you escaped. Your job should not have been to worry about me. If I had any idea you were looking for me, I would have come to find you. I thought... I thought you must have been killed."

Tears welled in his eyes too, and I could see he meant it. He had lost hope, and now, to him, I had just come back from the dead.

From the corner of my eye, I could see Arthur's beaming face, looking almost as happy for me as I felt about this reunion. It could not have happened without him, and I quickly realized I hadn't yet introduced him as I should.

Switching to the language they would understand, I introduced Eric first, mostly to get him out of the way, and then, holding my breath, I introduced my father to Arthur. The warm embrace and words he gave him were a complete surprise to me, and to Arthur too, but the more I thought about it, the more sense they made. Arthur's father had helped him get home, so of course he would already have warm feelings for the Lassarian royal family. Now that Arthur had brought me home too, he would have my father's loyalty for life.

Although I had much more to say to him, duty called him away. We would have a chance to speak again this evening and I couldn't wait to find out exactly what had happened while I'd been away. On my own part, I would have to gloss over many of the things that had happened to me, but I would share what I could without causing him too much distress.

The royal quarters were a maze of corridors, buildings and courtyards, but finally, we were led into a large room, this one with a small fountain in the centre of the cool tiled floor. The walls were made of stone, inlaid with intricate mosaic designs, and songbirds in cages sang merrily from one corner of the room.

On the settee, next to the cages, sat my mother.

She got to her feet in surprise at the sudden appearance of a half-dozen people in her home, most of whom were pale and obviously foreign. Her gaze passed over each of them in turn as she tried to decipher what was happening, but when she got to me, she stopped, her eyes squinting in disbelief.

"Zara?" She tried to take a step towards me but her legs gave way, and she collapsed onto the ground as the servants and Arthur both rushed forward to help. The commotion caused more people to enter the courtyard. I felt no recognition at the sight of the young women, but as they called my mother Mama, I realized these must be my younger sisters.

With my mother finally settled back on the settee and calmed, I walked slowly towards her, trying not to startle her again. "It's me, Mama."

Through her tears, she explained to my sisters who I was. As she said each of their names, I could see glimpses of the little girls they used to be. They were all women now and strangers to me, but hopefully, we could get to know each other again soon.

"Your head," my mother tutted as she looked me up and down. "Have you been walking around with it uncovered?"

I had to fight back a smile. It had been a long time since I had worried about that kind of modesty. "It is a long story, Mama, and I will share it with you, but if you don't mind, these men with me have been waiting patiently. Father promised them they could stay with us."

With that opening, the clerk quickly relayed the instructions my father had given and the servants went straight to work to prepare extra rooms for our guests. My sisters stared at the pale-skinned men curiously, hiding their mouths behind their hands as they whispered to each other, even though Arthur, Eric and the others couldn't understand them anyway.

The men were shown to their quarters where they could relax until dinner, while I sat down with my mother who kept staring at me as though she'd seen a ghost.

"How did you end up here?" I asked, unable to contain my curiosity any longer as I gestured to the grandeur of the room around us. "What happened?"

"The Actilians," she said simply, as if that explained anything.

I recognized the word from the men at the port, but I still didn't know what it meant; they said something about my father being promoted after the plunder of the Actilian kingdom. "Who are the Actilians?"

Once again, she gave me a look of disbelief, but this time it related to what I'd said, not simply my existence. "They are the people who took you from your father."

A memory stirred from somewhere deep inside me, of that trip with my father, sitting next to him as he reviewed the upcoming diplomatic visit with his men. Perhaps I *had* heard him speak about the Actilians then, I just hadn't paid close attention. Their prince had been the one who decided he wanted me, and who took me from my father through lies and deceit once my father refused to sell me to him outright.

Clearly, the story hadn't ended there, though. "What happened, Mama?"

In my childhood, she had always relished the chance to tell a good story, and it didn't seem that had changed as she settled back in her seat, placing her hands across her stomach. "You must remember that the Actilians falsely arrested your father and sold him into servitude?"

That had been the last thing I knew for sure about what happened to him, at least until Arthur had told me about his father helping to send him home, so I nodded in agreement.

"As soon as he returned to us, he requested an army to take back to Actilia to free you."

That, I never knew. By the time he arrived, I would have been long gone already, having made my own escape and gone in search of him.

My mother confirmed my guess in her next breath. "When they reached the port, he went ahead of the rest of the fleet to speak to the king and prince who had treated him so poorly. They told him you had run away. Your father believed they were lying to him, just as they had lied to him before. With no alternative, he commanded the rest of the emperor's forces to land and they ransacked the entire city in search of you. The king and prince were killed in the fighting, claiming to the end that they had no idea what became of you."

My father raided a city and killed a king for me? He had never been a violent man by nature, and I couldn't imagine how much guilt and pain he must have been carrying to do such a thing.

"He brought back gold, jewels, weapons and slaves, and as a reward, the emperor promoted him into his inner circle of advisors. Only two years ago, the emperor made him the chief minister."

So, in a way, our separation led to the life they all led now. There must be more to the story, but even this much would take some time to process.

"He offered a public reward to anyone who could bring you home," my mother continued, which explained the scene with the men from the port earlier. "But in his heart, he believed you were dead, that those men had used and killed you, and he blamed himself. He has not been whole since then, Zara. Having you back will be like a second chance at life for him. We can all start fresh."

Although she beamed at the idea, my heart twinged. As glad as it made me to see her and my father, everything else about this place no longer felt like home to me. Even my literal home had changed. After the years of searching and all I had been through, I did want a fresh start, certainly, but did I want it here?

Or perhaps, somewhere along the way in my search for my father, had my idea of home become tied to a different man instead?

~**Arthur**~

Although I had made many diplomatic visits with my father before, and a few on my own as well, I'd never seen anything like the Munisian palace. From the elegance and opulence of the buildings, the sheer size of it, the way the people spoke and dressed to the strict hierarchy of access, it all felt completely foreign and overwhelming.

Was this how Zara must have felt when she first arrived in the lands I considered familiar? My heart ached at the thought of her being there alone, with no resources at her disposal. At least I had her to guide me through this and translate for me, Eric and my men as backup, and all the respect that came with my position and wealth, while she hadn't had any of those things. My admiration for her only grew stronger with each new thing I learned about her and each experience we shared.

Seeing her reunited with her father made the long journey worthwhile, even if nothing else came of our trip. The joy on both their faces almost brought tears to my eyes, and I tried my best to be happy for her even if the thought of her staying here when I sailed for home in a few days' time made my chest tighten and my breath grow short.

While I continued to take a look around my temporary accommodation, a knock sounded at my door and I hurried over to it, hoping it would be Zara herself, materializing out of my thoughts. Instead, Eric stood there, pushing his way inside as soon as I opened the door to him. Aside from the bed, a small sitting area, and a large cabinet for storing clothes and bedding, the large room was empty, leaving plenty of room for Eric to pace the tiled floors, which he did now.

"I need to find out more about that woman," he began without any explanation at all, as if I should automatically know what he was talking about.

"What woman?" I asked as I closed the door behind him, making sure we wouldn't be overheard. The servants might not know our language, but it didn't hurt to be cautious.

"The one we saw in the courtyard. The one from the harem."

I almost groaned out loud. He had to be kidding. "You heard what Zara said: talking to the women in the harem isn't allowed, and nobody here cares that you're a prince. They have forty princes of their own, they don't care about you. You should forget you even saw her."

Maybe that sounded blunt, but we had to tread carefully here. The Munisians were known for being difficult to deal with and wary of foreigners. That explained why none of the other kingdoms had been able to ally with them, and why, if we could, it would be a huge advantage for us. We couldn't risk messing that up for Eric's curiosity over a woman he'd seen for half a second. There must be *some* women back in Silatria he hadn't bedded yet, he didn't need to start here.

He carried on as if I hadn't said anything at all. "I don't think she wants to be here. They're holding her against her will."

Where on earth did he get that from? "You can't possibly know that, and even if she is, it's none of our business, Eric. They have their own customs and their own beliefs. You were willing to marry my sister whether she wanted to or not; what gives you the right to be offended now?"

I disliked the idea of any woman being forced into sexual servitude, but I had to be realistic too. We lived in a world that condoned it in multiple ways, and it seemed to be the foundation of the whole harem system. The two of us weren't going to be able to change it, and certainly not in the limited amount of time we had here.

At least he made no argument on that point, but he didn't back down either. "I can't explain it, but I feel like I'm supposed to help her. Maybe that's the whole reason I felt compelled to come on this trip."

"I thought you came to redeem yourself in your brother's eyes." My words were still blunt and a little harsh, but he needed to hear it. If he did something rash like he had when he teamed up with Westley Eastam to try to get Dee in the first place, he could end up in a lot of trouble, and I would rather not have to explain to King Cassian why I'd returned without his brother.

"It can be about more than one thing," he muttered petulantly before finally ceasing his back-and-forth movements across the room and coming to stand directly in front of me. "Zara's father said you could have anything you ask for. Ask for a chance for us to speak with this woman. At least then we can find out who she is and why she's here."

Although Zara's father had made that offer, I had no intention of taking him up on it for something that felt like a fool's errand. "She probably doesn't even speak the same language as you, and she's more than likely here because her family wanted the prestige that came with having their daughter in the harem. Zara told us it's considered an honour."

"Zara can translate for us," he suggested, still unwilling to take no for an answer. "It's probably best that she's there anyway. I don't even have to speak to her directly, or look at her. I'm not trying to cause trouble, Arthur; honestly, I'm not. I just need to know who she is."

In the two months that Eric and I had spent together, I had never seen him as worked up about anything as he was right now, and against my better judgement, sympathy began to creep in. "I'm not making any promises, but I can ask. Perhaps if you're not talking to her directly, it would be alright. But *if* they agree to it, you have to follow whatever conditions they put on it. If they decide to cut out your eyes for looking upon her, I won't be able to do anything about it."

Zara had told me that actually could be one of the punishments handed out for looking upon the emperor's wives, gruesome as it sounded.

The mention of such a possibility didn't seem to throw Eric off, though. He simply clapped me on the shoulder in gratitude. "Thank you, Arthur. I'm going to go and rest now until we're needed for dinner."

He left me as quickly as he'd arrived, and on my own, I looked over at my own bed. I should rest too, to be as fresh as I could be for what the evening might bring, but the idea of lying down on my own, without Zara, held no appeal. We hadn't spent a night apart for the entire trip, and sleeping with her in my arms had quickly become normal for me. It would feel like something would be missing without her there.

When Zara's father had told me earlier that I could have anything I wanted, there had only been one thought in mind: I wanted Zara herself. I wanted her to return to Lassaria with me as my bride and future queen.

But before I could ask him for that, I needed to ask her first, and hopefully, at some point this evening, I would have the chance to do just that.

~Eric~

Arthur's promise that he would speak to Zara's father, Adil, about the woman from the harem helped to set my mind at ease a little bit, but only a little. Ever since I laid eyes on her, a restless feeling had taken up residence in my chest, making my heart race and my stomach tighten. What brought on this reaction mystified me, and although Arthur clearly assumed my interest in her was physical, as it always had been with me in the past when it came to women, it felt like more than that.

Something in her posture and the melancholic, detached air that surrounded her had spoken to me, as though something deep inside me had resonated with something inside of her. It almost felt like we had met before. I didn't believe in love at first sight or any of that romantic nonsense, but I had no other words to describe what I felt. I'd had feelings for Elodie, yes, but they were very different. This emotion felt completely new, and I had to find out what it meant.

The men working for the minister were efficient, and in less than half an hour, my belongings had been brought from the ship to my new lodgings. Among my papers, I had a list of the trade negotiations I hoped to accomplish during our stay, and I started a new list now to accompany it, identifying the people we had been introduced to so far and their relation to each other. I didn't want to miss any angle that might result in a better outcome for me and for Silatria.

At the bottom of the page, I added the words: *Harem woman, name: unknown, relationship: unknown*

Adil returned home another hour or so after that, I could tell by the flurry of activity outside my room. I had left the door open so I wouldn't miss anything, and I followed the noise back out to the main entrance hall where Zara and her mother were still sitting, along with the women that must be her relatives, and now, her father as well.

With no sign of Arthur or the other Lassarian men, I began to retreat, not wanting to interrupt a private moment amongst the newly-reunited family, but Adil caught sight of me and beckoned me over to join them.

"Please, come and sit down. We will eat soon. You must be hungry."

Actually, I was, and the promise of food and the chance to get to know Adil better enticed me to take him up on his offer. He gestured to the chair on his left, and the girl sitting there immediately got up to make room for me. Zara sat on his right, but she got up as well as I sat down.

"I will go and get Prince Arthur to join us too," she told her father, and he nodded his assent before turning to me.

"What do you think of the emperor's palace so far?"

"It's beautiful," I answered honestly. "I have never seen its equal."

"Normally, I don't like flattery," he warned me. "But in this case, it is the truth, so I will allow it."

He had the warm, charming smile of a man at home with small talk in any setting, every movement imbued with effortless grace, and I had to remind myself that this same man had been sold to Westley Eastam's father to provide manual labour. The idea seemed preposterous.

"Tell me about your own castle and kingdom," he invited. "Zara says you are from Silatria?"

"That's right. Have you been there?"

He shook his head with a wry smile. "I had no liberty to travel while in the area."

Of course. That had been rather tactless of me, but thankfully, he didn't seem to be offended.

"Is it similar to Lassaria, then?" he asked, encouraging me to continue.

"In many ways, it is. Silatria is bigger than Lassaria, almost four times the size, and we rely heavily on our farming and textiles, whereas Lassaria has their precious metal reserves which provide the bulk of their wealth. We work very closely with them, though, and that alliance will only grow now that my brother, the new king, has married Arthur's sister, Cordelia."

"The news of your father's death reached us just a few days ago," Adil said, inclining his head in sympathy. "My sincere condolences."

I accepted his sympathy, even though I still felt guilty about my father's death, brought on by Westley Eastam's scheming. Though I couldn't do anything to bring him back, I did want to try to make up for any damage I'd done to the kingdom, especially to our financial state, and that formed the main reason for my presence here.

Arthur and Zara joined us a moment later, Arthur taking the seat on Adil's other side with Zara sitting next to him. Adil asked Arthur about his father and family, and then he asked how Arthur and Zara got to know each other.

The two of them exchanged glances, Arthur's cheeks turning pink in a way that made the nature of the relationship between them completely obvious. Zara remained more collected. "It is a long story, Baba," she demurred. "Let's save it for after dinner."

The servants brought the food out soon afterwards, dishes I had never seen before made with thick sauces and fragrant spices. Zara's father insisted the conversation remain in the language of his guests, which meant that Zara's mother and sisters were unable to join in. Zara translated for them as best she could while trying to listen in on the conversation between her father, Arthur and I.

Adil asked Arthur the same question he had asked me, about his initial impressions of the palace and the Munisian capital city.

"Zara told us a bit about her home before we arrived, but seeing it in the flesh is something quite different. It is all very impressive." The Lassarian prince glanced over at me, as if debating whether to add something else, but since I had no idea what his look meant, I couldn't offer any guidance. A moment later, his train of thought became clearer to me when he continued speaking. "We noticed a young woman by the pool at the courtyard where we entered earlier. Do you know who she might be?"

Adil's open expression turned slightly more guarded. "Only members of the harems are allowed there. She must have been one of them. It is better if you pretend you did not see her."

"Harems?" I repeated, unable to stop myself from interjecting at the word in plural. "There's more than one?"

Adil nodded. "There is the emperor's harem, and there is one for his son, Malek, the crown prince."

Zara had mentioned that the emperor's eldest son might have his own harem now. It seemed she had been correct.

"Zara explained a little about the harems to us," Arthur said, giving her a smile of appreciation before turning back to Adil. "And we understand that we cannot see the women or speak to them. However, I wonder if Zara might be able to speak to this woman on our behalf."

"Why?" The question came not from Adil but from Zara herself, making it clear that they had not discussed this between them ahead of time.

"Prince Eric would like to know more about her," Arthur explained to both her and Adil. "He thought he recognized her. If it is possible to engage with her without offending anyone, we would appreciate it, as a personal favour."

Saying that I thought I recognized the woman was a bit of a stretch, but it did make more sense than simply saying I had a feeling I should speak to her. If the white lie would get me what I wanted, I wouldn't disagree.

"There are many women in the harem," Adil explained. "It might be difficult to determine which one you saw."

Frustratingly, he had a point. If I couldn't see them to pick her out, how would he know which one I wanted to speak to? I could explain her beauty, but I imagined that might not help to narrow it down. I would guess the crown prince didn't select many ugly women for his harem.

"I saw her as well, Baba," Zara spoke up. "I would recognize her. I would guess she is in Malek's harem, she seemed about my age."

Adil nodded thoughtfully. "That might work out, then."

The tightness in my chest eased just slightly at the idea that I would actually be able to speak to the woman, whoever she might be.

"You should meet Malek's wives anyway," Adil added, looking at his daughter.

Zara's brow wrinkled in confusion. "Why?"

Her father glanced over at her mother, who, of course, had not followed a word he'd said. Without any input from her, he had to offer his own explanation: "They are important women in the palace. Now that you are back, they should know who you are."

Zara looked wary, but when I shot her a pleading look, she sighed. "Fine. I can meet with them tomorrow morning, before the princes meet with the emperor."

With that agreed, talk turned to other things, and I gave Arthur a grateful nod. There weren't many people I liked, but so far, he had turned out to be a good friend. Hopefully, this visit would leave us both satisfied in the end.

CHAPTER FOUR

~Zara~

After dinner, my father invited me to his study so we could catch up properly. He did not invite my mother or sisters, perhaps guessing, correctly, that parts of my tale would not be appropriate for their ears. Eric excused himself, saying a respectful and rather charming goodnight to everyone. I still didn't know exactly what had brought on his interest in this woman from Malek's harem, but Eric seemed much happier after we agreed that I would try to speak with her.

After Eric had gone, Arthur lingered next to me, hesitantly. "Do you want me to join you?" he murmured, for my ears only.

Part of me would have liked to have him there, providing the kind and caring support that came so naturally to him, but truthfully, it would also be easier without him there. Speaking in private would allow my father to speak in his own language, which would be more comfortable for him, without either of us having to translate.

"Not tonight, thank you. Have a good night, and I'll see you in the morning, Your Highness."

I added the title since my father and others might still be listening, and I knew Arthur understood that even if he didn't like it. The little cocoon we had built for ourselves on the ship, where we were simply Arthur and Zara with no other considerations, no longer applied. Tonight, he would sleep in his bed and I would sleep in mine, missing the rocking of the waves and his warm arms around me.

My father bade Arthur goodnight before leading me to his study, a room down the hall that looked just as impressive as the other rooms in his new residence, but which still managed to feel warm and cozy too. It felt like my father, actually; like a visual representation of his essence with books scattered around and a half-dozen projects on the go. He always had an incredible amount of energy to go with his natural intellect, which explained how he had risen as far as he did. Now, he had climbed as high as he could possibly go. The only people above him in status in the whole empire were the emperor and his family, which I could still barely wrap my head around.

"There have been many changes since you left," my father said, as if he could hear my thoughts as I looked around the grand room. "I will tell you all about them, but first, I need to know what happened to you. How did you end up in the company of the Lassarian prince?"

That wouldn't be a short story, but I had promised I would tell him, and so I did. I explained how I escaped from the Actilian castle, though I did not know at the time who the castle belonged to. I told the story of how I had travelled across a continent in search of him, following the clues left behind, and how I had used whatever resources I had at my disposal to get by, including my own body. Not a stupid or naive man, my father would understand the dangers I had been in and that I did what I needed to. Aside from the occasional nod or tightening of his lips, he remained silent throughout my whole tale, not interrupting or even asking questions, until I got to the point where I met Westley Eastam and he promised to help me in exchange for my help against Arthur.

"You worked against the prince? And he knows this?"

I nodded, a smile playing at my lips as it did whenever I thought of Arthur. "Prince Arthur knows everything I have just told you. He knows that Eastam lied to me and he knows what I almost did in stealing his seal. He has forgiven me for all of it."

"And Eastam?" My father's tone made it clear that he already hated the man, though he had only learned of his existence in the last few minutes.

"Dead. We witnessed his execution ourselves the day before we set sail."

My father nodded in satisfaction. "Good. One less evil in the world."

The way he said it made it clear that he had dealt with a great many of them in his time, but his gaze softened as he looked at me, examining me almost as if he had never seen me before.

"Very few women could do what you did, Zara. Very few men either. You survived and you never gave up, and it breaks my heart to know that you went through all of this because of me. If I hadn't taken you on that trip..."

As if a dam had burst, his emotions seemed to overwhelm him and his eyes filled with tears. In a moment, I knelt on the floor at his feet, my arms around him.

"It's not your fault, Baba. I wanted to go with you and you had no way of knowing how evil those men were or what they would do. If I had simply accepted my fate, I would have still been there when you arrived, and it would have saved us both years apart. My own stubbornness is to blame as much as anything."

Cradling my head against his chest, his tears still falling, my father shook his head. "You stood up for yourself, you fought for yourself, as you should have. As I should have done for you. Do not ever be sorry for that."

Holding each other in the fading light of the study, we cried together, crying for the lost years and the time apart and all the hurt we'd been unable to spare each other from.

"Mama said that you went back there," I told him once my tears had started to ease. "She said you destroyed the whole city as retribution for what they did."

"I felt so much anger," he admitted, wiping the dampness from his own cheeks. "I am not proud of it, even though it's why I have the position I have now. When they told me they couldn't return you to me, I thought they must have killed you.

I thought they used and discarded you, and I wanted them to feel the pain I had felt, so I did the worst thing I could think of: I took their princess in return."

"What do you mean?" I asked, looking up at him in confusion. My mother hadn't mentioned this part.

"The king had a daughter, about your age. Before he died, I made sure that he knew that she would be brought here and given to my prince, just as his son took you from me. She would never be free so long as you were gone."

"Baba!" I couldn't contain my shock. My father had never taught me that kind of justice. Wrongdoers should be punished, yes, but committing another evil act did not make the first one any better.

"I'm not proud of it," he repeated softly, his gaze downcast. "My pain eased with time, though it never disappeared, and eventually, I spoke to the emperor about it. I suggested that enough time had passed and the girl could be returned to her own people, but he thought it would be a sign of weakness if I did not stick to my word. So long as you were missing, she would stay here."

That was a weight I did not want on my conscience, but at least there seemed to be a clear path to redemption. "So, she can be released now? Since I'm safe, there's no reason to hold her any longer."

"I will try to convince the emperor of that," he agreed. "Perhaps the princes can take her with them when they leave."

The idea of Arthur leaving while I remained here made my chest tighten in discomfort.

"Malek will need to be the one to order her retirement, though, since she is in his harem," my father mused.

The mention of the crown prince sent a shiver down my spine. Perhaps he had matured since the last time we met, but I didn't hold out much hope. Having their every whim catered for since birth would spoil most men, and Malek seemed to be even more rotten than most.

Arthur must have had nearly the same privilege, and yet, he turned out the complete opposite. He was a true gem, a diamond among the black coal of most noblemen's hearts.

"What is that smile for?" my father asked curiously, picking up on the way I couldn't help my lips curling whenever Arthur crossed my mind. "Are you looking forward to meeting Malek again?"

I started in surprise. "What? No. I have not thought about him in years."

Until Arthur and Eric had asked about him, I had put the prince out of my head entirely. He had never been worth thinking about.

For some reason, my father looked disappointed with that response. "Well, he will be glad to know of your return. He will want to see you."

I supposed that my family must be closer with the royal family now, thanks to my father's new position and the living arrangements here. I still wanted to know more about exactly how he got his new position, but the excitement and drama of the day, not to mention the draining release of emotion we had just shared, had started to catch up to me. Though I tried to stifle my yawn, my father saw it anyway.

"Go to bed," he commanded, exactly as he used to when I was a little girl. "In the morning, you can visit the harem, and then I will accompany you and the princes to meet with the emperor and Malek. It will be a busy day, and you need your rest."

I couldn't argue with that, so after one more embrace, I got back to my feet and returned to my new room. Despite being comfortable and having almost everything I could want, it lacked the one thing I wanted most: a certain Crown Prince of Lassaria in the bed. Missing Arthur with every part of my being, I climbed into bed and quickly relaxed into a deep sleep.

~Fatima~

Any morning that I woke up in my own bed, I counted as a good one. When Malek came into the harem's main hall the night before, I immediately shrunk back against the wall, trying to make myself as invisible as possible. If I had even a small chance of getting out of Munisia soon, I would rather avoid any more nights in Malek's bed than I had already spent there. Unfortunately for me, he seemed to like the chase despite having a building full of beautiful women who were bound to him. Somehow, he always seemed to know who would be the least interested in keeping him company and he'd choose that person. That perverse pleasure meant that he frequently chose me, since I didn't seem to be able to hide just how much I loathed him.

However, last night, luck favoured me. Malek seemed to be in a good mood, speaking with several of the women who regularly fought for his attention before taking Minsa herself to his room. That rarely happened, no matter how much she wanted it to, and I breathed a sigh of relief as the door closed behind them.

"I wonder what he wants," I overheard one of the other concubines mutter.

"What do you mean?" one of the youngest girls asked, one who had more curiosity than sense.

"He only takes the old cow to bed now when he wants something," the first woman explained. "My guess is he's got his eye on another woman."

As Malek's first wife, Minsa had authority over the harem, and traditionally, she had some say in approving new additions to it. In practice, she could do nothing to stop Malek if he'd made up his mind, other than making the new woman's life miserable when she arrived, but it looked better if she appeared to approve and welcome any new members.

Personally, it wouldn't affect me if he brought on another new face or not. Hopefully, this would all be behind me soon and none of it would matter any-more.

The concubines had to wait on the wives in the harem, so once I got up and got dressed in the morning, I went to help prepare Sade's bath. The second of Malek's wives and by far the least obnoxious one, it had been a godsend when I had been assigned to her rather than to either of the others. She also came from a foreign land, the daughter of the ruler there who had sold her to Malek in exchange for a trade treaty, but whereas my home lay to the north, across the sea, she came from the south, in the sunbaked desert lands beyond Munisia. Some of the other concubines made fun of her for the darkness of her skin just as they mocked me for my lightness, but I thought her rather beautiful. She kept herself apart from the drama of the harem, content to read her books, do her needlework, and go for long, slow walks around the palace gardens. I wouldn't go so far as to say we were friends, but we weren't enemies either. We shared an unspoken respect for each other as two women who didn't belong here but had no other choice and were bearing the indignity of it the best we could.

Malek did not spend much time with her. I suspected he found her quiet poise off-putting.

"I hear you may be leaving us soon." Sade's accented voice took me by surprise as I helped her into her bath. She rarely spoke to me, or to any of us.

"There are rumours," I admitted, well aware that the whole harem had been talking about it after Minsa shared the news with me of the minister's daughter's return. "I won't believe it until I am out on the open sea."

Sade nodded in approval. "It is better not to get your hopes up. Disappointment can sting all the worse when you expect too much."

"Why would you want to leave?" one of the other concubines interjected, although she hadn't been invited into the conversation. "No man will want you now. Better to stay here where you are provided for."

Although I saw her point, I couldn't agree with it. "I don't need a man to survive. I may not have as many things somewhere else, but I will have my freedom, and that is more valuable."

The concubine rolled her eyes and called me crazy, several of the other women agreeing with her, but in Sade's eyes, I saw only understanding.

When Sade was ready, we all made our way to the main hall where breakfast had been brought by the servants. The wives got to eat first, and only when they had finished could the concubines have their meal. Anything left over would be given to the servants.

Khalid stood next to the door along with one of the other eunuchs, and he gave me a bittersweet smile as I found a seat close to him with my plate of figs, cheese and honey. "When are you going home? I will miss you."

"Not you too!" People were jumping to a lot of conclusions. No matter how hard I tried not to get ahead of myself, everyone talking about it made keeping my hopes in check more difficult. "I haven't heard anything yet. I imagine the minister's daughter has to get settled first. I doubt I am at the top of her mind."

I had no idea what this woman had been through, or anything about her other than the fact that my father and brother had separated her from her father through some kind of trickery. Their crime provided the reason for my punishment, the crime for which they had paid with their lives, but what they'd done with her, I had no idea. I had never seen her before, nor even heard of her until the day her father arrived and destroyed the only world I knew.

So, when someone knocked on the door and the eunuchs admitted a beautiful woman in a pale purple dress, I didn't immediately make the connection. Everyone in the room watched curiously as she made her way over to where the wives sat, Minsa in the middle, Dalia on her right like a little lap dog, and Sade to the left, a short distance away from the other two.

"Your Highnesses," the newcomer greeted the women with an elegant curtsey which reminded me of the court where I grew up. Such manners were not common here in the palace. "Please forgive the interruption, but I would like to beg your indulgence to speak with a member of the harem."

"Who are you?" Minsa asked, scanning the woman's appearance with distaste. She disliked anyone prettier than her, and this woman certainly fit that bill.

"My name is Zara. I am the eldest daughter of Adil, the emperor's chief minister."

A gasp circled around the room as all eyes moved to me. Was this the moment I had been waiting for? I truly hadn't expected it to come so quickly, and my heart began to race with nervous excitement.

Zara turned to look around the room as the women whispered to each other, scanning the space as if looking for something in particular, until her eyes fell on me. "The woman there, in yellow. May I speak to her in private, please?"

She wanted to speak with me. After all these years, the time had finally come. Minsa seemed to relax as she realized the significance of Zara's request, and she gave her blessing, as eager to get rid of me as I was to go. Minsa ordered Khalid to accompany us, and together, we followed Zara back to the courtyard with the reflecting pool. Besides the three of us, no one else seemed to be around, but to my surprise, when we sat down next to one of the columns which surrounded the courtyard, Zara spoke over her shoulder, using a different language entirely, but one I recognized from my youth.

"We're here. What do you want me to say to her?"

A deep, masculine voice replied from behind the column, an unfamiliar voice that for some reason sent a flare of recognition through my body. "Ask for her name. Ask what she's doing here."

"Who is that?" I spoke the words aloud, in the same language they were using, and Zara looked back at me in surprise.

"You can understand us?"

I gave a curt nod, though it should be obvious. "It's not my native tongue, but I understand. What is happening? Who wants to know my name? Don't you know it, my lady? Aren't you here to release me?"

"Release you?" The look of confusion on Zara's face made it clear that she had no such intentions, and my heart sank painfully. Just as Sade had warned me not to, I had let myself hope too much. "I'm afraid there's been a misunderstanding, I can't..."

She trailed off, her eyes widening in surprise and, perhaps, understanding.

"Are you the Actilian princess?"

"Princess?" The voice from the other side of the column repeated. "She's a princess?"

Zara turned back to shush the unseen man before looking back at me again, her expression sympathetic and inviting.

"Let's start over, shall we? My name is Zara. My faceless friend behind the wall is named Eric. Who, exactly, are you?"

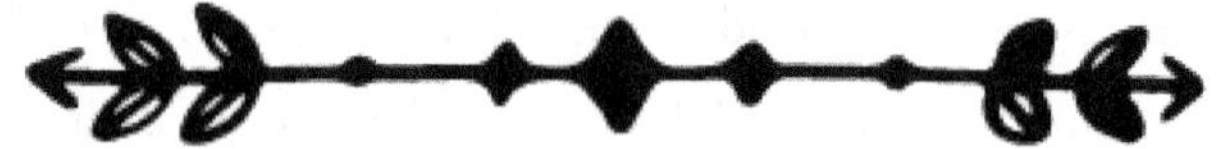

~Eric~

If Arthur hadn't been beside me, holding me back, I might not have been able to resist rounding the column and talking to this woman face-to-face. When she spoke out loud, that feeling of connection that I'd experienced when I first saw her grew even stronger. Even better, she knew my language. Zara didn't need to interpret at all, so I could speak to her directly were it not for the ridiculous rules of the harem.

However, I believed Zara when she said the rules must be taken seriously, and since I did quite value my eyes and would prefer not to have them gouged out by the emperor's son because I looked at his property, I managed to stay hidden, with Arthur's help.

When Zara asked the woman if she was a princess, as soon as she said it, I knew it must be true. Her bearing, her gracefulness, and her beauty all spoke to good breeding and good training. She must have been raised in privilege, somewhere far from here based on her appearance, so where did she come from and how did she end up in this place?

Thankfully, Zara asked the question before I had to tell her to.

"My name is Fatima," the woman replied in her beautifully-accented voice. "And you are right, I am from Actilia. My father was the king there, before his death."

She really was a princess. A princess in hiding, a princess in captivity, and somehow, I had been brought here to set her free. I felt more convinced of that than I had been of anything else in my life.

"So, my father brought you here," Zara said softly, and it didn't sound like a question. She already knew that, though I wasn't sure how, and from the look of confusion on Arthur's face, he didn't seem to know anything about it either.

"Yes," Fatima confirmed, the word clipped but strong. "How much do you want to know?"

"Everything." Though Fatima hadn't been speaking to me, I answered anyway, loud enough that she could hear me. "Please, tell us as much as you can."

For a moment, I could hear only silence, and I wished yet again that I could see her, that I could try to read her expressions and her body language rather than simply listening to the disembodied voice that came to me from the other side of the column.

"I was fourteen when the Munisians came," Fatima began, speaking louder after the reminder of my presence. "I didn't know anything about what had happened with you and your father. The first I learned of it was when the soldiers came to take me and my mother to safety. They said the castle had been attacked."

I had been in enough battles to understand the rush of adrenaline she must have felt, the strange, heightened awareness that came from realizing your life might be in danger. But unlike a battle, she would have had no way to defend herself, a young girl relying only on those around her to protect her.

"They tried to sneak us out through a hidden passage in the castle kitchens, but the Munisian soldiers were already there. They recognized that we must be people of importance, so we were taken to the throne room where my father and brother were already restrained and being questioned by your father."

Arthur winced, as if knowing somehow, without seeing her, that Zara would be wincing too.

"My father tried to lie and say he didn't know who we were, to protect us, but his men betrayed him. They identified my mother as the queen and me as their daughter, and your father said that unless they returned you to him, my mother and I would be taken to the emperor's palace here and subjected to the same fate that they had given you. We would be enslaved by the emperor in his harem."

Any respect I may have had for Adil burned away in the white-hot anger that raged through my body. What kind of a man threatened a woman that way? And not just an idle threat, either; obviously, he must have carried it out, for Fatima was here now, in the harem, just as he had promised.

"My father and brother swore that they had not harmed you but that you ran away and they didn't know where you were. He thought they were lying, and when they were unable to produce you, he had their heads cut off on the spot."

On the spot. In front of her, she meant, and though I had witnessed many executions in my time, a rush of sympathy still went through me at the thought of this young girl forced to witness such a thing, involving people she loved.

"My mother grew hysterical," Fatima continued, her voice strangely devoid of emotion as she spoke. Perhaps she kept the emotion hidden to defend herself against the pain of her memories. "She said she would rather die than be taken and her body abused, and she made good on that threat, impaling herself on one of the soldier's swords."

This time, Arthur and I both flinched. Fatima had lost her entire family in a matter of minutes, right before her eyes.

"I was not brave enough to do the same," she continued. "And so, they brought me here."

"I am so sorry," Zara said, and she certainly sounded that way, her voice heavy with regret. "None of it was your fault, and you shouldn't have been involved."

I could almost hear Fatima's shrug. "We are women. Life is rarely fair for us, Your Highness."

Your Highness? Arthur and I exchanged confused, silent looks as Fatima used that title for Zara, but it must be a matter of mistranslation. None of us bothered to correct her.

"All things considered, your father did not treat me cruelly. He spared me the worst on the return journey. He told me that there would be guards outside my door at all times, and there were. I have heard stories of what can happen to women on a ship full of men, but on my journey, they left me alone, and I am grateful for that."

I had spent enough time around sailors to know exactly what she meant, and I begrudgingly gave Adil my silent thanks for that consideration.

"When we arrived, your father presented me to the emperor, who gifted me to his son, Malek, instead. I have been in his harem ever since. That is my story."

That may have been the basics of what happened, but I had a feeling it barely scratched the surface of the whole story. I wanted to know so much more about her.

"You have borne Malek children?" Zara asked, and Fatima hummed in assent.

"Three of them, but I have not seen them since they were infants. They will not miss me when I am gone. I am ready to leave immediately. I hoped... well, when you came to speak with me, I hoped that's why you were here."

"I will certainly speak to my father," Zara offered. "I only learned about any of this last night, and he already said he would speak to Malek. I will have him do it today, if possible. I am sorry you have been through any of this, but hopefully, it will be over soon. In fact, we are meant to be meeting with the emperor in a matter of minutes. We must go, but I will try to speak to you again soon."

"Thank you, Your Highness."

The rustle of fabric told me that they were both standing up, and after a moment's silence, Zara spoke to us again.

"She's gone. You can come out now."

I had a dozen questions, at least, but I knew Zara was right that we were expected with the emperor soon, so I stuck to only one for now. "What did you mean that it will be over soon?"

"They brought her here in retribution for what happened to me," Zara explained, guilt clouding her expression. "Now that I've returned, she should be released, so long as Malek agrees."

Well, I hadn't expected freeing her to be quite *that* easy, but it also reaffirmed my belief that I had come here for this reason. With her entire family gone, she would need somewhere to go and someone to help her. She would need a prince.

"Let's go, then," Arthur suggested, offering Zara his arm. "It's time for us to meet the emperor and his son for ourselves."

CHAPTER FIVE

Though not everyone would have noticed, I could see just how much the conversation with Fatima had shaken Zara. The way her jaw tightened and the way her hand pulled at the fabric of her dress betrayed her inner turmoil even if outwardly, she looked perfectly composed to everyone else.

Zara liked to think of herself as tough, hardened from experience, and in many ways, I had to agree. However, she also had a natural compassion that she couldn't entirely hide. That empathy had led to her siding with me instead of Westley; once she got to know me, she couldn't go through with what she'd promised him. In the same way, guilt had started to eat away at her thanks to the idea that she had caused Fatima's suffering, however inadvertent the connection between them might be on Zara's part.

"Is it normal that the women in the harem don't see their children?" I asked under my breath as we made our way back to Zara's home. Her father would be waiting to accompany us to the meeting with the emperor.

She nodded distractedly. "They're raised by wet nurses, servants and tutors in the children's quarters. The women are meant to serve their 'husband', the head of the harem, and children would provide a distraction."

That seemed unnecessarily cruel, to both the mothers and their children. Surely, Malek could only make use of the women one at a time, and only when he had no other responsibilities. To have dozens of them at his beck and call at all times felt like overkill.

Zara's mouth twisted into a grimace. "She's had three children and nothing to show for it."

It couldn't be more obvious that she took Fatima's indignities personally, and I sought to reassure her as best as I could. "What happened to her isn't fair, but you didn't have it easy either, nor could you have known the situation here. None of it is your fault, Zara."

"I know." Though she said the words, regret still filled her voice. "But at least I can make it right today, and then you and Eric can take her back with you and help her start over."

Eric certainly seemed to want to do that, but the way that Zara spoke of Eric and I leaving without including herself made my chest tighten. Was that really what she wanted? We hadn't had a moment to ourselves to discuss how she felt about being home and back with her family, and with each passing moment, I grew more desperate to know what was going on in her head.

Now was not the time to ask, though, not with Adil waiting to lead us to the emperor's audience chamber. The emperor had been told we were here and that we had brought Zara back with us. Adil assured us the emperor would be open and willing to discuss trade agreements and whatever else we were interested in since we had acted in such good faith. A learned man, the emperor also knew our language and would speak to us in it, which we were to consider a great honour.

Adil reviewed the instructions Zara had already given us about keeping our heads down as we entered and not to speak until we were addressed. Because we were princes, once the emperor had acknowledged us, Eric and I would be allowed to look up, but Zara must keep her head down at all times.

"I remember, Baba," she confirmed, still sounding a million miles away in her head.

I could not offer her any support as we walked through the halls that led to the emperor's private receiving room. As far as anyone else knew, we were merely passing acquaintances, and we needed to maintain that facade in front of the emperor.

The room we were led into had a beautiful, tiled mosaic floor with splashes of colour in reds, oranges and browns. Keeping my head down as instructed while the man at the door announced our arrival, I couldn't see any of the room other than the floor at first. Adil kept his head down too as he walked further into the room, the three of us close behind him.

"Adil." A rough voice spoke from the far end of the room in front of us, and Zara's father bowed even lower.

"Your Majesty. These are the men I told you about. May I present Prince Arthur of Lassaria and Prince Eric of Silatria."

I dipped my head lower, mimicking Adil's posture, and Eric did the same.

"You are welcome, Your Highnesses," the same voice said, and since we had now been acknowledged, I cautiously raised my head to get my first look at the rest of the room.

Rather than a throne like my father used, the emperor sat on a long, low couch. Silk robes in vibrant colours covered his body and a large beard, streaked through with grey, covered the lower half of his face.

Behind him, servants stood ready with fans and food and drink, only a step or two away should the emperor decide he needed anything. A clerk sat to one side at a desk, his quill scratching quietly across the parchment as he made notes on the court proceedings, and to the other side stood a young man about my age. His clothes were equally as bright and luxurious as the emperor's, but they were fitted tighter, making him look ready for action while the man on the couch looked almost ready for a nap. The emperor's half-closed eyelids added to that impression as he gazed out on Eric and I with a look both curious and sleepy.

"Which of you is Arthur?" he asked, and I immediately stepped forward, inclining my head politely once more.

"I am Prince Arthur, Your Majesty. I bring wishes for health and long life from my father, the King of Lassaria, and he has sent this token of his esteem." From the pouch I wore around my waist, I withdrew the gold pendant my father had sent with me to smooth my introduction.

With a wave of his hand, the emperor instructed one of his men to come and take it from me, and once the servant had it, he took it to the emperor directly, kneeling down as he offered the item to his sovereign.

"Lassarian gold is highly sought after," the emperor wheezed, coughing a couple of times as he turned the pendant over in his hand. "We would be glad to hear of any opportunities to acquire more of it."

That was an invitation to discuss trade with his advisors, exactly as I had hoped for, and I bowed my head once more in gratitude. "Thank you, Your Majesty."

With that agreed, I stepped back, and the emperor called Eric forward. He, too, had a gift, in the form of a small but beautifully crafted dagger from the master metalworkers of Silatria. The emperor looked impressed as he turned it over in his hands.

"It means a great deal to us that you have travelled all this way to return the minister's daughter. Malek is particularly grateful for it, and he will personally oversee all the trade negotiations with both of you in thanks."

The man standing next to him acknowledged that with a nod, looking at both Eric and I with a cool, critical air as he addressed us, also in our own language. "I am sure we can find some common ground."

So, that was Malek, the emperor's son. Eric stiffened next to me, no doubt thinking of Fatima and what she had endured in his harem, and I shot him a warning glance. We were still guests here and we could not afford to offend anyone or start a fight over customs which differed from our own.

"Bring the girl forward," the emperor called out next, and both Eric and I stepped to the side to make way for Zara to step to the front. She kept her eyes demurely down, as instructed, but I could tell from the defiant strain of her shoulders that she found the position unnatural. "She has grown into a beauty, Adil, as you said."

Zara's father bowed his head down again. "It is in her blood, Your Majesty."

What did that mean? I had no idea and clearly Zara didn't either, her brow furrowing as her gaze stayed focused on the floor.

"You have not told her yet?" the emperor asked, still speaking about Zara as if she weren't standing right there in the room with us, and Adil shook his head.

"No, Your Majesty. There is a lot we still need to catch up on."

"Told me what?" Zara asked, and a gasp circulated around the room, shock registering on the faces of the clerk and the servants. Clearly, she should not have spoken.

"Your manners have not improved much with your time away, I see." Malek's tone remained cool but a glint of interest sparked in his eyes as he looked at Zara, which troubled me.

"Please, forgive her, Your Highness," Adil requested. "She needs some time to readjust to life in the palace. The world she has been living in is very different."

"Shall I tell her?" Malek asked, looking at his father who merely shrugged in response. Taking that as approval, Malek pressed ahead, speaking directly to Zara, who still did not look at him. "You know that your father was an orphan?"

She nodded, saying nothing. I could practically see her biting her tongue.

"It came out some years ago that he is actually the child of the late emperor's sister. She had a child stolen from the palace, and we have determined that your father is that child. He and my father are cousins."

Though Zara still did not speak, I could see her eyes darting back and forth along the ground as she processed that information, and my mind raced to put it together too. That meant...

"You are of royal blood, Zara, both your father and you," Malek continued. "That made his appointment to chief minister possible, and it is why you are eligible for the great honour that awaits you."

"Honour?" Zara couldn't stop herself from repeating the word, despite the restrictions on her, and I wanted to know exactly what it meant too. From the look on Malek's face, the smug self-satisfaction in his expression, I didn't imagine it could be anything good.

"You are technically a princess," he explained. "And as such, I am willing to make you my wife."

~Zara~

For just a moment, when Malek said my father descended from the late emperor and I had royal blood too, my spirits lifted. That explained why Fatima had called me Your Highness, which I thought strange at the time; it must be common knowledge throughout the palace. It also explained how my father had achieved his high position. Everything fell into place.

Most of all, to me it meant that as a princess, even a minor one, the idea of me marrying Arthur suddenly seemed far less ridiculous. For that split second, as I imagined it, my whole body filled with warmth and light and hope at the mere possibility.

But Malek hadn't finished, and as soon as he mentioned an honour, my stomach dropped, all the hope that had been rising in me sinking like lead as I tried to figure out exactly what he meant. I couldn't see the expression on his face since I wasn't allowed to look at him, but even just his self-satisfied tone of voice let me know that whatever he considered an honour would likely not be anything good for me.

He quickly confirmed as much when he said he would be willing to take me as his wife.

He would be *willing* to. He made it sound like he'd be doing me a favour, when there could be nothing in the world I wanted less. Under no circumstances did I want to be locked up in any man's harem, especially not one so obviously spoiled and self-indulgent as the future emperor. For years, finding my father and coming home had been all I thought about, all I lived for, and now, faced with this prospect, I found myself wishing I had never come at all.

A dozen responses danced on the tip of my tongue, including some rather colourful curse words I'd learned over the course of my travels, but all of them would endanger not only myself, but my family, and possibly even Arthur and Eric too. I had to remember that we were definitely not in Lassaria anymore.

"This is indeed an honour, Your Highness," my father replied on my behalf. From the corner of my eye, I could see him bowing once more, making my stomach heave. It seemed he had every intention of letting this happen, and on my other side, I could see Arthur growing more agitated, fighting his own urge to speak up.

Luckily, and surprisingly, Malek provided an opportunity for me to speak instead as he gloated in his presumed victory over me. "Of course it is, Adil. Zara may express her gratitude directly."

My gratitude? There were a few things I wanted to express, but gratitude was not one of them.

Having been given permission to speak, I raised my head, finally laying eyes on Malek for the first time since our one brief encounter all those years ago, back when we were both children. He had certainly grown since then, as had I. Dressed in his imperial robes, he looked tall and strong-looking, his dark hair cut short, even shorter than the beard that covered his chin. Dark eyes watched me from beneath his thick eyebrows, and full lips twisted into a smug smirk as he awaited my response.

He wanted my submission. I had seen that look on the faces of men before, including the Actilian prince whose actions had started all of this in the first place.

The fact that I had never seen that expression on Arthur's face just added to the things that made him so different from all the men I'd known before.

Thinking of Arthur and the life I could imagine with him, however faint that possibility may be, made it clear why I could not and would not submit to Malek, and thankfully, I thought I could see a way out. One thing I could tell him should dampen his ambitions, though I suspected it wouldn't be appropriate to talk of such things openly in the emperor's presence. However, Malek had left me little choice, so I spoke the words anyway, trying to keep my tone as humble as I could.

"Many things have changed in the years since I left Munisia, Your Highness, and I'm afraid you will no longer find me the virginal girl you once knew. I understand that purity is required of all wives of the royal blood, so it is with regret that I must decline your kind offer."

That should do it. I had laid on my false humility thick enough, and I had been as delicate as I could be. In my eyes, the situation seemed clear: I was no virgin, and the emperor's son could not take such a woman as his wife. At that moment, I could almost be grateful for the circumstances that had led to my deflowering.

Despite my delicacy, the clerks and servants around the room were still shocked by my statement, almost as shocked as they had been when I spoke out of turn earlier. This news would definitely be making the rounds within the servants' quarters this evening.

Malek, meanwhile, went rigid, his eyes filled with anger. "These men?" he demanded, his gaze moving to Arthur and Eric, and I quickly shook my head.

"No, Your Highness. The princes have been only kind and respectful to me." I didn't lie, technically. Though Arthur and I may have done other things together, we had never had sex. "I spent years on my own before I met them and I did what I needed to survive."

"Did you know of this, Adil?" the emperor demanded, and my father's shoulders drooped in dismay. He had all but accepted Malek's offer a moment ago, and if it transpired that he had known of my state and tried to pass me off as a virgin and a suitable bride for the emperor's son, he could be in a great deal of trouble.

To save him the trouble of lying, I did it for him. "No, Your Majesty. I had not told him, as I know that no father would like to hear of such things. I did not intend to tell anyone and definitely not to make such a public announcement of it, but in light of Malek's proposition, I could not keep it from you. I would never attempt to deceive you."

That seemed to mollify the emperor somewhat, though he still looked unimpressed. "You are dismissed, then."

Gratefully, I bowed my head again, and took a step backwards, eager to get away completely after my narrow escape, until I remembered one additional thing: Fatima. I had promised to speak to Malek about her today, and I couldn't go back on my word after all she had already been through.

"Your Highness, there is one more thing."

Malek stared down at me, his gaze fierce and intense, obviously unhappy about the way this had played out.

"The Actilian princess in your harem was brought here because of my abduction. Now that I have returned, I humbly request that you allow her to retire. Her debt has been repaid."

In truth, the debt had never been hers to begin with, but I wasn't about to try to argue that in a room full of men.

Malek regarded me silently for a moment, his eyes still burning in frustration at not having gotten his own way, until a new light sparked in his eyes, making my stomach turn once more. "She may go, but only if you take her place."

Yet again, a round of gasps and whispers circulated around the room as I stared at the prince in disbelief. "But I just said..."

"I heard you," he cut me off snidely. "Obviously, you cannot be my wife, and normally, it would not be appropriate to offer a woman of your blood a position as concubine. However, given the circumstances, I believe we can make an exception. You can take Fatima's position as concubine if you want her to be released. If you choose not to, if you want to find a man who will marry you even in your condition, then you are free to do so, but Fatima stays. That is my final word on the subject."

I opened my mouth to protest, shock still coursing through my body, but my father took my arm to pull me away before I could make things worse. "We will consider your generous offer, Your Highness. Come, Zara."

Arthur and Eric bowed as well, all four of us walking backwards with our heads down until we reached the door, my heart still racing all the while. What in the world was I supposed to do now?

~Eric~

Arthur and I were both worked up by the time we finally got back to the relative privacy and security of Zara's father's home, but I suspected our agitation had completely different sources. He was concerned about Zara while I worried for Fatima. My earlier optimism about how easy it would be to get her released had started to look like a rather cruel joke.

Zara didn't exactly look happy either. "You knew about this, didn't you?" she demanded of her father once he had taken us all into his study where we could speak without constraint. "You knew Malek wanted to marry me?"

"I suspected it," Adil confirmed, grimacing beneath the weight of his daughter's anger. "Even as a child, he showed interest in you. I'm not sure exactly when you caught his eye, but you did. That was the reason why the emperor wanted to meet with you just before we went on our trip. There were rumours of you joining Malek's harem, and to be honest, that chatter was one of the reasons why I took you with me on the voyage. I thought you should have a chance to see some of the world before being locked away from it. Of course, I could not have predicted what would actually happen on that journey."

Zara had certainly seen a lot of the world now, but clearly, the idea of joining the harem appealed to her no more now than it might have been then.

Adil continued his explanation. "Once we discovered the truth of my heritage, Malek bemoaned the fact to me, on more than one occasion, that if you had not been lost, you could have been his wife. When I delivered the news of your return to the emperor yesterday, Malek heard it too, and it obviously piqued his interest. So yes, given all that, I suspected he would make you an offer, and it would not have been appropriate for me to refuse it."

Unfortunately, that was the way these things worked, and Arthur had made a good point when he compared it to the marriage contract between his sister and the crown prince of Silatria. Cordelia had been contracted to marry my brother, sight unseen, and when everyone thought him dead, the contract transferred to me instead. Cordelia's personal preferences were not taken into account any more than Zara's were now, or Fatima's, for that matter.

"We can't leave Fatima in there," I announced to the entire room. Although Zara had been trying to help by bringing her up, Malek intended to use her as a bargaining chip now, and I feared what the consequences would be for her. Zara's return might be her only chance to get out.

"Zara can't sacrifice the rest of her life just to free her either," Arthur argued back, his whole body tense, which put me on the defensive too. I understood he had feelings for Zara, but she planned to stay here anyway. What difference did it really make if she joined the prince's harem or married another random man? As far as I could see, it didn't affect Arthur personally at all.

"It is not such a bad life..." Adil offered weakly, but he didn't even finish the sentence when we all glared at him, making it clear that none of the rest of us agreed.

"What is the difference between a wife and a concubine?" Arthur asked, the muscles in his jaw still tight as he tried to understand all the intricacies of the situation.

Zara answered that one. "The prince's wives have a higher status. Their children are officially recognized as heirs, and as princes or princesses in their own right. The wives are given special privileges within the harem where the concubines serve them. He can have an unlimited number of concubines, if he wishes, but the number of wives is limited and is considered a greater honour for the woman's family."

She grimaced at the word 'honour', just as she had in the throne room.

"However, in reality, there is not much difference," she continued. "All of them are stuck there, subject to the prince's whims. Their lives are not their own. In every way that matters, they are the same."

"Malek said it wouldn't have been appropriate to make you a concubine because of your royal status," I pointed out. "And yet, Fatima is a concubine, though she is also a princess?"

"Because she is a prisoner of war," Zara explained. "Her royal status can be disregarded, just like mine can be now that I have told him I am not a virgin."

"At least he has given you a choice now," Adil interjected, still trying to calm everyone down. "You don't need to accept his offer if you truly don't want to."

"But if I refuse, Fatima must remain," Zara countered. "It is not fair, to her or to me. How could I live with that guilt?"

"There is no reason for you to feel guilty," her father assured her. "Many things in our lives are the result of the station we are born into. She had the misfortune to be born to a family that cheated and disrespected us, and that is why she is here. It's not your fault."

As sorely tempted as I might be to point out that Fatima's presence here was much more Adil's fault than anyone's, we still needed him on our side. I couldn't afford to alienate the man just yet, so I tried to look for another solution instead. "What if Arthur and I ask for her release, as part of our negotiations?"

"On what grounds?" Adil asked in confusion. "It has nothing to do with either Silatria or Lassaria."

Technically, that might be true, but I tried to spin it another way. "She is still a princess enslaved against her will. Our code of chivalry demands that we provide our assistance."

Though it might be a stretch, my claim wasn't entirely implausible. The Actilian culture had much more in common with our own than with that of Munisia. We could claim that we were acting on behalf of our shared brotherhood with the Actilian people.

"You could try," Adil said, not sounding particularly convinced. "But he will not let her go for nothing, as we have already seen. You must be prepared to make concessions."

That frustrated me since I had come here to try to strike a good deal on behalf of Silatria and help to rebuild our tattered finances, but I also felt that my brother, Cass, would understand my actions once I explained them to him. Even if the trade deal I came back with wasn't as good as it might have been, he would not leave an innocent woman behind here either.

"We should begin negotiations as soon as possible, so we can see what the potential for a deal is," Arthur suggested, his eyes fixed on Zara. "Don't make any hasty decisions, please."

"I won't," she promised. "There is a lot I still need to think about."

Something profound but unspoken seemed to pass between them as they stared at each other, but at the moment, I couldn't be bothered to try to figure out what it might be. We had too much to do.

"Come on, then," I said to Arthur. "Let's go and get started."

Adil sent one of his men to take us back to the administrative district where the clerks would be waiting for us, and hopefully, where Malek himself would soon join us. My negotiation skills were about to be put to the test, and there had never been quite so much riding on them before.

CHAPTER SIX

~Fatima~

Only after I returned to the harem's main hall, ignoring Minsa's grimace at my return, did I realize I still had no idea why Zara wanted to speak to me in the first place. She asked about how I ended up in the harem and promised she would speak to Malek on my behalf, but she gave no explanation at all about why she wanted to see me before she knew my identity.

For that matter, she also hadn't told me anything about the man behind the column, why he listened to us, or why he seemed so invested in my responses. The whole encounter made little sense to me, but I clung onto the sliver of hope she had given me anyway. The chief minister had great influence, both by virtue of his position and his princely blood, so hopefully, Malek would listen to his daughter when she argued on my behalf.

"I have friends who serve in the emperor's receiving room," Khalid murmured to me under his breath a short while later, when no one could overhear us. "I'll try to find out what is said."

"Don't go to any trouble," I urged him. "I'm sure that Minsa's spies will report back as well. One way or another, I will find out."

Though the women were confined to the harem's lodgings, gossip flew freely between the harem and all other parts of the palace. With little else to do, the news we got from outside provided the only real entertainment for many of the women here.

However, neither Khalid nor Minsa shared the news with me in the end. Instead, Malek himself came into the hall, in a foul mood even by his standards.

Minsa and Dalia immediately got to their feet, trying to get his attention, but he ignored them entirely as his eyes scanned the room, looking for someone in particular. Unfortunately, it seemed to be me, as his eyes narrowed when he found me sitting next to one of the trees, trying to make myself invisible.

"Come." The order might be curt, but I couldn't ignore it. He rarely visited the harem during the day, but when he did, it usually meant something had happened to upset him and he wanted a quick fix to make himself feel better.

With no other choice, I got to my feet and followed the prince out of the hall and down the short corridor that led to his personal chambers.

"Kneel," he commanded as soon as the door closed behind us, making me grimace.

I didn't enjoy being intimate with him in any way, taking no pleasure from anything that we did together, but this had to be my least favourite thing and he seemed to know it. He would use it as punishment for me or when he wanted to feel powerful. What he wanted to achieve this time, I couldn't say, but it didn't really matter. The end result would be the same either way.

"I know you can hear me, Fatima." He growled my name, getting closer as he pulled his cock through the opening in his robes. Though I had never seen another one in person, I'd heard the other women in the harem say that Malek's couldn't be called impressive. Some suggested that might explain why he felt so hard-done-by all the time, even though, by most standards, his life was a charmed one. "On your knees."

Either I did as he said or I would be punished as he saw fit, and with my freedom so close at hand, I couldn't afford to mess up. Reluctantly, I bowed my knees and opened my mouth as Malek took hold of my head with his hands and shoved his sweaty cock down my throat as I tried not to gag.

Some men, I'd heard, were mostly silent during intimate acts, but not Malek. The sound of his own voice seemed to turn him on, and he frequently used the opportunity to flaunt his authority, as he did now.

"No matter how much you glare at me, you'll still take what I give you, won't you? You're a lot less high-and-mighty when you're on your knees. She'll learn that too. I'll see her beg."

Who did he mean by 'she'? I had no idea, but I couldn't have asked even if I wanted to, not with my mouth full of him and my eyes watering as he slammed into me harder.

He continued muttering until his cock swelled with his imminent release, and I braced myself for its unpleasant arrival. The first time he had done this to me, I had made the mistake of spitting it back out, choking in my surprise, and for a week afterwards, he confined me to my room. He expected all of us to pretend that we loved it, and shockingly, some of the other women in the harem swore they actually did. I thought they must be lying, or they had just convinced themselves that they did to make it more bearable. I had never mastered that particular skill of self-deception.

He groaned as his orgasm hit and I did my best to swallow it down without breathing, trying not to taste anything. His cock looked even smaller when it started to go limp, so as he always did, he tucked it back within his robes before I could see it in its natural state.

I expected that to be the end of it; these daytime encounters were always brief since he had other places he should be, but to my surprise, he took a seat as I wiped my face clean and got back to my feet.

"The minister's daughter asked me for your freedom today."

My heart skipped a beat as hope rose within me. She had really done it. Did that mean this encounter had been some kind of farewell gift from Malek, one last humiliation to remember him by?

"I heard she had returned," I said quietly, doing my best to sound meek and not too invested in his response. "I'm glad she is safe."

Although I desperately wanted to know if he had agreed, I couldn't simply ask him. I would have to wait for him to tell me, if he intended to.

"Why should she care so much about you, I wonder? A woman she has never even met before?"

Was this some kind of test? It would be easy for him to find out what happened in the harem this morning, so I made no attempt to hide it. "I spoke with her earlier this morning, Your Highness. She came looking for me. She seemed very kind and humble."

Malek snorted in derision at my comment. "Humble is the last word I would use to describe her. That glint in her eye... she has always thought herself better than she is."

I had nothing to say in response to that. That didn't match the impression I'd got from Zara, and even if it did, I would rather not talk about her. I wanted to know what he had decided about me.

At last, he satisfied my curiosity, but hardly in the way I hoped. "For your sake, you had better hope she is as kind as she seemed. I told her you could go if she took your place."

My stomach lurched in disbelief as the room spun around me. Though I wished he was kidding, I knew Malek too well for that; he never joked. He took everything, and himself, far too seriously.

If he presented me with that choice, if I had a chance to be free, I couldn't imagine choosing to give it up for someone else's sake, and especially someone I barely even knew. Zara sympathized with the unfairness of what happened to me, but the blame didn't lie with her, and I couldn't expect her to pay such a steep price to make it right.

The disappointment that flooded my body hurt nearly as much as the desperation I'd felt when I arrived here in the first place. It seemed my hopes had all been for nothing, and as I returned to the harem alone, I almost wished Zara had never returned at all. At least that way, I wouldn't have let myself dream.

~**Arthur**~

Not being able to speak to Zara freely was driving me crazy. I had grown so accustomed to knowing every thought that passed through her head, and telling her all of mine, that to be cut off from her at a time like this left me feeling empty and incomplete.

I could try to guess how the meeting had affected her based on how it made me feel, but it couldn't compare to hearing it from her own lips. Lips that I hadn't kissed in far too long. Lips that Malek wanted for his own.

"Stop scowling," Eric whispered to me as we sat in the room where we'd been taken to await Malek's arrival. "You'll scare him off."

Right now, I wanted to do a lot more than scare Malek, but Eric had a point. We were here to try to make diplomatic overtures, not create enemies, and perhaps we could still find a way to charm or bribe Malek into changing his mind. People usually had a price; I'd taken that much away from my encounters with Westley Eastam. Find the thing a person wanted more than anything, give it to them, and you could have almost anything you wanted in return.

There must be something that Malek wanted more than Zara or Fatima. After all, he had no shortage of women. We just needed to find out what that thing might be and hope that we could offer it to him, and maybe we could all leave here happy and satisfied.

Some of the men who had accompanied us from Lassaria had come along specifically for these negotiations, and the Munisians had their own bureaucrats too. They would sort out all the details once Eric, Malek and I had agreed on the principles, and they were busy laying out the foundations of any possible arrangement now while Eric and I sat there uselessly, waiting for the Munisian prince to appear.

Another half an hour passed with me fluctuating between anger, indignation and trying to remain calm and collected, until finally the door burst open and Malek walked in, followed by two of his personal bodyguards, as if we might try to do him harm.

That could be taken as a sign of bad faith in negotiations like this, but in this case, injuring him definitely crossed my mind, especially when he sat down and adjusted himself in his robes crudely. "My apologies for keeping you waiting. Sometimes, having a harem to satisfy can be a demanding job."

Gritting my teeth, I had to remind myself that he didn't know Zara meant anything to me beyond a passing acquaintance, or that Eric had become obsessed with Fatima for reasons beyond my comprehension. I still hadn't laid eyes on the woman myself. Malek's words were simply meant to show off in the way that men often do to each other, exaggerating their prowess in the expectation that it would create camaraderie, or perhaps to inspire jealousy.

"I'll take your word for it," I replied coolly but levelly. "Princes of Lassaria do not keep a harem."

"I have heard that," Malek replied, equally mildly. "It seems a flawed system to me, to put all your eggs in one basket, so to speak. What if the wife you take doesn't please you? What if she can't bear children?"

Some kings had indeed faced that issue, but it seemed like a stretch to use that as an argument for abandoning the entire institute of monogamous marriage. "Then that is what is destined."

Malek snorted in disagreement. "Fortune favours the brave. Those who succeed make their own destiny."

Sensing that we were unlikely to come to an agreement on this, Eric stepped in. "I can see the benefits both ways," he told Malek with an easy smile, which in reality, couldn't have been all that easy for him. He must know as well as I did that it could have been Fatima that Malek had been visiting just before he joined us. "Neither Arthur nor I are married yet, but I've had my fair share of women. There are plenty of willing candidates, I just don't keep them all locked up in one place."

That made Malek laugh, as Eric meant it to, breaking the tension that had been simmering at the table. "Sometimes it's better when they're not so willing," he said with a smirk, putting my back up once again as Eric tensed beside me.

Eric might be a rake, but he had never forced himself on a woman. I had seen plenty of them go to his bed freely, and the idea that Malek might force either Zara or Fatima had us both on edge.

Malek, however, seemed oblivious to our response, still chuckling at his own 'joke'. "So, what is it you want from Munisia then?"

We spent a couple of hours going over the trade agreements that we hoped to put in place. Knowing that they wouldn't give us everything we asked for, we asked for more than what we actually wanted, and Malek knew how to play the game as well as we did. He whittled our requests down until we reached an agreement that seemed suitable on both sides.

Only when we were almost ready to mark our agreement did Eric step in with his other request. "Earlier, when we were with the emperor, Zara asked about releasing the Actilian princess who joined your harem following Zara's disappearance."

Malek's expression immediately turned guarded. "Yes, and I gave her my response."

"Of course," Eric agreed smoothly, doing his best to appear as indifferent as possible. "However, there are rules of chivalry which guide Arthur and me, as princes, and one of those is to provide assistance to women who are in need of it. That is the reason that we brought Zara back to you, unharmed, and for the same reason, we would like to return Fatima to her own people, now that her debt has been repaid."

"Fatima is not in need of assistance," Malek countered. "She is well provided for."

"Zara would have been provided for in Lassaria as well," I added, trying to provide Eric with some backup. "But as she wished to return here, we honoured that request."

At this point, I wished we hadn't, not with Malek's ultimatum hanging over her, but I could hardly say that to the man in question.

I stuck to speaking of the other princess instead. "If Fatima wishes to return with us, she should have that choice. It would be seen as a great gesture of peace and goodwill from Munisia towards all the northern kingdoms. If she chooses to stay, then of course that is her right as well."

The flare of Malek's nostrils told me more than any words could that he knew exactly what Fatima's choice would be if it were put to her.

"Your customs and rules do not apply here," he pointed out, entirely correctly, no matter how much we might wish it would be otherwise. "You may take her with you if she's retired, but that decision is in Zara's hands."

He began to get to his feet, clearly not willing to discuss the matter any further, and Eric leaned forward, his voice low and desperate, as if he felt the opportunity slipping away from him. "What do you want for her?"

My stomach sank as interest flashed in Malek's eyes. The question had been too open-ended, too frantic. It gave away just how important this was to Eric, which we had been trying hard not to do, and of course, Malek picked up on it.

"Have you seen her?" he asked in reply, a question that seemed innocent enough but held a great deal of danger. We were not supposed to have seen any members of the harem, since looking at them was forbidden.

Thankfully, Eric didn't fall into that particular trap. "No. I have no personal connection to her, but her story, as related to me by Zara, has moved me. I can't help imagining how I would feel if my own sister were in her position, far away from the world she knew. I would hope that another of my fellow princes would offer their support."

Eric had no sister, but thankfully, Malek didn't seem to know that. He eyed Eric suspiciously anyway though. "That is very soft-hearted of you."

He really meant that Eric sounded weak, which he did. Infatuation did that to a man.

"I assure you, it's quite out of character," Eric replied drily. I had to smile, and Malek did too, but he didn't back down nor make any concession at all.

"If it means that much to you, then I suggest you speak to Zara directly. She holds the key. Excuse me, Your Highnesses."

With that, Malek and his entourage swept out of the room, leaving us with a potential trade deal but no further along with sorting out the mess of Malek's harem.

"So much for that," Eric muttered beneath his breath. "I guess we'll have to move on. First, we need to talk to Zara, as he said."

It sounded like Eric had no intention of giving up, but if he honestly thought I would let him try to convince Zara to give up her freedom in exchange for Fatima's, he was delusional. "She is not joining Malek's harem."

Eric gave me a grim smile. "I never said she would, but she may be able to help anyway. Maybe it's time to get a little creative."

~Zara~

While Arthur and Eric went to negotiate with the emperor's men, I received an invitation from Malek's wife, Minsa, to join the women of the harem for honey cake and wine.

Instinct told me that the invitation had not been made out of the goodness of her heart. From the very brief encounter I'd already had with her this morning, I could tell she fell into the category of women who viewed everyone else around her as competition. In her position as Malek's first wife, she should feel more secure than anyone, but she obviously didn't, and her wanting to spend time with me suggested that she already knew what took place between Malek and me in the emperor's receiving room this morning and Malek's subsequent proposition to me.

None of that surprised me either. The harem walls had never stopped gossip coming in, or going out, for that matter, when it suited the women inside.

"Be careful she doesn't poison you," one of my sisters said as I prepared to return to the harem. Although I had no desire to go, refusing the invitation would have been considered rude, and perhaps, if nothing else, I could speak to Fatima further during my visit. "I heard about one concubine chosen by Malek who had no family at all, some street urchin that he saw and lusted after. Within a week, she died; by accident, officially, but no one believes that."

I didn't believe it either. With no family to complain about her death, there were no repercussions for any scheming that might have led to the poor girl's demise. Imagine having to share Malek's bed in the first place and then having to pay for it with her life. I could hardly imagine a worse tragedy.

The afternoon air hung hot and heavy as I made my way through the palace, the heat melting into my skin in a way the colder air of the northern countries never had. I had missed the sun and heat while in Lassaria, but now, I almost missed the chilly breeze that made sitting down in front of a fire afterwards such a pleasure. I especially missed sitting next to Arthur in front of that fire, the flames reflecting in his sweet blue eyes as they had in the brief, quiet moments we had together at his castle.

The harem door was opened for me by a handsome young man who kept his eyes respectfully down as he greeted me. He wore the blue and green loose-fitting garments of the emperor's guard, and his feet were bare. "Good afternoon, Your Highness."

That title would take a lot of getting used to, as would speaking in my native language again. "Please, call me Zara. What is your name?"

"Khalid, Your Highness." He repeated the title even after I'd told him not to, but the hint of a smile on his lips told me he knew how ridiculous the rules were that forced him to do it. In his refusal to take things too seriously, I thought I could see a kindred spirit.

"Where are you from, Khalid?"

As I used his name, he raised his eyes to me. They were a dark brown, even darker than his skin, and full of intelligence and no small amount of good humour. "I am the seventh son of a fisherman. I grew up just north of the city."

His response explained a great deal, as he must know it would. Sons were a blessing, but too many of them meant splitting and diminishing the family fortunes. Daughters could be bartered for financial gain but sons must be provided for, and if the chance came to gift one of them to the emperor, many families would jump on it. Khalid must have been a boy when he was chosen for the harem and castrated, as required by all in his position; now, he was a young man but probably older than he appeared, and slighter than he might have been if life had worked out differently for him. Still, he seemed to have accepted his lot with good grace.

I would not go so quietly. Deep down, I probably fell closer in temperament to Fatima's mother who had killed herself rather than accept her fate, though that kind of permanent solution didn't appeal to me either. I was a survivor; I always had been, and those instincts still flared inside me as I regarded the gilded prison in front of me.

"You there! Stop wasting the princess' time." Minsa's imperious call made Khalid wince. "Let her pass."

"I've been here for seven years and she doesn't know my name," he whispered to me conspiratorially as he stepped aside. "Good luck."

Trying not to smile, I gave him a nod of understanding and made my way further into the hall where Minsa waited along with Malek's other two wives. Their names were a mystery to me, but I smiled at them all politely as I took a seat. Minsa offered me a drink but I refused, remembering my sister's warning. It would be bold to attempt anything on me given my father's position, but it still didn't seem worth the risk.

We made polite small talk as their drinks were poured and cakes were placed in front of each of us. The conversation could only be described as inane and pointless, reminding me of why I rarely spent much time talking to other women in the first place. Arthur's sister, Cordelia, had been a pleasant exception.

"You must be pleased to be home," Minsa suggested after we had exhausted the usual pleasantries, putting words in my mouth that I wouldn't necessarily have said on my own. "We have all heard the stories of the way women are treated in those foreign lands. It must have been very difficult for you."

Of course she referred to the loss of my virginity, which she must have already heard about from the servants in the emperor's hall. Clearly, she saw me as defective. "Life can be difficult no matter where you are, Your Highness. I did what I had to in order to survive, but overall, I cannot say that women are treated any worse there than they are here. It is simply different."

She seemed unconvinced as she gestured around at the opulent surroundings of the harem. "Here, we are treasured and protected."

That was one way of looking at it, but not one that I agreed with. "Do you never miss speaking with other men, Your Highness?"

The idea seemed to scandalize her. "Why should I want that? The affairs of men are none of my business."

The youngest wife who sat next to her nodded enthusiastically, but the other one, the elegant, darker-skinned one, regarded me curiously. "You spent your time in the company of men while you were away?"

Minsa looked at her in surprise, though whether her surprise stemmed from the question or the fact that she had spoken at all, I couldn't be sure. I answered her honestly anyway. "Almost exclusively, Your Highness. Some were bad, some were decent, and some... some were very good."

One in particular leapt to mind, but my thoughts of Arthur were disrupted by Minsa's horrified huff. "Shameless!"

Belatedly, I realized what my words sounded like, and tried not to laugh. "I am not speaking of the time I spent with them in bed, Your Highness. Although, now that I think about it, that fits as well."

The one who had asked the question in the first place raised her fan to her face, and I could have sworn she hid a smile behind it, but Minsa still looked unimpressed. "That kind of talk might have been appropriate in whatever heathen places you have been staying, but it doesn't belong in the harem."

"Of course not, Your Highness." I inclined my head in mock deference. "The harem has nothing to do with sex, after all."

This time, there were giggles from around the room, making it clear just how many people were listening to us. As I took a quick glance around, my eyes landed on Fatima, sitting against the far wall, close to Khalid. Not only did she not laugh, it didn't seem like she had been listening to us at all. Her shoulders drooped as she wrapped her arms tightly around herself, looking far more defeated than she had when I spoke to her earlier.

Belatedly, I realized she must have also heard what happened in the emperor's room today. If she guessed that I did not want to take her place, then she must think she had no chance of leaving after all, and my heart went out to her. More than ever, I was convinced that I couldn't leave her to this fate, even if I still had no idea how I might stop it.

Minsa, meanwhile, silenced all the titters in the room with a glare. The muscles in her cheek twitched as she looked back at me. "It sounds like you don't wish to join us, then."

"I am considering His Highness' proposal," I replied, knowing full well that anything I said here would make its way to Malek's ears. I couldn't give anything away just yet, not until we had a plan. "But I do appreciate you making me feel so welcome."

No one witnessing that exchange believed that I meant it, or that Minsa had been trying to make me feel welcome in the first place. It seemed fairly clear that if I *were* to join the harem, they could anticipate a significant clash of personalities between me and Malek's first wife.

Lucky for Minsa, then, that I had absolutely no intention of ending up here. Now, I just needed to figure out how to avoid it, while still helping Fatima to get free at the same time.

For that, I needed to talk to Arthur.

~Eric~

I knew I had blown our chances with Malek as soon as the words were out of my mouth: "What do you want for her?"

His lips quirked into a self-satisfied smile that made my stomach sink and my blood boil. Obviously, he liked having the power to deny what we wanted, and I could imagine he behaved the same way with the women in the harem too. He got off on the power imbalance, as his earlier comment had already made crystal clear when he talked about it being 'better' when his partner wasn't willing.

Sure, I had slept with plenty of women, probably quite a lot more than he had if the size of his harem provided an accurate reckoning, but all of them came to my bed willingly and left satisfied. We both knew what we were giving and getting. The idea of forcing a woman was repugnant to me, especially coming from a man who could have his pick of women who would happily submit to him in exchange for the security he could offer them.

Instead, he seemed to take pleasure in trying to bend to his will those who would resist him, whether that applied to me in this negotiation or to the women in his harem. Women like Zara and, I suspected, Fatima too. From the conversation she'd had with Zara, it seemed pretty clear she disliked being here, and the man in front of me had to be the reason why.

By making it clear to him that I wanted Fatima's freedom, I had only made our path more difficult.

When he left, I told Arthur that we were going to need Zara's help, and we left our men there to continue to flesh out the trade agreement while the two of us returned to the royal family's private quarters.

"What are you thinking?" he asked me as we walked the seemingly empty corridors.

I simply shook my head at him. "Not here." Even within my own castle, the walls sometimes had ears, and I suspected the emperor's palace had even more than normal.

When we returned to Zara's home, we couldn't find her or her father. Adil had gone to work while Zara, we were told, had gone to visit the harem.

"Why?" Arthur asked the servant who translated for us. He didn't like the sound of that at all, his face gone ashen.

"Because the women invited her," was the unhelpful reply, and in the face of it, we could do nothing but withdraw to Arthur's room to wait for her return. The night before, I had spoken in here freely, but this time, I checked the walls carefully, looking for any open spaces where sound might carry.

"You're looking a little paranoid," my princely counterpart pointed out, though I knew his emotions ran just as high as mine did. He just did a better job of hiding it.

"We have to make sure we can't be overheard." What I had in mind could get us in a lot of trouble.

At last, a knock sounded at the door and Zara entered, her purple dress dusting the ground at her feet. "Did you have any luck with Malek?" she asked before the door had even closed behind her, and I ushered her further into the room before answering, making sure we were secure.

"No. He's sticking to his decision from earlier: he'll only release Fatima if you take her place."

Zara grimaced in distaste. "That will never happen."

"So then…" I began.

"In which case…" she said at the same time.

We both completed the sentence together: "We need a different plan."

At least we were on the same page, and we shared a small smile of understanding. Arthur, however, remained more cautious.

"What options are there? We can't just go in and take her." I raised my eyebrows in disagreement, and Arthur groaned. "Be serious, Eric. We have a handful of men and no weapons between us. We'd have to make it through a half-dozen gated checkpoints between here and the harbour. It's not possible."

When my expression didn't change, he appealed to Zara instead.

"Zara, has anyone ever escaped from the harem before?"

She shook her head slowly before answering. "No."

Arthur gave me a pointed look, but Zara hadn't finished yet.

"However, there's a first time for everything."

That was more like it. "So, you have a plan?" I asked her eagerly, but she quickly tempered my enthusiasm.

"Not yet, but I agree with you that there might be no other choice. It would have to be very carefully done, in a way that doesn't draw any suspicion to the two of you."

"How would that be possible?" Arthur asked incredulously. "Malek knows we're interested in her, Eric basically just offered him anything he wanted in exchange for her freedom."

Zara shot me a disapproving look, which, I had to admit, I deserved, and I owned up to it. "I made a mistake, but if I understand you correctly, you're suggesting we get her out of the palace while we're still here, so they can search us and our ship and not find any trace of her?"

Zara's look of annoyance slowly turned to a more pleased one as I demonstrated I understood the gist of her plan. "Precisely. You will need strong alibis for the time of her escape and nothing to tie you to her disappearance in any way."

"But how will she get out?" Arthur wondered, and here, Zara had to shrug.

"I'm not sure yet. We'll need a better understanding of exactly what the obstacles are, and I thought perhaps I could ask for us all to be taken on a full tour of the palace. You are, after all, my father's honoured guests."

"Would he be willing to help us?" Arthur asked hopefully, but when Zara hesitated, it didn't surprise me.

"I'm not sure, and I think it would be better not to risk telling him. If any word of it got back to the emperor…"

She didn't need to say it. We all knew what the consequences would be, not just for Adil, but for all of us. What we were talking about amounted to theft, if not treason.

"Fatima might know people who would be willing to help," Zara continued instead. "I spoke to one of the harem guards briefly and he seemed reasonable. If he or any of the other eunuchs also wanted freedom…"

Once again, I understood her perfectly. "I could provide well-paid positions within the Silatrian court for anyone who wanted a new life. They would be taken care of."

Arthur looked between the two of us as if we had completely lost our minds. "And if all of this worked somehow without blowing up in our faces spectacularly, how are we supposed to take Fatima away? Surely our ship will be watched if they suspect us at all."

"She would have to be taken out of the city, somewhere that you could pick her up after leaving. Perhaps a fishing village up north."

That seemed to mean something in particular, but I wasn't going to get weighed down in specific details right now anyway. A sense of purpose flowed through my veins and I couldn't wait to get started. "When can you speak to her again?"

"I will try this evening," Zara suggested. "We need to find out if she even wants to try. After all, if she is caught, she will be punished."

That thought cooled some of the fervour inside me, but only part way. "She'll be willing to try." I couldn't say why I felt so certain of that, but I did.

"I will find out," Zara promised. "And I will see about getting you a tour of the palace. Now that your trade talks are completed, there won't be a need for you to stick around much longer. We can't waste any time."

I didn't intend to. The sooner we could come up with an actionable plan, the better, and I would be more than happy to put the Munisian court behind me for good.

CHAPTER SEVEN

~Fatima~

Khalid did his best to cheer me up as the afternoon went on, but inside, I felt numb. As I looked around the room, I could see the endless days to come, each one just like the one before: the inane gossip of the other women followed by quiet nights alone in my small room or nights spent lying beneath Malek's clammy body as he used me for his own gratification.

Occasionally, that routine would be broken up by pregnancy and giving birth, but then my child would disappear and things would go right back to the way they had been.

Nothing would ever change. Life would go on like this forever, or at least until I got old enough that Malek no longer desired me. Then, I would be given an allowance to go and live in the countryside with all the other retired concubines, with no prospect of love or family of my own.

I would live my whole life and die here, and I hadn't even realized until now just how deeply I held the hope that it wouldn't come to that. Only now, when that hope had been extinguished once and for all, did I understand how much I had been relying on the chance that my fate might still be changed.

"You need to eat something," Khalid urged me as the others all took their dinner but I didn't move from my spot against the wall. "Starving yourself won't help."

Wouldn't it? Maybe it would be better to put an end to everything. At long last, I could understand what drove my mother to run that sword through her body. In my youth and inexperience, I thought anything would be better than death. Now, I felt a lot less certain.

"The princess seemed nice," Khalid continued, ignoring the fact that I hadn't responded at all. "I'm sure if there's a way to help you, she will."

Zara had given me the same impression, but the issue lay with the first part of what he said: *if* she could help, and as far as I saw it, she couldn't. Unless she gave up her own freedom, her hands were tied, and I wouldn't ask that of anyone who clearly hated the idea as much as I did.

When I still remained in place, he went and got me some food on his own, sitting next to me to make sure I ate it, despite the disapproving looks Minsa threw in our direction. The food all tasted the same to me, each bite tasteless and bland, but I ate it anyway simply so that he would stop hounding me about it.

I had almost finished when another knock sounded at the door, and Khalid reluctantly got up. "Keep going," he instructed as he moved towards the door to answer it. The harem certainly had more than its usual share of visitors today.

Whoever stood on the other side didn't come in, but they left a message with Khalid, who relayed it to Minsa. Lost in my own apathy, I missed what he said, but I heard Minsa's offended reply. "She can't dictate the comings and goings of this harem and its members."

Khalid's response was murmured and respectful. "She is simply asking your permission, Your Highness, as is proper."

That did little to mollify Minsa, but with a huff, she conceded anyway. "Make sure it is quick. Malek will not be pleased if he wants her and she is not here."

I didn't realize they were talking about me until Khalid came to stand in front of me. "Princess Zara has asked to speak with you."

Again? What could she possibly have to say to me now? If she intended to offer condolences or an apology, I didn't particularly want it. Even so, as a request from a princess, and since Minsa had already approved it, I had little choice. Just like everything else in my life, I simply had to do what others wanted me to.

Khalid accompanied me out of the room and back to the courtyard where Zara and I had spoken earlier today, though it seemed like a lifetime ago already. She sat next to the pool, away from the columns this time. It seemed her mystery friend hadn't accompanied her this time, though I still had no idea who he might be or why he had come along the first time.

While Khalid kept a respectful distance, I took a seat next to Zara, our images reflecting in the pool below us: one darker and richly dressed and the other lighter in the traditional dress of the harem. Despite our differences, we still had quite a lot in common as two princesses whose lives had not worked out as we expected, and as the wind danced across the water's surface, the images mixed and mingled.

"You have heard about what Malek said to me when I asked about your freedom?" she began with no introduction, speaking in the same language we had conversed in earlier this morning. Khalid did not understand it, and neither would most people passing by. She had obviously chosen to use it for that reason, and even with that precaution, she kept her voice low and quiet.

"I have," I agreed dully.

A sympathetic smile flashed across Zara's face. "And you know that I have no wish to join the harem."

"I assumed as much, Your Highness. I can't say that I blame you."

Again, Zara's smile seemed empathetic and kind. "Well, that answers my first question. I wanted to double check if it really meant that much to you to leave, and it seems it does. Now, I just need to know how badly you want it."

For the first time since I left Malek's room this afternoon, the weight in my stomach eased ever-so-slightly, and I blinked at her in surprise. "What do you mean, Your Highness?"

Zara waved her hand, pushing the title away. "Please, just call me Zara, and I will call you Fatima, if that's okay?"

"That's fine," I replied, but she still hadn't answered my question. "I thought Malek said that he will only release me if you take my place."

"He gave that condition, but I am talking about something else, something which doesn't rely on Malek's mercy."

She kept her words guarded as she sounded me out, trying to determine my level of commitment without incriminating herself too much, but I had no interest in beating around the bush. "Please, Zara, speak plainly. What are you suggesting?"

Seeming to appreciate my candour, she returned it with her own. "I'm talking about breaking you out."

It sounded that way to me, but I didn't understand. "How is that possible?"

"I don't have all the answers yet," Zara warned me. "And I will need your help to find them. But I have others who are willing to help too, men with the means to get you safely away, far from Munisia itself, so long as we can get you out of the palace. I need to be clear with you about the dangers, though: if you are caught, it could mean imprisonment or even death. Malek will not take it well."

She didn't need to tell me that, nor did I fear death after all my thoughts on the subject earlier. If even a chance of freedom remained, I had to take it. As Malek liked to say, fortune favoured the brave.

"Who are these men?" I asked curiously. Not only *my* life would be in danger if we were discovered, but so would the life of anyone who dared to help me. Why would strangers put themselves on the line that way?

"They are foreign princes," Zara explained, lowering her voice even further so I had to lean forward to hear her. "One from Lassaria and one from Silatria."

Silatria? A memory hit me so strongly and completely unexpectedly that for a moment the courtyard around me completely disappeared. In my mind, I could see the throne room of the Silatrian castle as my father spoke to the king. A large fire burned in the fireplace, warming my skin, and I could smell the citrus of the small orange tree we had brought as a gift for the royal family. Everyone around us spoke in the language I had just learned specifically for that visit.

The trip had been one of the few times I ever travelled outside Actilia, our whole family travelling together, and on the journey, I overheard my parents talking about laying the foundation for a marriage between me and the Silatrian crown prince. That explained why they brought me along, so he could see me for himself, though I couldn't have been more than eight years old at the time.

They didn't know I'd heard them talking, but when we met the royal family, I peered at the crown prince curiously, trying to imagine what it would be like to be married to him. He was a teenager, almost a young man already, handsome but serious-looking. He bowed to me politely when we were introduced, but said nothing else. His younger brother, on the other hand, seemed far more light-hearted. He impersonated his princely brother behind his back, making me giggle, and when he realized I appreciated it, he did more impressions of both my father and his, until my mother had to admonish me to stop laughing and behave like a proper princess. With a flushed face, she apologized to the king on my behalf.

I had not thought about that visit in many, many years. It belonged to a part of my life that had died a long time ago, but the idea that one of those princes might be here now and wanted to help me brought me to sudden tears, as though the world hadn't completely forgotten about me after all.

Maybe my story didn't need to end here. With a new fire in my heart, I nodded at Zara eagerly. "I am willing to take the risk. Tell me exactly what you want me to do."

~Arthur~

Once we had finished eating dinner, Zara excused herself from our company. She told her father she would be going for a walk in the gardens, but Eric and I knew that she actually intended to go and speak to Fatima again. I pointed out that it might look suspicious if she kept speaking to her before she suddenly disappeared, assuming this plan could work at all, but Zara assured me she had considered that. She promised she would squeeze as much information as she could into this meeting to limit the number of subsequent meetings required before making some kind of attempt.

She also promised she would come and speak to me privately tonight to tell me how things had gone. It annoyed Eric not to be included in that meeting, but once again, we had to consider how things would look. If the three of us were seen whispering together all the time, someone might notice. Instead, Eric had been tasked with keeping Zara's father company while I retired early, and then Zara could sneak into my room with no one knowing. Whatever she shared with me, I could tell Eric in the morning.

I couldn't wait to finally speak to Zara alone again, but what we had to talk about weighed heavily on my heart. In helping Fatima, she would be taking an enormous risk, and she still hadn't said a word about leaving with us herself. I needed to know how she felt after all the events and revelations of the day, but it scared me too, worrying that she had made up her mind to stay here.

I had no idea what she was thinking at all, and I didn't like it. I wanted us back on the same page as we had been for so much of the last month. I wanted her to choose life with me over the future she could see here, now that she had seen for herself that her family was safe.

It terrified me that on that last point, we might not be on the same page at all.

Adil invited Eric and me to his study while the women occupied themselves after dinner, and we spoke about the trade terms that we had negotiated with Malek that afternoon, and about Adil's travels, including his memories of Lassaria. His gratitude towards and respect for my father felt sincere, and I appreciated his actions too. Hopefully, the consideration my father had shown Adil would ease the path for what I intended to ask Adil before we left, so long as Zara herself agreed.

After an hour, I claimed that my head had begun to ache from the unaccustomed heat, which made Adil chuckle. "It is very different from your Lassaria," he agreed. "Have a cool drink before bed, that will help you to sleep."

Thanking him for his consideration, I bid him goodnight, exchanging a nod of understanding with Eric as I did. Eric would keep Adil occupied as long as he could so that no one would question Zara's whereabouts when she returned.

Only a few minutes after I returned to my room, a gentle knock sounded on my door and Zara swept in, still wearing the stunning purple dress I had been admiring on her all day. She looked every inch a princess, regal and beautiful. All things considered, I couldn't blame Malek for wanting her, even if he went about trying to claim her in a completely despicable way.

We both knew what this meeting was for and what we were meant to be talking about, but as soon as I saw her, I couldn't resist. My arms were around her and my lips against hers before I even fully realized what I meant to do, and to my great relief, she returned my embrace with equal desire and fervour.

"I've missed you so much." The words were murmured against her mouth since I didn't want to take my lips away for even a second.

I thought she might tease me and tell me that we had seen each other regularly since we arrived here, which might be true but was not the point. However, she knew exactly what I meant and she must have felt it too, for her hand went to the front of my breeches, pressing against my cock that had already begun to swell for her.

Her whisper, when she spoke, sounded just as full of need and desperation as I felt. "I want to be with you, Arthur. I want to make love to you. Properly. Completely."

Blood rushed to my groin even faster as her words sank in. Of course the idea of taking that step with her appealed to me, but the reasons we hadn't done it before still remained. "What if you get pregnant?"

"There are a million 'what if's," she shot back, making me groan as her hand stroked my entire length through the fabric of my clothing. "What if we fail in our plan and are imprisoned? What if Malek insists on claiming me even if I refuse him? What if the ship sinks on the return voyage to Lassaria? What if we never get another chance?"

The last possibility frightened me most of all, weakening my already lowered resistance as she continued to caress me. "I want to be with you too, Zara. If you're certain, then yes. That's what I want."

She smiled as she squeezed my stiff cock, making me groan once more. "We'll need to remain as clothed as possible, in case anyone comes looking for either of us."

There would be no time for exploring each other as we had done on the ship, our hands exploring every inch of each other. Instead, she unlaced my breeches, pulling me forward with the laces until her back hit the wall, and raising her skirt. Her skin lay completely bare beneath it, the warm air here making any kind of undergarments unnecessary.

"Right here?" I glanced over at the bed, thinking she would be more comfortable there, but Zara nodded.

"If someone comes in, we can make up an excuse. On the bed, it would be more difficult to explain."

She had really put some thought into this, or perhaps, she had simply been in this situation before. Either could be possible, and right now, I didn't really care. All that mattered was that she wanted me and I wanted her, and we had this moment to make each other happy, no matter what awaited us later on.

Hooking her leg around my waist, Zara guided my cock to her warm, wet entrance. My fingers and my tongue had been inside her before, but never my cock, and it pulsed with anticipation, every part of my body hot and ready.

"Fill me, Arthur." Her words were both an instruction and a plea, urging me not to stop. "I need you inside me. I want to feel all of you."

I wanted that too, more than anything. The connection between us had already been sealed in every other conceivable way; only this remained and then she would truly be my first.

My eyes locked on her dark ones, I leaned forward, pressing my hips towards her and driving my cock deep inside her.

"Oh, God." It felt even better than I could have imagined. Being in her mouth had been spectacular enough, but this felt even better. She fit me like a glove, her body warm and welcoming, wet enough that I could glide in but still providing enough friction that I could feel her on every inch of me.

I couldn't imagine what it felt like for her, but her eyes closed as I pushed in as far as I could go, her lips parting as she exhaled. "Arthur."

Though she gave me no further instruction, somehow, with my name on her breath, I knew what to do anyway. With each thrust of my hips, my confidence grew and so did my speed, driven on by the need inside me and the eager way Zara bucked back against me, letting me know she found fulfillment in it too.

"You're incredible. You feel incredible," I whispered to her in awe, watching her face as my body shoved hers back against the wall, over and over again. Her hands never stood still, gripping my hair, curling around my neck and smoothing over my shoulders. I kept one hand on the wall behind her to steady myself and the other hooked around her leg that rested on my hip, holding her in place. When it felt that she might be getting close to her release, I let her leg go and moved my hand to the sensitive skin just above where we were joined, and she immediately began to tremble.

"Yes," she moaned, biting her lip to try to keep from crying out too loudly. "Just like that, Arthur, yes!"

Her eyes closed as the pleasure took hold of her, and as soon as I felt her contracting around me, my body jolted too. Collapsing against the wall and her, I emptied myself deep inside her, both of us shuddering with gratification and deep satisfaction. The pleasure overwhelmed me, and so did the knowledge that she had given it to me willingly and enthusiastically. She had wanted it just as much as I had, and she had taken just as much enjoyment from it.

My breath came out short and heavy as I pushed myself back up, worried I might be crushing her, but her smile told me she felt no pain. "I didn't come in here for that," she said with a laugh, pushing me gently back so that my cock slid out of her and she could lower her skirt again. "But I have no complaints."

I certainly had none either. "I love you, Zara."

Those words hadn't been said between us yet, and I hadn't planned to say them now. I didn't want her to think I had only said it because of what had just happened between us, but at that moment, there were no other words I could think of to adequately sum up the way she made me feel. I loved her, and she deserved to know it.

"You are too good to be true," she murmured back, her eyes soft with affection as she tucked my cock back into my breeches and tied them back up again. "Let's get back on track, shall we? I still need to tell you about my conversation with Fatima."

Indeed. That was why she'd come here in the first place. I swallowed down my disappointment that she hadn't said anything about loving me in return, and invited her to take a seat instead. "What did you find out?"

~Zara~

I truly hadn't set out to seduce Arthur that evening. As I made my way to his room, my thoughts were focused on Fatima and everything that needed to be done to make her escape possible, but as soon as I arrived and he held me with such need and desperation, I made up my mind. I wanted him, right there and then, consequences be damned. Even if I became pregnant, even if my father or mother or Malek himself should walk in on us, I didn't want to face our uncertain future knowing that I had the chance to show the man I loved just how much I wanted him and didn't take it.

I loved him. What we had went beyond lust and far further than friendship. Though I couldn't say for sure when I knew it for certain, I felt it with every fibre of my being. Had it been his principled, honourable reactions to everything he encountered here in the emperor's palace? Was it the sweet moments and the private conversations we'd shared on the voyage on the way here? Or did it go back even further, to the moments when he broke down my walls and truly saw me in a way no other man had ever tried to, all the way back in Lassaria?

I couldn't be sure, but the fact remained that I loved him, and the frantic, intense intimate moments we had just shared had only made that feeling grow stronger. His lovemaking had been so hesitant yet determined, enjoying every sensation but always aware of my needs too, making sure I enjoyed myself. He didn't need anyone to teach him how to do it. It came entirely naturally, his caring and loving nature guiding him in this as it did in everything else.

And yet, when he uttered the words to me, when he told me that he loved me too, those sweet blue eyes of his full of adoration and fulfillment, I couldn't bring myself to say it back to him.

No words had been spoken between us about what the revelation about my father's parentage might mean for us, but I had been thinking about it, and I would bet everything I owned that Arthur had thought about it too. As a princess, he could marry me if he wanted to. There would still be obstacles, of course, his mother and the prejudices of his people chief among them, and we would require the approval of my family and my emperor too, but it would be possible. A chance existed, a very real one, that the future I'd dismissed as a fantasy could actually come true.

And if I said those words out loud right now, if I told him that I loved him too, which I absolutely did, that possibility would suddenly become a lot more real. It could easily sweep us away, making everything else seem insignificant, and before I lost myself in it, I still had to take care of Fatima. I couldn't embrace any potential happiness for myself until I knew that she wouldn't suffer any further for something that had always been completely out of her control.

So, when Arthur said he loved me, I simply told him how sweet he was, and then I moved on to the real reason I had come to see him in the first place: to tell him what Fatima and I had spoken about.

"Fatima wants to leave. She's willing to do whatever is necessary and she understands it may endanger her life. She asked me to make sure that everyone else involved understood that as well and to tell them that she understands if they aren't able to make such a sacrifice; she doesn't want anyone to have to suffer on her behalf."

Those comments were what confirmed to me that I would do anything necessary to help her succeed. Despite her desperate situation, she still thought of others besides herself, which confirmed to me that she deserved our help.

"And does she have any ideas or resources that might help with that?" Arthur didn't have Eric's enthusiasm for this whole endeavour, but I understood the reason why. Although Arthur hated Fatima's situation as much as the rest of us did, he had grave concerns about my safety and security and what could happen to me if we were discovered. I was afraid of that too, since it would be stupid not to be, but I had learned a long time ago that there were times when you needed to take the chance if you wanted the reward.

"She does, actually. I mentioned the possibility of enlisting the help of some of the eunuchs in exchange for their freedom as well and she thought she could count on at least one of them. She knows the routines of the women in the harem and there are times of day she can often slip away for a little peace and quiet. If she were to disappear at one of those times, it might be hours before anyone will notice she's missing."

Arthur nodded thoughtfully. "And what about actually getting out of the palace? How will she get past the gates?"

That would be the most significant obstacle, certainly. Each person going in or out of each area of the palace had to stop at the checkpoints, and there were four of them between the harem and the palace exit. Slipping through one unnoticed would be risky enough; we couldn't rely on it working four times. We were going to have to be more creative than that.

Luckily, I had an idea that I thought might work: "She will pretend to be me."

Arthur clearly hadn't expected that, his brow lining in confusion as he tried to understand. "But people will know she isn't you."

"Will they? Who has seen me since we arrived? Those men from the port, the clerk in my father's office, the people in the emperor's hall, and the women in the harem. None of those people will be manning the gates. The men working there have only heard that the chief minister's daughter has returned, but they have no idea what she looks like."

Arthur still looked unconvinced. "What about the men at the gates when we arrived? They saw you."

True, but it had only been for a matter of seconds and I wouldn't expect them to remember me. Besides, he had forgotten one important fact. "They didn't know who I was then. They were focused on you and Eric, while I blended into the background with your other men. Besides, Fatima can cover her head and wear my clothes. She can't leave wearing the costume of the harem anyway."

That would definitely attract unwanted attention.

"And the men will just allow her to walk out if they think she's you?" Arthur's question contained both curiosity and a hint of disbelief.

"I am not currently bound here in any way," I pointed out. "A woman should not leave the palace unattended, but Fatima won't be alone. She'll have at least one of the men from the harem with her, and an excuse about where she is going. There's a market that takes place in the city that she could claim to be visiting."

Arthur's lips pursed again. "But won't they recognize the eunuch?"

"Perhaps," I had to admit. "But we can come up with a good reason why he would be accompanying 'me'. If we do it at a time when my father, the emperor and Malek are all occupied, the men at the gates won't dare to interrupt them over something as insignificant as a woman going shopping."

That made him smile, just for a second. "It could still go wrong," he argued, and I couldn't disagree with that. Things could always go wrong, but if we never took that chance, we wouldn't get the things we truly wanted either.

I kept my counter-argument simple: "And it could go right. Fatima is willing to take that risk."

I held his gaze as firmly and as confidently as I could, trying to pass some of my own resolution on to him. I truly believed this plan was sound, and his support for it would mean a great deal to me.

At last, Arthur sighed. "You know the way things work here better than I do. If this is what you want to do, and you're sure it won't cast any suspicion on you, I'll help in any way I can."

I felt certain we could keep the risk to a minimal level. "I can't be blamed simply because Fatima pretended to be me. We'll make sure that you and Eric and I are all accounted for at the time of the escape. Fatima can be taken out of the city to a predetermined spot where you can pick her up on your way home. It could work, Arthur. I truly believe it could."

"If you believe in the plan, then I believe in you. You're clever, and courageous, and beautiful. A perfect princess." He took a step towards me, looking for all the world like he was ready to take me up against the wall again, but before he got a chance, a knock rang out, startling us both.

"Your Highness?" My father's voice drifted through the closed door. "I'm sorry to disturb you, but I'm looking for Zara. Have you seen her?"

CHAPTER EIGHT

Although I did my best to keep Adil occupied, eventually, he glanced at the darkening sky outside his window and noticed how much time had passed. He mumbled something beneath his breath in his own language, most of which I couldn't understand, but I did distinctly hear the name Zara, and he got to his feet before I could protest. "Please excuse me, Your Highness."

I couldn't blame the man; after all, he'd only just got his daughter back. Naturally, he would be concerned about her safety, but since I knew that she would be meeting with Arthur to share the details of her conversation with Fatima, I didn't want Adil to interrupt them before they'd finished.

"Wait," I called out, standing up and hurrying after him. "Zara said she would visit the gardens. I'm interested in seeing your native plants anyway, so perhaps we could go take a look now? We'll likely find her there."

"Another time, Your Highness. It's nearly dark and she should be back by now."

Adil checked the room where Zara's mother and sisters were gathered but they all shook their heads when, I assumed, he asked them if they'd seen her. Her own room looked empty, the door standing open, and one of the servants, when questioned, pointed Adil to Arthur's room as I followed behind uselessly.

She must still be in there, but I couldn't do anything to stop him now. Would Adil be suspicious about them speaking in private and what they might be discussing? Or would he simply assume they were doing what men and women usually did when they were alone? That might be preferable at this point to him discovering the truth.

Adil knocked sharply on the door, calling out to identify himself to Arthur and explain what he wanted, and a moment later, Zara herself answered the door.

"I'm here, Baba. I saw something in the garden that reminded me of Lassaria and I came to tell Prince Arthur about it. I didn't realize you were looking for me."

Not a stupid man, Adil looked suspiciously between his daughter and the Lassarian prince. They were both fully clothed, but unless I was much mistaken, Arthur's breeches were tied looser than before. Perhaps they *had* been fooling around with each other, which normally wouldn't bother me except that they were supposed to be focused on helping Fatima. I hoped they hadn't completely lost track of that fact.

Whether Adil noticed the same thing or not, I couldn't be sure, but he still looked unhappy with the situation. "I understand that customs are different abroad, but you cannot be in a room alone with a man, Zara. Now that you are home, you must consider your reputation."

She raised her eyebrows in amusement. "I have already told the emperor himself that I am no virgin, Baba. What reputation do I have left to protect? Besides, the prince and I were simply talking."

Arthur's guilty reaction completely undermined her words, his eyes falling to the floor as he cleared his throat. Hopefully, we wouldn't need to rely on his deception skills to secure Fatima's release or she would have no chance at all.

Zara's reasoning did not satisfy Adil anyway. "Still, the servants knew you were in here, and if Malek heard of it..."

"Malek has no claim on me," Zara told her father firmly, cutting him off. "He has made me an offer, that is all. An offer that I have no intention of accepting."

Adil's gaze moved warily between his daughter, Arthur and me. "Come to my study and we can discuss it further there. This doesn't concern the princes. Have a good night, Your Highnesses."

Zara's lips pursed but she made no further argument, following her father from the room, leaving me and Arthur alone. I quickly stepped inside and closed the door behind me. "Well? What did she find out?"

"You were supposed to keep her father occupied," Arthur grumbled, taking a seat as I followed suit.

"I did. Long enough for you to get your prick out, clearly, but did you actually find out anything useful?"

A bright flush crept up Arthur's cheeks. "I don't know what you're talking about."

"You're a terrible liar," I told him bluntly. "Fortunately for you, unlike Zara's father, I couldn't care less what went on between you in here. That's entirely your business. All I want to know is what happened with Fatima. Please, Arthur. Tell me what you know."

My voice broke slightly on the 'please', the strain of the day and my worry for Fatima getting to me, and Arthur's expression melted into one of sympathy. He didn't understand why it meant so much to me that we help her, and I couldn't explain it either. It simply did, and at least he appreciated that.

He got down to business, telling me everything he and Zara had discussed. The plan sounded good to me as I turned it over in my head, trying to examine it from all angles. Whether Zara or Fatima had come up with it, the reliance on the guard's assumption that a woman couldn't be up to anything too devious was a clever twist.

"So, we're supposed to make sure we've got an alibi for the time?" I confirmed, and Arthur nodded.

"I think it would be best if we were actually with Malek. If we claimed to be anywhere else, he might doubt it, but he wouldn't be able to refute what he saw with his own eyes."

That made sense to me, even if the idea of spending more time in the Munisian prince's presence couldn't be less appealing. "Zara as well?"

Arthur's grimace told me he didn't want Zara anywhere near Malek, and once again, I couldn't blame him. "No. On the off-chance the guards do report to Malek that 'Zara' is leaving the palace, if she is sitting there with him, Fatima would be immediately compromised."

I hadn't thought of that, but he had a point. Zara needed to be out of sight, yet also have an alibi so no one suspected she had helped Fatima. "Where will she go, then?"

Arthur's face contorted once more. "The harem. Dozens of people will see her there, but she will still be out of the public eye."

I nodded in agreement, seeing the logic of it. "When is this taking place? We don't have much time."

"I know, Eric," he assured me. "It will have to be tomorrow. Hopefully, Fatima gets away and they can search our ship and clear us to leave the following day, as planned. I think it's safe to say that if they realize after we're gone that we had anything to do with this, our trade deal won't be worth the paper it's written on."

That thought had already crossed my mind too, but at this point, I really didn't care. "Forget the trade deal. Right now, I care a lot more about getting us all out of here safely."

Arthur winced, and my eyes darted back towards the door, remembering the other woman involved in all this, the one whom Arthur had clearly fallen in love with.

"What about Zara? Will she stay, or will she return with us?" I had a hard time imagining the headstrong woman I'd come to know being content in the restricted life we'd glimpsed within the palace walls. Even if she didn't agree to join the harem, her options seemed limited.

"I don't know yet," Arthur admitted. "I hoped to have a chance to speak to her about this evening, until her father interrupted."

"Well, if there's anything I can do to help, say so. You are putting yourself on the line for me here, both of you, and I appreciate it. I will return the favour if I can."

"Thanks, Eric." Arthur gave me a smile of camaraderie and perhaps even friendship. In our desire to help both Fatima and Zara, we had discovered a common ground that hadn't been there before. "This trip hasn't turned out at all the way I anticipated."

"You and me both." Returning his smile, I got to my feet. "I'll go to my room now, and in the morning, we can decide under what pretext we'll meet with Malek again."

With Arthur's agreement ringing in my ears, I returned to my room alone, hopeful for what the day ahead might bring. Things might yet go wrong, but now, at least we had a chance that we might succeed.

~Fatima~

Everything Zara and I had spoken about still swum around my head as I returned to the harem. First things first, I needed to speak to Khalid, but that would be easier said than done. Although people were used to the sight of us talking to each other, we always spoke in public, in front of the other members of the harem. Generally, no one paid us any attention but they easily could, and this time, the things I needed to discuss with him were far too sensitive to risk being overheard. Even if it seemed like no one listened to us, the risk of even a stray word reaching the wrong ears was too great.

We would have to speak in private, but that carried its own risks. The eunuchs were not allowed to be alone with the members of the harem unless they were accompanying us from one place to another. Even though, thanks to their mutilation, they could not receive sexual pleasure the usual way, the possibility still existed of them touching the concubines and bringing satisfaction to the women. Of course, in the eyes of the Munisian rulers, that would be a terrible crime, in the same way the women were not permitted to be alone together for fear they would find pleasure in each other.

The women of the harem existed solely for Malek's use, and nothing more.

The punishment if Khalid and I were caught alone together would be accordingly severe. If Khalid wanted to refuse, I wouldn't blame him, and that was before he even knew the full extent of what I wanted to propose.

"Can you come to my room when everyone is asleep?" I murmured to him as we made our way back through the corridors to the harem's main hall. "There is something I need to talk to you about."

Khalid gave a small huff, his eyes straight ahead rather than on me. "I am glad to see the light back in your eyes, but I have a feeling it means trouble."

"Almost certainly." I had no intention of lying to him, not after our years of friendship and not when we needed to have total trust in each other if he agreed to what I intended to propose. "I'll understand if you say no, Khalid. You must consider your own safety."

He huffed louder, nervously but intrigued, torn between curiosity and fear. "I can't make any promises on when it will be, but if the opportunity arises, I will come."

"I will wait."

Malek chose one of the other concubines for the night, apparently having had his fill of me earlier that afternoon, so after helping Sade prepare for bed, I returned to my own room to await Khalid's visit. The women all wore soft shoes and the eunuchs went barefoot, so there were no footsteps to warn of anyone's approach. Hours passed in silence, but I had no trouble staying awake, my thoughts continuing to race, until finally, my door was quietly pushed open.

"Fatima?"

Khalid couldn't see me in the darkness, so I quickly whispered back, "I'm here," and just as quickly, he came the rest of the way in, closing the door behind him.

"I told the others my stomach felt unsettled. I should have a few minutes before anyone gets suspicious."

In that case, we couldn't waste any time. My eyes were better adjusted to the darkness than his were, so I went to the door and took his hand, bringing him to sit on my bed so we could whisper quietly, close together as I turned to face him.

"What I am going to tell you is in the strictest confidence, Khalid. You can refuse to have anything to do with it, but you must not tell anyone what I share with you. Can you agree to that?"

I didn't really have any doubt that he would agree; if I did, I wouldn't have involved him in the first place, and thankfully, he didn't let me down. "Of course. What is it?"

Speaking the words aloud gave me a bit of a thrill. "Zara wants to help me to escape."

As succinctly as I could, I filled him in on the conversation I had with the princess and the tentative plan we'd come up with. We both knew time was of the essence; the longer we waited, the more things could go wrong. The element of surprise would be vital.

Finally, I got to the point, at least so far as it concerned Khalid. "Even posing as Zara, I won't be able to leave the palace on my own. I need someone to accompany me and it would be safer for that person not to return. I know that it's no small favour I am asking, but..."

"I'll do it." Khalid's firm, assured words cut me off mid-sentence.

"You don't need to answer right now," I tried to tell him. "Take the night to think about it. It would mean completely changing your life. Zara says you would be given a new position and provided for, but the language, the culture, the food, the people, everything would be completely different to what you have known. I know what a shock I had coming here from Actilia."

"I don't need to think about it," he promised. "You are the closest thing I have to family since coming here, and if there is a chance for you to be free, I will help you however I can."

"But one of the other men could go instead..."

Again, he didn't let me finish. "I don't want to stay here without you. You are the only one who treats me like an actual person, Fatima, and not just a body to carry out whatever tasks they need done. I'd rather take my chances with you. And before you say it, I know what the penalty would be if I am caught."

I couldn't help shuddering at the thought. The Munisians were creative when it came to torture, and a eunuch who betrayed his master's trust would be subjected to the worst of it to set an example for the others.

"That is why we will make sure we are not caught," he promised. "I know how to blend into a crowd, and I know exactly where we could go to meet the ship. Stop arguing with me. You want me to come or you wouldn't be telling me all this."

As usual, he knew how to make me smile. "You're right. Of course I want you to come; I just want to make sure you know the risks. Even if you choose not to, I will always be grateful for the friendship and support you've given me here."

"There's no need for those words," he admonished. "We will have plenty of time to reminisce on our time here later. Now, let's make a plan. I am allowed one day a month to go and visit my family, but I rarely use it. I can claim some special occasion that I had forgotten, and that I need to go for a few hours. No one should question my absence until the late evening."

That should work perfectly. My own disappearance would be noticed sooner than that, but so long as it happened after we were out of the palace, the precise timing made no difference.

"Zara will send me a coded message in the morning once she has confirmed the best time. I will need to reply to her with where they can find me. If I don't hear from her, then we make no move. She will leave clothes for me in the courtyard where we met today so I can change before we leave."

"She is taking a risk as well in helping you," Khalid pointed out. "As are the princes."

He had that exactly right. I could hardly believe so many people were willing to help me with such a fraught endeavour, but I appreciated it more than I could ever say. Hopefully, I would have a chance to convey that gratitude properly once we were all safe.

Taking a look around my dark, tiny room, almost like a cell, I gave my friend one last chance to back out. "This may be the last night we ever spend here, Khalid. If we are caught, it may be the last night of our lives. Are you completely sure about this?"

His hand found mine once again in the darkness. "There is life outside these walls, Fatima, a life that you have been denied for far too long. Let's go and find it."

~Zara~

My father had never been a naïve man. One of the reasons he did his job so well and had risen so far even before his royal connections were revealed was because he understood what drove people. Besides greed and lust for power, plain old lust could often be one of the main drivers, and he broached the subject as soon as we were alone together in his study.

"Whatever your relationship with the Lassarian prince has been, it needs to end now, Zara." I opened my mouth to protest, but he shook his head, cutting me off. "I don't need any denials, or any details for that matter. I have seen the way you look at him and he at you. I believe you do care for each other on top of whatever intimacy has occurred, but you need to be realistic. He will be leaving in a matter of days and you will remain here, and your reputation *does* need to be considered. It's one thing to say that men forced you into unmaidenly situations in foreign lands, it is another to go to a man's bed willingly within the emperor's own home. Malek will not like it, and whatever Malek dislikes, he finds a way to punish."

There he went talking about Malek again, as if the prince had any say in my life whatsoever. Bristling at the implication, I did my best to set the record straight. "During my time away, the men themselves never forced me. *Circumstances* forced me, in much the same way Malek is trying to force me now. Arthur, on the other hand, has never done anything of the sort. I do care for him, Baba, you're right about that, and he…"

I swallowed, buying myself some time as I tried to decide how much to share before Arthur and I had a chance to discuss the situation properly. In the end, though, I wanted my father to know I had not simply fallen victim to lust. The bond that had formed between the two of us went far deeper, and since he needed to appreciate that, I told him the truth.

"Arthur loves me. He is serious about a relationship between us, so much so that he must have spoken about me to his parents before we left Lassaria. His mother felt threatened enough to try to warn me off, and I don't believe she would have if he hadn't made his own feelings clear."

My father's brow furrowed, trying to follow my logic. "But if that is the case, why did he bring you back here?"

"He brought me because he knew how much it meant to me to know that you were safe. He would leave me here if he thought I wanted it. That is how much he loves me. However, given the choice, I believe that he would like me to return with him, and to be perfectly frank, I want that too. I am so glad that I got to come here and see you and Mama and to let you know that I am safe, but the truth is: this no longer feels like my home. I don't know exactly what Arthur's intentions are now, but I know what I feel, and I want to return with him, no matter what the situation will be upon our return."

These feelings had been building inside me over the course of the day, but I had not even fully realized them myself until I spoke them out loud. Now that I had said the words, however, they seemed obvious: I wanted to return to Lassaria with Arthur. Returning as his wife would be ideal, of course, but if that turned out to be impossible, I would take however much of himself he could give me. His mother had said I would be too proud to be his mistress, but if it came down to that or never seeing him again, I would choose his love.

What good was being a wife to a man I didn't love? What good was being a princess if I couldn't have my prince?

My father, however, shook his head almost sadly. "If that is the case, it would have been better for you not to come back at all."

I disagreed. "If I hadn't returned, you would still think I had died. I wouldn't have learned of my royal blood. That will stand me in better stead no matter what happens next. The regret of the past can be lifted, Baba. You will know that I am happy and we can write to each other. Perhaps you can even come and visit me in Lassaria someday."

"You do not know Malek as I do." Regret played across my father's face as he looked away from me. "His refusal to release the Actilian princess is only one example of his character. He believes that whatever he wants is rightfully his, and now, he wants you. You said you had no intention of accepting his offer, but the simple fact of the matter is that it is not truly an offer. He will find a way to make you accept it. I have seen him do it time and time again. Where his father has honour, Malek has none. It would be better for you to accept his offer willingly and negotiate the best deal for yourself that you can. You have already been downgraded from wife to concubine, and he won't hesitate to make your position even worse. The one thing he will not do is let you go."

Once again, my father surprised me, and not in a good way. "You think I should willingly surrender my freedom and any chance of happiness to satisfy the prince's selfish whims?"

His pursed lips made it clear he thought I had twisted his words. "I'm saying you have no real choice. There can be a good life for you in the harem, even as a concubine. You are a clever woman, Zara, you always have been. Malek could provide you with the means to study whatever you want. You would be free to correspond with other scholars, including in foreign lands. So long as Malek is kept happy, it's not a terrible life. I understand the intimacies may not be particularly pleasant, but it is such a small part of your day. You would have security and any material things that you wanted. You could still visit with your mother and sisters, and perhaps even with me if you add that as a condition of your agreement. Many women would sell their souls for such an arrangement."

He had a point and I knew that, but he had forgotten that I had grown very used to surviving without material comforts. I had lived through things most of the women in the harem could not imagine, and I did not survive them all only to step willingly into a cage of my own making.

And that didn't even take into consideration the fact that I was in love with someone else.

I tried to soften my tone as I responded, recognizing that my father was truly trying to help, in his own way. "I understand what you are saying, Baba, I honestly do. But haven't you always said that there is no force in the world greater than love? For your love of me, you brought down a kingdom. For my own love, I only need to refuse to give myself as an offering to a spoiled child masquerading as a prince. It seems simple in comparison."

"Zara!" My father glanced around the room nervously even though we were completely alone.

I would not stop there though. "If you are worried there will be repercussions for you or Mama or any of our family for me refusing, then come with me. The Lassarian king spoke highly of you, I am sure he would find you a place within his own administration. None of us are helpless, and there is nothing I can think of that Malek could threaten me with that would make me change my mind."

My father sounded far from convinced. "I hope you are right about that, and I am not worried for myself. The emperor would not let Malek punish me, so don't think that I am encouraging you this way for my own personal benefit. My concern is only for you."

"I didn't mean to suggest otherwise, Baba." I gave him a smile, trying to smooth things over. "I know you mean well."

Recognizing he had little chance of securing my agreement, my father sighed. "We'll see what tomorrow brings with the princes' trade agreement being finalized, and once they are ready to depart, we can see where things stand. In the meantime, stay out of Malek's way as best you can, and I'll do my best to distract him too."

That sounded like the best course of action, and I readily agreed. "Things should be a lot clearer by the end of the day tomorrow."

By then, we would know whether Fatima's escape had worked, and then Arthur and I could discuss the future properly. The following day would settle a great many things.

I could only hope they would be settled in our favour.

CHAPTER NINE

The next morning dawned bright and sunny once again. We hadn't seen a cloud in the sky since we arrived here, and Zara's complaints about the cold and damp in Lassaria made a lot more sense to me now. Hopefully, the other benefits of life there would outweigh her concerns about the weather when I made my proposal to her.

After thinking about it alone in my bed last night, remembering all the time we had spent together and especially the incredible moments that evening when I finally gave up my virginity, I had to believe that Zara loved me in the same way I loved her, even if she hadn't felt comfortable saying it out loud. She knew the reasons why I hadn't been with a woman before and she had never pushed me to go further than I felt ready to go. For her to ask me last night to go the rest of the way with her, it *must* mean that she felt ready to commit to me too. And if I had that right, then in my eyes, the way forward seemed perfectly clear.

As soon as this business with Fatima had been settled, I would ask Zara to be my wife.

My parents might not appreciate being cut out of the decision-making, my mother especially, but their own criteria allowed me to choose a foreign princess as my queen, and I had the benefits of the trade deal with Munisia to back it up. They would have to accept it, if only because I didn't plan on giving them any other option.

On the other side, Zara's father had promised me that anything I wanted; I had only to ask for it. Perhaps he hadn't meant to include his daughter in that equation, but I planned to ask anyway.

In the morning, Zara arranged for us to be taken on a tour of the palace as she had suggested the day before. We saw people moving in and out of the gates, being stopped by the guards for questioning but ultimately being let through, and hopefully, things would go just as smoothly for Fatima and whoever she found to accompany her. Eric, Zara and I were able to exchange a few words about the proposed escape during the tour without drawing too much attention to ourselves, enough for Eric to give his blessing to the entire endeavour. Zara promised that she would take care of letting Fatima know.

As soon as we returned to her house, Zara also sent a message to her father, telling him that Eric and I would like to share the midday meal with the emperor and Malek. The emperor often ate in public with people who were in favour, so the request wouldn't seem unusual, although Malek didn't often join him. Having him there would be key to our plan, though, so we all breathed a sigh of relief when he agreed.

Zara would visit the harem at the same time, eating with the women there while Fatima made her escape. Everything seemed to be falling into place.

When the time came for us to part ways, I wished that I could take Zara in my arms to wish her luck, but of course, that kind of public display of affection wouldn't be possible. All I could do was give her a nod of encouragement, and she did the same to me as we went to our respective meetings.

Rather than the receiving room where we had met the emperor the day before, this time, we were taken to a dining room adjacent to a large courtyard. No doors stood between the outside space and the indoor, just columns joined by arches, creating a frame for the beauty of the courtyard beyond where fruit trees grew along with flowers and a marble fountain provided fresh water that sparkled beneath the sun. I could barely tear my eyes away from the beautiful and peaceful view, but neither the emperor nor Malek seemed to notice it. I supposed that was human nature; eventually, even the sublime became routine when you were exposed to it long enough.

"I understand you have reached a deal that's acceptable to all of us," the emperor said as trays laden with food were brought out and placed down in front of him. He went through each one, picking out the things he wanted to eat before the servants brought the trays over to us.

"Prince Malek has been very helpful, Your Majesty," I replied, trying my best to butter them both up despite my dislike of the prince. "I hope it can be the beginning of a long and prosperous partnership between our three kingdoms."

The emperor nodded thoughtfully. "It is fortunate that both my chief minister and his daughter ended up in your kingdom. Other princes we've encountered are not nearly so honourable."

Once again, pride filled me at the way my father had treated Zara's father, and I could only agree that their visit to Lassaria had indeed been fortunate, though of course I meant it for a different reason. I simply felt grateful that Zara had come into my life at all.

Malek asked how we had enjoyed our tour of the palace, which meant he had been kept well-enough informed of our movements to be aware of the tour, since we hadn't said anything about it.

"Your security is impressive," Eric told him. "Recently, we had a breach at the Silatrian castle where intruders took my brother's new bride from her chamber on their wedding night. I don't imagine that could happen here."

Malek and his father exchanged amused looks. "Certainly not," the emperor huffed. "No one can get in or out of the palace without us being aware of it, and never from our personal quarters."

We had to hope they were exaggerating, especially when Malek made a rather ominous addition to the emperor's statement. "Getting in is easier. Getting back out again can be much more difficult."

Did that refer to Fatima or to Zara? Either way, I didn't like the implication.

Part-way through the meal, a servant came up behind him and whispered something to the prince in his native language. I couldn't make out many of the words, but I could have sworn I heard 'Zara'. Unless I imagined it in my paranoia, which could also be true, but when I glanced over at Eric, his lips had tightened. Had the moment come? Had Fatima made her move, and Malek just been informed of 'Zara' leaving?

The prince began to rise to his feet. "Please, excuse me, Your Highnesses."

We couldn't do that, so I quickly blurted out my prepared excuse. "Actually, there is something I still wanted to discuss with you, Your Highness. As we intend to leave tomorrow, it's rather urgent. Can you spare me a few more minutes?"

"I will return shortly," he said, pushing his chair back.

"It has to do with the Lassarian gold mines," I added, dangling my biggest carrot in front of him. "I'm sure you don't want to miss this opportunity. I can't guarantee that we will be able to wait for your return, since we have a lot to do to prepare for our departure tomorrow."

Malek's nostrils flared, making it clear he didn't appreciate being told what to do, and he glanced over at his father who gave him a short nod. Reluctantly, the prince returned to his seat. With a crook of his finger, he called one of the servants over to him and gave some instructions before returning his attention to me. "What about the gold mines, Your Highness?"

As slowly as I could without making it too obvious that I was stalling, I laid out the history of the gold mines for him, their discovery and the methods of mining used, information that was of absolutely no value or interest to him, but which he wouldn't dare to interrupt with the prospect of a sweetened deal in front of him.

His fidgeting grew stronger as I began to give an overview of the other king-doms we currently traded with, his body growing more and more tense until the servant he had sent away returned. Again, the man spoke quietly to Malek in their own language, but this time I felt certain I caught not only the words 'Zara' but 'harem' as well. Malek got to his feet once more.

"I need a moment," was all he said, not waiting long enough for me to make any further protests as he spun around and left the room.

The emperor's eyes narrowed as he watched his son leave. "My apologies, Your Highnesses. It must be a matter of importance. He means no disrespect."

I had no doubt that he had received important news. What stage things were at and what Malek might find when he got to his destination, however, I could only guess.

~Fatima~

Every inch of my body felt alive and on edge as I went through my regular morning routine. The loose clothing I wore had been designed to show off my body, letting Malek see what belonged to him, and the idea that I would never have to wear it again or have him look upon me or touch me nearly made me giddy. After washing myself, I helped the others get Sade ready and went to the main hall for breakfast. Though I wasn't hungry, my stomach feeling far too jittery with nerves to want food, I forced myself to eat anyway. It might be some time before things were settled enough to eat again, and I needed to keep my strength up.

I didn't seek Khalid out, nor did he pay any special attention to me. We both seemed to agree without discussion that it would be better for us not to be seen together too much. He kept his usual position at the door, and as the morning drew on, each noise from outside the room, the chatter of servants as they passed by or even the call of the birds, had me on edge. Was this the moment that the message from Zara would come? Or would it be the next one?

By the time the knock finally sounded, I had imagined a hundred different scenarios about why she might have had to change her mind, and I tried not to get my hopes too high until I knew for sure it had anything to do with me. Khalid opened the door and spoke to the person there before returning to the room and addressing Minsa, loud enough so that we could all hear him.

"Princess Zara would like to join you for lunch in half an hour's time. She would be glad to eat with the entire harem or with Your Highnesses privately, as you wish."

My lips pressed together in appreciation, trying not to smile. A clever move, the message showed Zara understood the rules of hospitality very well. Now that the idea of a private meal had been suggested, it would be an insult for Minsa not to offer one whether she wanted to or not. With Minsa and the others occupied and out of sight, it would be easier for me to slip away unnoticed.

Zara really had put some thought into this.

As expected, Minsa sent the offer for Zara to dine with the wives in private, and as Khalid moved back to the door, he caught my eye. I gave him the smallest of nods to let him know I still intended to go through with what we'd discussed, and I assumed he gave that message, along with the official one, to whoever stood on the other side of the door.

Once Minsa, Sade and Dalia left the room to go to lunch, I made my move.

"I would like to take a walk," I told Khalid, loud enough for the other concu-bines nearby to hear, should they want to listen. "Will you accompany me?"

"Of course, my lady, but it will have to be short. I have the afternoon off to visit my family."

"I understand."

As we left the room together, I felt convinced that nothing in that exchange would have seemed unusual to everyone. So far, everything had gone to plan.

Without a word between us, we headed immediately for the courtyard where Zara had promised to leave me a change of clothes, and I found the small sack tucked next to the pool, just as she'd said. With Khalid standing guard, I ducked into one of the small rooms adjoining the courtyard and put on the dress and scarf Zara had left for me, on top of my harem clothes. Once again, she had clearly considered what would work best. The blue dress was fine enough to suit a princess, but not special enough that it would draw too much attention. The scarf for my head, in the same shade of blue, would shade my face well enough that no one should guess from a glance that I was anyone other than who I claimed to be.

As for the empty sack, I tucked it beneath the bodice of the dress, thinking it may come in handy later on. Even if we found no use for it, leaving it lying around might seem suspicious. The last thing I wanted would be to leave any clue that would point fingers to someone having helped in my escape.

"Khalid?" I opened the door a fraction and whispered his name, checking that the coast was clear.

"Ready, Your Highness."

It had been a long time since anyone had called me that, and when I stepped out of the room, a warm smile lit up my friend's face.

"I would hardly recognize you myself. It's perfect. Come, quickly."

He didn't have to ask me twice. Together, we headed to the gate that separated the emperor's private quarters from the rest of the palace. This marked the farthest I had travelled from the confines of the harem in years, and each step felt like a victory even though I knew we still had a long way to go.

Khalid spoke for us both, as we'd agreed, greeting the guard at the gate by name. "Good afternoon, Akeem. I'm accompanying Princess Zara to the market."

He handed over the small token which signified his supervisor's approval for him to leave. Of course, it had been given to him for the purpose of visiting his family, not to accompany me anywhere, but the guard at the gate wouldn't know the difference.

He did, however, peer over at me curiously as I kept my head down, not making eye contact. "Has the prince given permission for her to go?"

The question made my stomach drop. Did Zara need permission from Malek to leave? She hadn't said anything about it.

Khalid, however, replied confidently. "Of course. That's how I got assigned to her. And I wouldn't look at her too closely if I were you. She may not be in the harem yet, but you know that His Highness has suggested it."

There were few secrets among the palace's employees, and Akeem immediately averted his gaze, understanding the danger. "Enjoy your day."

He opened the gate for us and it took all my effort not to grin as I stepped through it, one step closer to freedom.

"We must go quickly, but not too quickly," Khalid whispered beside me. "If Malek is watching Zara's movements, Akeem might send him a message. We need to get out of the palace before he acts upon it."

Once again, I needed no further encouragement. I walked as quickly as my soft shoes would allow on the cobbled path that led through the administrative section of the palace to the next gate. There, Khalid did not know the guard personally, but he showed the brand upon his skin that identified him as one of the eunuchs, and he explained who we were and where we were going in the same confident, firm tone. They searched him to make sure he had nothing concealed on him that he might be stealing from the palace, and I had a momentary panic that I would be searched too and they would find my harem clothes beneath my dress, but thankfully, my status as either a princess or simply as a woman seemed to make that unnecessary. We were allowed to pass unimpeded.

A queue had formed at the third gate and we had to wait to get through. Each shout from behind us or the sound of approaching footsteps made my heart thump harder in my chest, but no one approached us, and when Khalid repeated his story, this time, the guards handed him a weapon before we were let through.

"These belong to the eunuchs, to defend ourselves when we leave the palace," he explained under his breath as we made our way down the steep hill that led to the final palace gate. "Let's hope I don't need to use it."

"You are doing wonderfully," I breathed back to him. "I couldn't have done this without you."

"We're not out yet," he warned me. "Don't thank me until we get out of the city."

The last gate was the busiest, but also the least thorough check. People at this level either hadn't had much access in the first place or had already been checked at the other gates, so less scrutiny took place, and when we were allowed through, I nearly cried in relief as well as a touch of frustration. Was it really that easy? Could I have done that at any point over the last years and been free a long time ago?

Khalid quickly rid me of that illusion. "That went well, thanks to your friends," he told me, allowing himself a brief smile of satisfaction. "But we're not done yet. Now, we need to make you disappear."

Taking my arm, he led me quickly away from the palace, the walls disappearing behind us as we ventured into the city itself. I had never been outside of the palace gates besides the march from the ship to the palace in the first place, but we had no time to sightsee. I kept my head down, following Khalid's lead, until he pulled me down a side street where a woman sat with her two young children, begging for coins.

"We can't offer you money," Khalid told her. Although we had some, we would need all of it to make our escape. "But you can have this fine dress the lady wears if you give her your clothes instead."

The woman eyed my dress with keen interest and a bit of suspicion. "What's the catch?"

"No catch," Khalid promised. "We just need it immediately. If you don't want it, we'll find someone else."

The woman beckoned me into the small, run-down building behind her, containing only some rags to lay upon and a small cooking vessel over a fire, and inside, we quickly exchanged clothes. A shrewd look crossed her face when she saw my harem costume beneath the dress. "Are you from the palace?"

"No," I lied quickly. "But you can have these too if you promise not to tell anyone that you saw us."

I handed over Zara's beautiful dress and my own silk garments in exchange for the plain black dress she wore and the head covering to go with it. Khalid knew what he was doing: I would certainly blend in more now. She even gave me some sturdier shoes which, even though they were nearly worn through, were still better than my soft-soled ones.

"Take these as well," she said, offering me some oranges to put in the sack which I still carried. "Running away is hungry work."

I tried to protest that I had not run from anything, but she simply shook her head. "I ran from a husband who mistreated me, which is how I ended up here. Your dress will keep us alive for a month, at least, and I'm grateful for it. Your secret is safe with me."

We exchanged a small smile of understanding, the understanding of two women who had been misused by men, and I returned to the street where Khalid nodded in appreciation. "Much better. Let's keep moving."

In the next street, Khalid found a man willing to give him different clothes too in exchange for his garments so he no longer looked like an employee from the palace. He also took some dirt from the street and rubbed it on his face to mimic the stubble of a beard, if no one looked too closely. With our new looks, we continued down the hill towards the harbour.

Just as we reached the base of the hill, soldiers from the palace appeared and my heart raced once again. We tried to keep our heads down, but one of them approached us anyway. "We are looking for a lady from the palace. Have you seen anyone?"

Khalid shook his head slowly. "No, sir. My wife and I have been to the market and we haven't seen anything."

He showed my bag of oranges as proof of our market visit and the soldier huffed in frustration before moving on to the next person on the street.

"It sounds like they've noticed you're gone," Khalid guessed beneath his breath. "Let's get on a ship, as quickly as we can."

Again, we moved as fast as we dared without looking like we were trying to get away. Khalid bypassed the larger ships and headed for the small fishing vessels where the fishermen were dropping off their catches for the day. He spoke to several of the men before he found one that would be heading to the town he wanted, and he offered the man a sizable sum to take us there and to house us overnight. The princes were meant to come and pick us up the next morning, so one night should be all we needed.

When everything had been agreed, the man opened a hidden door in the bottom of his boat. "One of you can fit in there if you need to hide, but you won't both fit."

That was for sure. The space barely looked large enough for even me, and the thought of being trapped inside there if the ship should happen to go down sent a wave of panic through me.

"It is better than returning to the palace," Khalid murmured to me under his breath, as if he had heard my thoughts, and I couldn't disagree with that. Gathering all my courage, I stepped down into the small space and slid my legs beneath the floorboards, shimmying down until I lay flat on my back. The door above me closed and empty fish vats were placed on top of it. The scent of the sea, salty and fishy, filled every breath I took as the ship creaked around me.

"How quickly can we leave?" Khalid asked the fisherman. I could still hear them clearly, which relieved me. At least Khalid could keep me updated on what was happening.

"I'm just waiting for the final tally for the day," the man replied. "Ten minutes, no more."

I could handle ten minutes, I told myself, taking another deep breath to keep myself calm as the boat rocked around me. In another circumstance, the gentle swelling of the waves might actually be comforting, but at the moment, I just wanted it to be over.

They chatted a bit more about the man's haul for the day and fishing in general, until suddenly, they both fell silent.

"Damn," I heard Khalid mutter before he leaned down closer to the floor. "The palace soldiers are coming. Stay there, I'm going to get off the boat just for a moment."

"No, Khalid, don't go!" Fear raced through me as I whispered back to him, but he made no response. The boat swayed as he stepped off it, back onto the pier, and my heart began to pound again, even harder than before.

"What are you doing here?" a harsher voice rang out, loud enough for me to hear.

"I'm a fisherman," Khalid claimed. "Delivering fish, like everyone here."

The first voice sounded unconvinced. "You're not dressed like a fisherman. Check him!"

Scuffling sounds reached me, and it only took a matter of seconds before they found Khalid's weapon. "This bears the emperor's mark," another man said, and a moment later, he added: "And this is the eunuch's brand. He's the one we're looking for!"

I clamped my hand over my mouth to keep from shouting out as my heart thudded painfully hard and bitter tears stung my eyes. This couldn't be happening! We had been so close. It couldn't really come to nothing, could it? There must still be something we could do. Hopefully, Khalid would have one more trick up his sleeve.

"Where is the woman?" the first man asked, his voice harder and threatening now. "It will go easier for you if you cooperate."

That was a lie, and Khalid knew it as well as I did. There would be no mercy for him whether I returned or not, and so he lied on my behalf. "She is already gone. I put her on a ship twenty minutes ago. You'll never find her."

A cry of frustration rang out, but the soldier wouldn't take his word for it. "Search the boats! All of them!"

Heavy footsteps sounded along the pier as the soldiers spread out, and the boat swayed again as others stepped onto it, two pairs of boots walking directly above my own feet. "Is there anything back there?" one man asked as vats were shoved aside. If they moved the one directly over my head, they would see the door, and I could do absolutely nothing about it. Pressing my lips together, I tried not to cry as I waited to be discovered.

But just as the noises above me moved perilously close, they suddenly stopped. "There's nothing here," yet another soldier replied. "Let's go."

The boat rocked once more as the soldiers left. In silence, I lay there with only the steady drumming of my heart for company, until finally, we began to move.

Several more minutes passed before the fisherman spoke to me. "We're safely away. The soldiers have gone but they've taken your friend. It's best you stay down there until it's dark. I'm sorry."

All my earlier optimism felt like a cruel irony as the sobs I had been holding in broke free, tears streaming down my face as I imagined what awaited Khalid back at the palace. He had literally given his life for mine, a choice I would have never wanted him to make. Even if I made it out of Munisia, which still felt far from certain, would the price ever be worth it?

What had I done?

CHAPTER TEN

With Arthur and Eric having lunch with the emperor and Malek, and Malek's wives accepting my offer to have lunch with them in the harem, everything seemed to be going to plan. I sent one of my father's servants to the harem with my message; just in case anyone paid attention, it seemed safer not to make an appearance there myself before Fatima's escape. I told the servant to pay careful attention to any message from the man at the door as I would ask her to repeat it back to me word-for-word, and she didn't disappoint.

Along with the acceptance of my offer for lunch, she told me the man said that it looked like a beautiful day to head outside and he thought the town of Hinport on the coast would be a great place to spend the day, if only it weren't so far away.

"What does that mean, Your Highness?" the woman asked me curiously.

"I have no idea," I lied. "He must have simply been making conversation, but thank you anyway."

Of course, I knew exactly what the message meant: Fatima was prepared to leave and she and her accomplice would be waiting for Eric and Arthur in Hinport.

On my way to the harem for lunch, I stopped for a moment at the reflecting pool where Fatima and I had spoken the day before, placing the small package with the dress for Fatima at my feet and then 'forgetting' it when I got up again. I couldn't see anyone around who would have noticed me, but even if someone had, my actions shouldn't seem too suspicious.

Minsa and the other two wives were waiting for me in a smaller side room of the harem quarters when I arrived, seated around a circular table. As I took my place at the table with them, a shudder ran through me at the idea of this ever being my life, sharing every minute of my day with the other women who also shared the same man's bed. Yes, I would be willing to be Arthur's mistress, if necessary, but in that case, at least I knew he truly loved me, and he would never expect me to break bread with the woman who would legally be his wife. Even though I had grown up with the idea of the royal harems, being here with the women in question still made the concept seem very foreign and unnatural to me.

I did my best to get them talking about themselves, which didn't take much prompting for Minsa. With great pride, she told me how she and Malek met and how he had chosen her as his first wife. Dalia, the youngest one, acted as Minsa's parrot, using many of the same phrases the older woman had used as she relayed her own story. Sade, on the other hand, gave away very little, and I got the distinct impression she would have chosen a different life for herself if she had the option. Unfortunately, as a princess, many things were decided for you; that was simply a fact of life. Sometimes it worked out, as it had for Arthur's sister, Cordelia, and sometimes it didn't, like Sade's life here. All she could do was bear it gracefully.

Each minute the meal lasted marked another minute that Fatima should be getting further away and out of Malek's reach, so I did my best to draw out our lunch as long as I could.

We were still at the table when Malek himself burst in and immediately stopped short at the sight of the four of us sitting at the table.

"Malek!" Minsa flushed with pleasure at the sight of him, her hands immediately moving to check that everything about herself would be displayed to her maximum advantage. "Your Highness. What a lovely surprise to see you."

Her fawning made my stomach turn, but Malek paid her no attention. His eyes were fixed on me. "You're here."

Keeping a serene expression on my face, I answered as calmly as I could. "I'm getting to know your wives. I hope that is alright."

Of course, I knew exactly what he actually meant: he must have heard that I had left the palace. My heart beat faster as I prayed that Fatima had already gotten far away, and that Malek suspected nothing about the rest of us.

Unfortunately, he put the pieces together much more quickly than I had hoped he would. "Gather the others," he barked at the eunuchs who had followed him. "I want the whole harem assembled, now."

With narrowed eyes, he turned back to us.

"You as well. Come to the hall."

"Actually, we just finished," I demurred, rising to my feet as gracefully as I could, as though I wasn't desperate to get away now that my work here was done. "The harem's business doesn't concern me, so I will return to my father's house."

The stormy expression in Malek's eyes only grew stronger. "You will stay here until I dismiss you. I can force you if you want it that way."

A gleam of excitement crossed his face with those words, making it clear that he found that idea appealing, and with a great effort, I kept from grimacing in distaste. Perhaps it wouldn't hurt to stay a little longer and see what his next moves were, so I simply gave a polite nod. "That won't be necessary, Your Highness. I can spare a few more minutes."

With a grunt, Malek left the room while I and the others followed him back to the main hall where the concubines and eunuchs were already being assembled. Malek ordered the women to be lined up in front of him, me in line along with the others, and it didn't take him long at all to realize who was missing.

"Where is Fatima?" He shouted the question at the whole room, making many of the women flinch. When no one answered, he stalked over to Minsa, lowering his face to speak directly into hers. "You are in charge of all the women here. Where is Fatima?"

Minsa's face had gone pale and her hands trembled as she clasped them together. "I don't know, Your Highness. I saw her this morning. She often spends time by herself. Perhaps she's in the garden?"

Without looking away from his wife, Malek addressed the head of the eunuchs. "Have you searched the garden?"

"Yes, Your Highness," the man replied. "We have checked the entire harem."

"Check it again!" Malek shouted, directly into Minsa's face as she winced, her whole body tense and unhappy.

No one spoke as the men scattered to conduct a thorough search. Malek took a step back, his eyes darting around the room and landing frequently on me. I did my best to appear calm and unconcerned since, as far as he knew, this had nothing to do with me, and when the men returned without Fatima, Malek's expression grew darker. He looked nearly ready to snap.

"Come with me," he said to me, turning on his heel and leaving the room as the women exchanged uneasy glances with each other.

With little choice, I followed Malek out of the harem and into his personal study where his own guards were waiting for him. "One of my harem is missing," he informed the guard, his voice filled with anger. "Tell me exactly what happened at the gate."

The man cleared his throat, pointing to another man at the back of the room, wide-eyed with fear. "Akeem worked the gate. The eunuch, Khalid, accompanied the woman who claimed to be Princess Zara. They said they were going to the market. The eunuch had his token to leave, so they were let through, and Akeem reported the departure to you, as you requested, Your Highness."

As he requested? Was Malek keeping tabs on me? I barely had time to process that before Malek grabbed the guard's sword from his side and ran it straight through the unlucky man who had been at the gate. His eyes widened in surprise and disbelief as the sword pierced him and I turned away as his body hit the ground. He never had a chance to say a word.I had seen plenty of violence and death before, but the responsibility for this man's death rested at least partially on my shoulders. Guilt made me look away as I whispered a silent apology to the man and his family in my mind.

"I want them found, now!" Malek shouted. "They can't have gone far. Check all the roads out of the city and the harbour."

He paused for a moment, and when I turned back to see why, I found him staring right at me.

"Check the ship that the northern princes arrived on."

Though my stomach sank at those words, I did my best to keep a straight face and not give anything away. We had expected they would check Arthur's ship; for that reason, Fatima wouldn't be going there, but I didn't like the way Malek looked at me when he said it, as if he were putting far too many things together already.

When the other men had all left, leaving only me and Malek and the body of the dead guard on the floor, still bleeding out onto the mosaic tile of Malek's study, he continued to stare at me, daring me to speak.

At length, I had to say something, so I bowed my head politely. "If you don't need anything further, Your Highness, I will return to my father's house now."

The last thing I expected was for Malek to smile, but smile he did, giving me a look that could almost be considered appreciation. "You're very sure of yourself. There are few men who could pull this off as well as you are."

"Pull what off, Your Highness?" I blinked at him in feigned confusion even as my heart raced. Exactly how much had he figured out?

My words only made him smile more, and the sight couldn't be called pleasant. His smile was tinged with cruelty, his dark eyes glinting coldly as he looked me up and down. "That is what I mean. That innocent act could fool a great many men, I'm sure, but not me, Zara. We are alike, you and I. We always have been."

This time, I couldn't stop my lips curling in disagreement or my nostrils flaring at the offensive comparison. "I am nothing like you."

A sharp, cold laugh burst from Malek's chest, like a barking seal. "So much pride," he sneered, his eyes still holding that same sickening look of appreciation.

"So much self-importance. And yet, when it came down to it, when you were on your own in those foreign kingdoms, you did what had to be done. You spread your legs for any man who would help you, didn't you? So why don't you see that I'm the man who can help you most of all? I am the only one who can give you what you want, and if you don't give *me* what I want, you will have to suffer the loss."

I understood his insults at the beginning well enough, but he had lost me at the end, and I told him so: "I don't know what you're talking about."

The smile fell from his face as his expression turned deadly serious. "After all her years in my harem, Fatima did not suddenly decide to leave on her own. You asked for her freedom and so did the princes with you. Now, she has suddenly disappeared. Did you truly believe I wouldn't know you had something to do with it?"

"I don't know anything about Fatima going missing," I lied. "All I've done today is dine with your wives, as you saw. You're speaking to me in riddles."

"Then let me be plain." He moved closer, his face inches from mine, just as he had been when he shouted at Minsa earlier, but rather than shouting now, his voice had gone low and dangerously quiet. "I said she would only be free if you took her place. If she is gone, then you are mine."

"That's not fair." Cold anger and indignation swept through my body as he twisted his own rules to suit his whims. "I had nothing to do with her leaving and you can't force me to accept your offer against my will."

"I can do anything I want, Zara. That's what it means to be the prince." His eyes were hard and full of determination. "But in this case, I will not force you. You're going to accept my offer, in front of everyone."

He must truly be delusional. "I had no interest in it before, Malek, and I'm even less interested now. I will not accept you. Ever."

Using his name rather than his title was an insult, but it only made the corners of his lips turn upwards. "Not even if it means the life of your Lassarian prince?"

The chill in my veins grew stronger as I struggled to remain calm. "Prince Arthur is not 'mine', and you have no power over him. If you harm him, you'll start a war. Many of the northern kingdoms are only waiting for an excuse to attack you. You're not stupid enough to give them one."

"You see? You are clever." His hand brushed against my cheek and I turned away, my disgust plain on my face, to Malek's amusement. "But not as clever as I am. In front of witnesses, the two princes asked me for Fatima's freedom. Their motive is clear. I suspect we'll find her on their ship now, and even if we don't, it won't be difficult to plant the evidence needed to convict them anyway. The punishment for interfering with the harem is death, as you well know. Will the world go to war over two princes who overstepped and interfered in the custom of our court? I don't believe they will. Arthur's father has other sons who could take his place, and the Silatrian prince is only the second son anyway. If I decide they're guilty, whether or not they actually are, they're both as good as dead."

At that moment, as my stomach turned to lead and my throat closed up, I saw clearly that we had underestimated Malek. As someone who held his position by virtue of his blood, I thought that he would have respect for other royal blood too, and in that, it appeared I'd been mistaken.

"What do you want?" I whispered. Clearly, he wasn't telling me all this just for the sake of conversation. His comment about being the only one who could give me what I wanted became clearer with each new word from his mouth.

He shook his head in disapproval. "You already know the answer to that, Zara. Don't pretend otherwise."

He was right. I understood, no matter how sick the idea made me. "You will let the princes go if I agree to join the harem."

That same smile of appreciation crossed his lips once more. "That wasn't so hard, was it?"

My mind raced as I looked for a loophole in the deal he offered, a way that I could keep my freedom and Arthur could keep his, but in every scenario, Malek held all the cards. Here, his word was law, and I had lost sight of that in my eagerness to help Fatima in the first place.

"And Fatima?" I brought her up now to be sure I understood his negotiation entirely.

"She has sealed her own fate in leaving. If she is caught, she will be put to death, along with the eunuch who helped her. That is non-negotiable."

"Nothing is non-negotiable," I argued back. He said we were alike, hadn't he? I would prove it to him. "If your men don't find them now, then you will call off the search. And if they do find them, the punishment will be more lenient. They will be imprisoned, not killed."

Imprisonment always left the possibility of release or escape. In that, it would always be preferable to death.

"Fatima can be imprisoned," Malek compromised. "The boy must die as an example to the others."

"You can tell the others he died," I pointed out. "Have his cell attended by a deaf and blind man. No one needs to know he is still alive. And no torture!"

Malek laughed again at the final stipulation, enjoying the negotiation as if the lives of other people weren't hanging in the balance. "Very well. We have pits in the dungeons. He can be put in there. Fatima will be imprisoned. The princes will be exiled from the empire but will be free to leave. That is my final offer, Zara. Will you accept it or not?"

~Eric~

Malek never returned to our lunch with the emperor and eventually, we had to give up on him. The emperor apologized on behalf of his son and tried to get Arthur to finish what he had been saying about the gold mines, but Arthur politely refused to go any further. That had all been a distraction technique anyway; he had no plans to offer the Munisians anything further than what he had already negotiated, so, in a way, Malek's absence spared him from having to make any false promises.

We could only hope that his prolonged absence meant good news for Fatima and, by extension, the rest of us.

When we left the emperor and returned to Zara's family's house, she hadn't returned yet, and neither had her father, so Arthur and I retired together to his room to discuss how things had gone. Although my stomach had tied itself in knots of worry for Fatima, I tried to remain optimistic.

"It's not as bad as chasing after Westley Eastam for weeks," I said, only half-serious. "At least we'll know by the end of the day how things will end."

"At least with Eastam, we always had another chance to find him if we failed," Arthur pointed out, his mood uncharacteristically dark. "If we fail here, multiple lives could be affected. Zara should be back by now."

He glanced at the door again, as if he could make her appear through sheer force of will.

"You don't know that. Who can say how long lunch in the harem takes? Or she may have gone to visit her father. We don't need to panic just yet."

For the next hour, we tried to distract ourselves even though every little noise made us jump. Eventually, even my hopefulness started to wane. It felt like something had gone wrong.

At last, someone knocked on the door. Arthur rushed to it, hoping to see Zara on the other side, no doubt, but one of the servants stood there instead and Arthur's shoulders slumped so hard that it would have been comical if the situation weren't so serious.

However, the servant's words buoyed him back up again. "Princess Zara is in the minister's study. She would like to speak to you both."

Without a second's hesitation, we followed the servant to Adil's study where Zara waited, along with her father. Adil's presence made me frown since we wouldn't be able to speak as freely in front of him, but surely Zara would find a way to tell us what we needed to know anyway.

Her posture and facial expression gave nothing away as she stood next to her father's desk, her hands clasped in front of her. Adil, on the other hand, looked downcast, though what he should have to be upset about, I couldn't begin to guess.

Zara spoke first, speaking to us far more formally than she ever had in the past. "Your Highnesses, thank you for coming. I have been granted a short time to say goodbye to you before you depart tomorrow, and I wanted to be sure that you knew just how much I appreciate all the kindness and consideration you have shown me."

Her eyes darted to Arthur, for just a moment, before returning to their previous position, looking down at the floor between us.

Her words made as little sense to Arthur as they did to me. "What are you talking about?" he asked, his voice filled with concern. "Granted time by who?"

"By Malek." Zara glanced down at her father, whose lips tightened unhappily. "I have accepted his offer to join his harem and I will be moving there tonight. You won't see me again."

"What?!" The word burst out of me and Arthur at the same time, but with more force from him, naturally. His face drained of colour almost instantly, his eyes wide with distress.

"You heard me," Zara said quietly, still not looking at either of us. "It seems that Princess Fatima has disappeared. In her absence, I am to take her place. It is all agreed."

My spirits lifted at the news that Fatima seemed to have gotten away, but I had never intended for Zara to have to give up her freedom in exchange. We had gone to the rather extreme lengths of this whole convoluted plan to try to avoid it.

"No." I had never heard a word carry as much desperation as Arthur's simple plea did. "Zara, you can't do this. What happened? We'll find another way."

"It is all agreed," she repeated simply, her voice completely devoid of emotion in contrast to Arthur's misery. "He has offered me a life better than I could have elsewhere. I have always been a practical woman, you know that."

"I don't believe that," Arthur replied firmly, taking a step towards her. Zara immediately moved back, and her father rose from his seat as if he meant to protect her, making Arthur stop on the spot. I put a hand on his arm to try to help calm him as he tried to catch Zara's eye. "There's something else going on here. Tell me what it is and we can work it out together."

"Your Highness, my daughter has made her decision." Adil's voice sounded firm, though tinged with sadness. "You cannot bully her out of it."

"Bully her?" Arthur cried in disbelief. "I love her, and I know this isn't what she wants."

When Adil made no reply, Arthur turned to Zara instead, who still refused to make eye contact with him.

"I love you, Zara. I know you love me too. I want you to come back to Lassaria with me. I want to marry you..."

Zara shook her head, finally looking at Arthur with an expression that I could not name. "You've been deceived once again, Your Highness, this time by yourself. I would have killed you at Eastam's command but you offered me a better deal. You brought me back here and you helped me to make Malek jealous. Now, he has offered me everything I desire. I have acted only in my self-interest at every step. If you have believed otherwise, that is your own doing."

Arthur's brow furrowed as he stared at her, unwilling to believe a word she said. "That's not true. I believe in you, Zara. I always have. You're not the person you're describing."

"I'm not the woman you would have me be," she argued back, calm and passionless. "The truth is: I don't love you, Arthur. I never said I did."

The words were so jaggedly painful that even I winced, though they weren't directed at me. I had been on the receiving end of similar words from Lady Elodie, when she told me she didn't care for me in the same way I did for her. That hurt bad enough, and we had never been as close as Arthur and Zara were. My gaze returned to Arthur with sympathy as Zara's words pierced into him.

"You don't mean that," he whispered, as if his breath had all been stolen.

Zara didn't respond. Instead, she turned to her father and gave a nod, and a few seconds later, the door to the study opened and several strong, armed men appeared. Adil gave them a command in his own language before turning to Arthur. "They will accompany you back to your room. Dinner will be brought to you there. In the morning, you will depart."

"Zara, please..." Arthur tried, stepping towards her again, but she simply turned away. It took all of the men and Adil to drag Arthur from the room, and the sound of their struggle continued down the hall.

Left alone, Zara turned to me. "Shut the door, quickly. There are things you need to know."

That sounded much more like the woman I had gotten to know and, intrigued by the sudden change in her, I did as she said, closing the door so that we could speak privately.

"We don't have much time, that much is true," she began. "Fatima will be waiting for you in the town of Hinport. The man who helped her to escape the palace has been apprehended, but as far as I know, she got away safely. She'll be on her own though, so the sooner you can get to her, the better."

That was excellent news, though not so much for the man who had helped her. "What will become of the eunuch?"

Zara grimaced. "I've successfully argued against his torture and death, but the alternative isn't much better. There's a pit in the palace dungeons where he will be kept in complete solitude. A blind and deaf man will lower food to him but he will live in darkness with the vermin and his own filth. Many people choose to starve themselves rather than remain in it for long."

I couldn't see how that would be much better than death, but Zara quickly explained her reasoning.

"Although it won't be easy, there may be a chance of escape. I will work on it from my new position within the harem. Please tell Fatima that I won't forget about her friend, but that she should move on in the meantime. There's nothing for her here."

"And this new position? What is the real reason for it?" I didn't buy Zara's explanation for it any more than Arthur did, even if I took the whole thing less personally.

Her lips pursed as tears gathered in the corner of her eyes, and she quickly dabbed them away. "Malek threatened to charge both you and Arthur in Fatima's disappearance. He has no evidence, none at all, but he made the completely valid point that he doesn't need any. He can create false charges, just as Fatima's father did against my father in the first place. When you are the law, truth doesn't matter."

I understood immediately. The kings of Silatria were bound by the rule of law because sovereigns in the past had taken advantage of their position one too many times and the people imposed restrictions on them, but Munisia hadn't yet reached that stage. What the emperor ordered, or in this case the crown prince ordered, would be carried out even if it defied all reason.

"You're trading your freedom for ours," I surmised.

She nodded firmly. "Arthur would never accept it, which is why I have to lie to him, but I know that you're a practical man, Eric. It's no good for all of us to pay the price when I can secure your freedom. Once you are far enough away that he won't be tempted to return, you can tell Arthur the truth."

I couldn't imagine that would go over well no matter how much distance lay between us, but I understood Zara's reasoning completely. "And what will you do?"

She shrugged in her elegant way. "I'll do what I've always done: survive. I'll find a way to free Khalid and then I will work on my own freedom. Malek forgets that I'm trained in several kinds of combat. If he thinks he'll have his way with me without coming to harm, he will find he's mistaken. I'm not out of options yet,

Your Highness, but if I have to worry about Arthur's safety at the same time, it will make things more difficult. He is my weakness, as Malek has already realized. You need to leave as planned tomorrow, pick up Fatima, and get to safety, and I will follow when I can."

"We are in pretty much the same boat as if you had simply accepted Malek's proposal in the first place," I pointed out. "Fatima's entire escape was unnecessary."

"That's the way of it sometimes," Zara agreed ruefully. "Just as if I had stayed in the Actilian castle in the first place, I may have spared myself years of wandering. With hindsight, a great many things are clearer, but we can't go back. We can only move forwards, and this is the best plan for now. Keep this in confidence between us until you can safely tell Arthur. Make sure he is safe. Please."

Her eyes watered once again and I knew that, no matter what she had said, she truly loved Arthur just as much as he loved her. Hopefully, that would help to ease the sting of her words when the time came to share the truth with him.

"Good luck then, Zara." I offered her my hand, as I would to a prince rather than a princess, and she shook it firmly.

"And to you. Take care of Fatima as well. She's earned some good fortune for herself after all this time."

With that, I could certainly agree, and Zara and I parted in mutual respect, not knowing if we would ever see each other again.

CHAPTER ELEVEN

Of all the things I'd done in my life to survive, lying to Arthur had been the most difficult of all, but I couldn't see any other option.

If he knew the truth, he would never leave me. It would go against every loyal and brave bone in his body, and though I loved those things about him, in this case, it would only work against us. I needed him to be safe so that Malek had nothing to hold over my head anymore. Getting out from under Malek's thumb wouldn't be easy, but I would find a way; so long as Arthur drew breath, I would find a way back to him.

I also knew that he wouldn't believe that I had simply changed my mind, and so I had to be brutal. I had to tell him to his face that I didn't love him, that I never had, and that I'd been using him all along. The pain and confusion in his sweet blue eyes pierced my heart, but I forced myself to picture those same blue eyes lifeless after Malek ordered his execution, and the choice became crystal clear again: to save him, I had to break his heart, and mine in the process.

There might be a chance he wouldn't forgive me for this, even after Eric told him the truth. He wouldn't appreciate that I had lied to him and pushed him away, but so long as he stayed alive, I would do whatever I had to do. I had survived so much and hadn't lost my fighting spirit, but without Arthur, there would be no reason for me to even try. His safety mattered more to me than anything else in the world.

Love had that kind of power, and Malek had done his best to exploit it. However, in his calculations, he'd forgotten the other side of the equation: yes, I would do anything to keep Arthur safe, including binding myself to Malek, but I would also do whatever it took to get back to the man I loved. Malek had just put a very large target on his own head, whether he realized it yet or not.

Knowing one of the harem eunuchs would be coming any moment to accompany me to my new 'home', I quickly returned to my room to pack. I suspected they would search my belongings to be sure I didn't try to sneak anything dangerous in with me, so only clothes and books and writing material went into the trunk. I would need to carry out the first part of my plan here in my room.

Pulling out the small sword which had accompanied me throughout my travels, I gritted my teeth and very carefully made a small incision into the delicate skin between my legs. Blood began to pool and I pressed my legs together to smear it around, wincing at the sting of the sliced flesh.

That should buy me a couple of days. Munisian custom forbade sexual intercourse during a woman's monthly courses, so if I could convince the servants who would check my suitability that I had my monthly menstruation, Malek would have to find someone else to fill his bed until I had recovered. During that time, I could figure out what to do next.

I had only just lowered my skirt and hidden the sword away beneath my pillow when someone knocked at the door and my mother entered to see if I had everything I needed. When I told both my parents together about accepting Malek's offer, my mother appeared to be delighted. "I always thought you were too stubborn to submit as you should," she admitted to me. "I'm glad to see the time away has changed you."

It certainly had changed me, though not in the way she meant, but I didn't bother to dispute her delusions. It would make no difference. My father, on the other hand, looked as though he had swallowed something bitter.

"I am sorry it's come to this," he told me when we were alone in his study and he had sent someone to fetch the princes. "I wish I hadn't been right in this case."

He had warned me that Malek would do whatever it took to secure my agreement, and he had indeed been right. But as my father had also suggested, I had used the opportunity to negotiate. Along with calling off the search for Fatima and commuting Khalid's punishment, Malek had agreed to include the stipulation that my father would be allowed to visit me. At least I would not be completely cut off, and hopefully, I could find a way to use it to my advantage.

"I'm ready, Mama," I told her, indicating my small trunk.

"I'm proud of you, Zara," she said, giving me a firm embrace. "Serve Malek well and please him and you will have a happy, settled life. It is what we all want. I only hope your sisters will find such a beneficial situation."

If I had ever needed further proof that my mother and I were not cut from the same cloth, that would have clinched it. She saw my situation as something to be celebrated, which I never could.

Two eunuchs from the harem arrived to collect me and they carried my trunk between them as I followed them to the harem entrance, accompanied by my mother and sisters. Not knowing what might come in handy, I paid attention to everything I could, including the position of the rooms and the way the men spoke to each other. Fatima had found a friend in the harem who had helped her to escape and I could use all the help I could get too.

After embracing my mother and sisters one last time, I followed the men into the harem itself. The small room they led me to already had a trunk full of clothes in it, and a grim irony settled over me as I realized what it must mean. "Did Fatima use this room?" I asked the men, but neither of them answered me, averting their eyes. Perhaps after what happened with Khalid, fraternizing with any of the harem women seemed too risky. That might make my own plans a little more difficult, but not impossible. Somehow, I would find a way.

No sooner had I begun to unpack than two servants appeared at my door, wanting to bathe me. "His Highness has requested your company this evening," one of them told me, keeping her eyes lowered. "We'll make sure you're ready."

I said nothing as I followed them to the bath where several of the other concubines had already gathered. Malek's three wives had their own private baths but the rest of the women shared a communal pool. They all eyed me, some wary, some suspicious, and some merely curious, and I gave them all a friendly smile. These women weren't to blame for my situation so it cost me nothing to treat them kindly.

As the servants removed my dress, pulling it up over my head, one of them caught sight of the blood between my legs. "You didn't tell us you were unclean," she admonished me, still not making eye contact.

"It must have just started," I lied. "I didn't know."

If it had just begun, I could draw out the excuse for a few days at minimum. The more time I could secure away from Malek, the better.

In my state, I couldn't sully the common bath so the servants took me to a separate room instead where they gave me some cloth to clean myself. I took that as a good sign. Normally, a new concubine would be cleaned and anointed with oils and perfume before being taken to the prince's bed. Since the servants left me on my own with none of those traditions, it must mean the deception had worked, at least temporarily. They were likely sending a message to Malek that I would not be available tonight after all. Left alone, I examined the wounds I had inflicted on myself. The skin had started to heal, so I pulled it apart again to keep the blood flowing.

Once I had dressed again, dinner was announced in the main hall. Everyone seemed subdued during the meal, with Minsa keeping a firm eye on everyone. If anyone spoke louder than a whisper, she called them out, ordering them back to silence. Fatima's escape reflected badly on her, as Malek had pointed out, and she responded by punishing those beneath her, as petty people so often did.

When the servants brought my plate to me, I glanced up to see Minsa watching me carefully, and my sister's warning came back to me. "I'm not hungry," I told the servant, even though my stomach protested as the food disappeared. Perhaps my sisters could find a way to smuggle me some food until I could make my own escape. Becoming the victim of some small-minded woman's misplaced jealousy didn't appeal to me in the least.

After dinner, the women in the harem would normally spend the evening together, talking or playing music, but tonight, Minsa ordered everyone to their rooms as a further punishment, which worked fine for me. Or so I thought, until I crawled into the tiny single bed on my own and thought about Arthur, so near and yet impossible to reach. Tomorrow, he would set sail, away from me and away from harm, and then, my true plotting could begin.

Tonight, however, I had only regret to keep me company, regret that I had come back here at all and regret at the hurt I'd caused the best man I'd ever known. With its bitter sting in my chest, in the privacy of my room, I finally let myself grieve, whispering into the stillness of the room through my tears.

"I will come, Arthur. Keep well until I can see you again."

~Arthur~

When Adil's men shoved me into my room, forcibly restraining me, I knew that whatever had scared Zara must have truly spooked her to her core.

If she had spoken the truth in her father's study when she said she had never loved me and she had wanted this all along, there would be no need to lock me up. If I went and argued with Malek, it would make no difference to her at all.

Instead, she arranged my restraint in advance; I saw the signal she gave her father and his men were already waiting to remove me from her presence. She knew I would be upset and she set this up; that much, I understood, but I didn't know what she would be so afraid of and why she thought I couldn't handle it with her. Though her words hurt me, I knew deep down she didn't mean them. What hurt far more was that she wouldn't trust me with the truth. Up until now, we had been a team, so what had changed?

Her father followed us down the hall to ensure his men locked me safely away, and as he stood in the doorway of my room, I called out to him in desperation. "Adil! Please, I beg you, talk to me. Tell me the truth."

His face somber, the older man stepped inside my room and gave his men some further instruction in their own language. At his order, they released me and left the room, closing the door behind them as I straightened out my clothes that had been ruffled in our struggle. No doubt the men would be just outside, ready to grab me again if I tried to flee, but at the moment, my priority was getting answers. If Zara wouldn't give them to me, I would appeal to her father, man to man.

"You must respect her decision," Adil told me, his expression uncharacteristically subdued, just as it had been in his study. "Compose yourself, Your Highness. A prince does not beg in this way."

"Right now, I am not a prince," I argued back, my misery clear in the strained timbre of my voice. "I'm just a man, and the woman I love is pledging herself to a man I know she despises. Why is she doing it, Adil? What's going on?"

Her father's dark eyes, similar to Zara's in a lot of ways, studied me carefully. "You really do love her, don't you?"

"I really do." I kept the words simple, hoping in their purity, he would hear their truth. "She is the most extraordinary woman I have ever known. I've never felt anything close to this for another woman. I wanted to speak to you about this privately rather than blurting it out like that, but under the circumstances…"

Adil grimaced, making it clear he understood what led to my outburst. "Were you serious when you said you would marry her? Is that even possible?"

"It won't be easy," I admitted. "My mother has some reservations and there are others in the kingdom who would also be against it. Before coming here, although I wanted it, I had my doubts that it could happen. But when you revealed that she's a princess, that removed the biggest obstacle. My father will agree, I am certain. As long as it's what Zara herself wants, we could find a way to make it work, and no matter what she said just now, I do believe it's what she wants too. She doesn't want to be with Malek. I have seen her true heart, I know I have, and it is far softer and more beautiful than the picture of herself she tried to paint. Life has made her hard and practical at times, but it is not who she truly is. She is strong but she also feels deeply. She has the heart of a queen."

Conflicting emotions swam in the depths of Adil's eyes as he considered my words. "And yet you brought her back here, knowing she might choose to stay."

I couldn't deny that, and I explained my reasoning to him. "I did it because she wanted to come. I would never force her to do anything that she didn't want to, and if I truly believed that she wanted to remain here as a trophy for Malek, I would accept that. But I *can't* believe that's true. Zara values her freedom far too much. The woman who escaped from Actilia and travelled across a continent on her own to find you would not willingly choose to enter the harem. Please, Adil: tell me what Malek has over her. Help me to help her."

"There is nothing you can do, Your Highness," he began, and when I went to protest, he held up his hands to stop me. "I don't mean there is nothing to be done, but there is nothing *you* can do. You asked what Malek has over her, and you are the answer. He has guessed that she cares for you and he has threatened your life."

"She told you this?" Why would she share it with her father but not with me?

"Not in so many words. She told me that Malek made threats against something she couldn't afford to lose, and my own spies in the prince's household filled in the rest."

"Spies?" Adil had my full attention now, even more than he had before.

"The Munisian court is full of people playing both sides," he told me ruefully. "I have spies in the prince's rooms and he has spies in mine. No doubt that is how he knew of the relationship between you and Zara. Very little that goes on here stays hidden for long."

His words were disturbing, but they also gave me a sliver of hope. "So, you must have information on him? Something that could be used on Zara's behalf?"

"It's not that easy," he warned me. "Malek needs to feel that he's won, at least for a while. When he's moved on to his next obsession, when his guard is down, I may be able to maneuver a deal for her."

"How long will that take?" The idea of Zara having to spend even one night with the prince made me sick, and the idea that she would do it to protect me made me feel even worse.

"Weeks. Maybe months." Adil knew his answer wouldn't be what I wanted to hear, and once again, he held up his hands to stem my disagreement. "I know that when you are young, that seems like a lifetime, but trust me, it's the best way. The most important thing for now is that you leave tomorrow, as Zara requested. So long as you are here, Malek can continue to use you to demand even further concessions from her."

Of course I didn't want to put her in that position, but how could I leave her behind? It simply seemed impossible. "I need to speak to her myself. There has to be another way…"

"It's too late," Adil told me simply. "She has already gone to the harem while we've been talking. Now that she's there, you cannot see her."

My stomach twisted painfully at the thought, and at the knowledge that she had planned this all ahead of time, putting my wellbeing ahead of her own. What must she be feeling right now? I couldn't even imagine.

"However, she managed to secure the concession that I will be able to see her from time to time," her father added. "It could be vital if we are to work together to free her."

What he said made sense, but I couldn't accept being shut out of all of it. "There must be something I can do. Malek cannot simply imprison or kill me. I'm the crown prince of Lassaria!"

I very rarely pulled rank, but if there had ever been a time for it, that time had come.

Adil, however, remained unmoved. "It makes no difference, Your Highness. He could easily make you disappear, you and your entire party, and send word back to your family that you were lost at sea. Hardly anyone would know the difference, and those that did would keep their mouths shut lest the same should happen to them. This is the way Malek operates."

"And you would serve such a man? Have you no honour?"

As he just pointed out, I had no leverage to make any demands, but I couldn't help asking the question anyway. What happened to the honourable man my father had been so impressed with, and the man that Zara looked up to?

Adil gave me a sad smile. "As Zara has already learned, when the life of your loved ones is at risk, honour quickly goes out the window. I will do what I can for her, but you and Prince Eric must leave tomorrow. There is no other way."

With that, he went out of the room, leaving my door guarded and me essentially locked in for the night. My eyes were drawn against my will to the spot where, just the night before, Zara and I had finally been joined as one against the wall, and I told her that I loved her. How, in less than twenty-four hours, had things gone so wrong?

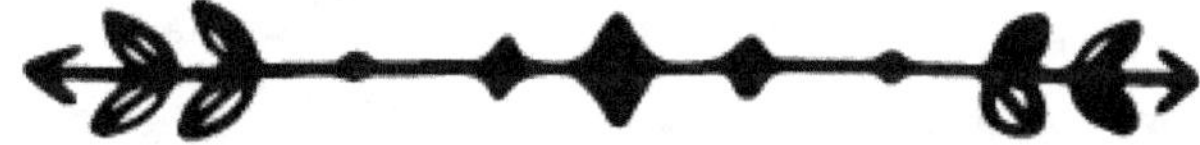

~Fatima~

The fisherman's home was little more than a wooden shack that smelled of fish and saltwater, not far from the port of a small fishing village. He gave me his own 'bed' of rags while he slept on the dirt floor next to me. A far cry from the luxury of the emperor's palace, I would have still embraced it happily if the thought of Khalid's fate didn't weigh so heavily on my heart. Try as I might, I couldn't imagine a scenario that didn't lead to his suffering and death, and as the fisherman snored loudly and wind whistled between the wooden slats of the walls, I stared up into the darkness, my earlier tears replaced by a helpless numbness.

Although Khalid had assured me he understood the risks and took responsibility for his decision, I couldn't help berating myself for my selfishness. If I could have simply accepted my lot, he would still be safe, giving me his warm smile as we sat together in the harem's hall. Was my freedom really worth more than a man's life?

And that assumed I even got away at all. If Malek tortured Khalid, as he almost certainly would, would Khalid tell him about the rest of the plan, about Zara and the princes and where they could find me? I couldn't blame him if he did. The emperor's soldiers could show up in the town at any time.

Or what if the princes never came? What if I had escaped simply to end up with no money and no food, stranded in a foreign land that I knew nothing of beyond the palace walls? Everything had seemed so clear and certain the night before, and now, it all felt dark and murky.

Eventually, I must have fallen asleep, worn out by the emotional strain of the day, for when I opened my eyes again, daylight streamed into the shack and the fisherman had gone.

A piece of bread and some fish were left on the small table near the door. The man must have gone to work and left them for me. With the orange I still had in my bag from the day before, it made for a decent breakfast, if not quite the breakfast I usually enjoyed. Khalid had chosen a kind and honourable man to help us and I whispered a silent thanks to my friend as I forced the food down my throat that felt tight with fresh tears.

Once I had eaten and tidied the small room as well as I could, I let myself out, trying to memorize the location of this shack among the other nearly identical ones that lined the beach just in case I needed to come back here. Though I didn't even know the fisherman's name, he would be my only friend in the world if the princes' ship did not arrive.

Hardly any activity could be seen in the small port with the fishing boats already gone out for the day. Unlike the harbour in the capital city, there were no officials overseeing each arrival, and I could see why Khalid had chosen it for a meeting point. Finding a spot with a clear view over the entire bay, I sat down on the ground to wait.

With each hour that passed, my mood grew darker. The princes could have been delayed for any number of reasons, or they may not be coming at all. If Malek suggested they were involved in my disappearance, they could be punished as well. Every possible worst-case scenario ran through my head, forming a large pit of despair in my stomach that threatened to swallow me whole, until, at last, a large ship appeared in the distance.

My heart began to pound as I watched it approach. Could it be the princes, or had Malek's men come to find me?

Too large to come into the small port, the ship weighed anchor some distance away while the men aboard lowered a small tender to row to the small pier. Some of the men inside wore uniforms, but they were unlike any of the emperor's colours I had seen before, and tentatively, hope began to rise in me.

Keeping my eyes on the small boat's approach, I got to my feet and walked to the pier slowly, conserving my energy in case I needed to run away at the last minute. As the boat drew level to the pier, a tall, dark-haired, light-skinned man leapt out. Though it had been years since I'd seen him, I recognized the Silatrian prince immediately, the younger of the two brothers I had met on that long ago day in a faraway land. My heart leapt into my throat as relief and anticipation flooded through my body.

He walked briskly down the pier, his eyes scanning the shore, and when he looked in my direction, I raised my arm tentatively. Though I couldn't be sure he even knew who he was looking for, to my surprise, his face lit up as he saw me, almost as if he recognized me too, and he broke into a jog as I moved quickly towards him as well.

"Fatima," he breathed, his eyes bright with relief as we got closer together and a warm smile that lit his face. "Thank goodness. My name is Eric, I'm…"

I couldn't help grinning back at him, despite the circumstances. "The second prince of Silatria. I know. We have met before."

"We have?" His eyes searched my face curiously, examining every feature as I drank in his appearance too. The charming, slightly goofy boy I remembered had been replaced by a strong, handsome man, but his bright, playful eyes were the same, and as his gaze moved across me, something I had never felt before stirred inside me. It felt like hope, but stronger too. I didn't know how to explain it.

"Many years ago," I explained, trying to jog his memory. "I came to your castle to meet your brother, along with my parents and older brother. I was just a girl at the time."

It took a second, but eventually recognition crossed his face. "Of course. The Actilian royal family. I had forgotten about that visit. The idea of marrying a little girl infuriated Cass, and your brother was a jerk."

The mention of my brother reminded me of everything that had happened that led to me being here in the first place. "Yes, he could be," I agreed, my lips tightening as I tried to hold back all the emotions fighting for priority inside me, the lost years and the cost of my freedom.

Eric winced, cursing beneath his breath. "I'm sorry, that was insensitive. I just… you took me by surprise. I felt a connection with you when I saw you the other day, but I didn't realize we had actually met before. It makes so much more sense now."

"You saw me?" I repeated curiously. That shouldn't have been possible. "When?"

"We have a lot to catch up on and we shouldn't linger here," he told me, gesturing towards the small boat he had arrived in. "Please, come with me."

I wanted nothing more, and when he offered me his arm, for the first time in years, I felt like a princess again.

Once we were safely settled in the boat and heading back towards his ship, I shared the story of Khalid's capture with Eric.

"He protected me to the very end," I said, my eyes dotting with tears, though it surprised me that I had any left by this point. "I'm so grateful to you and the Lassarian prince for helping me, but I wish it hadn't come to this."

Eric grimaced as he looked towards the ship. Following his gaze, I could see another man on the deck, fairer than Eric, his shoulders stooped miserably. "You are not the only one leaving someone behind in the palace. Things have not gone entirely to plan."

As he told me what happened to Zara, a fresh wave of guilt washed over me. How many people needed to suffer on my behalf?

Eric seemed to know the thoughts in my head without me saying a word. "None of this is your fault, Fatima. Malek is responsible for all of it. He is the one to blame."

Accepting that would be easier said than done, but Eric also told me what Zara had told him about Khalid, about how his punishment had been commuted to imprisonment in a pit, but I couldn't see how that would be much better. It definitely didn't make me feel any better.

The men aboard the ship raised our small boat back to the deck of the larger ship, and once we had alighted, Eric introduced me to Prince Arthur.

"It's a pleasure to meet you," he said, bowing politely, but the sadness in his blue eyes outweighed any happiness his words implied. "I'm glad we could help you."

"I'm so sorry about Princess Zara. I never intended for things to go this way."

"It's not your fault," Arthur told me, unconsciously echoing Eric's words. "Zara knew what she risked in helping you. It's simply the kind of woman she is, and she would want us to complete what she started. That's the reason I forced myself to leave, as she requested."

His face tightened miserably, and I could see in his expression just how hard it must have been for him to leave her there. It appeared there might be more than merely friendship between them.

"The two of you are a sorry sight," Eric told us both bluntly, looking between Arthur's sad face and mine. "And I don't intend to put up with it for the weeks it will take to return home."

Arthur's expression darkened to a scowl. "Just because you got what you wanted doesn't mean that all is right with the world."

"Of course it doesn't," Eric replied. "Which is why we need to make it right. That's why I intend to return to the Munisian palace tonight. What I need to know is: who's coming with me?"

~**Eric**~

The looks on Arthur's and Fatima's faces switched almost in perfect sync from misery to confusion.

"What do you mean you're going back?" Arthur asked, his brow furrowed in concern. "You're the one who spent half the morning convincing me we had to leave!"

When I went to speak with him first thing that morning, pushing past the men who were still standing guard outside his room, I found that Zara's secret wasn't such a secret after all. Arthur already knew nearly as much about the situation as I did, so I quickly told him the rest, everything that Zara had told me about why she had said the things she did and why Arthur needed to leave.

"How am I supposed to just leave her here?" he asked me in agony. "With *him*?"

We could agree that the situation couldn't be called ideal, but I had been forced to leave Fatima in the harem for two nights after first seeing her, so I repeated his words back to him, sarcastically. "They have their own customs and their own beliefs. We shouldn't interfere."

His scowl made it clear he recognized the words and didn't appreciate hearing them any more than I had. "I helped you as much as I could, Eric, and Fatima is free now."

"She is, but she's still relying on us to come and meet her today, and Zara has asked you to leave. She says that's how you can help her. Aren't you the one who's always going on about letting women make their own choices? This is what she wants, at least right now."

We argued back and forth a while longer, but finally he had to concede that, with no other plan, following Zara's instructions made the most sense.

That explained why he looked so completely flummoxed by my apparent change of heart, but my decision wasn't quite as impulsive as it seemed. I'd been observing things carefully for the whole of our stay, and knowing the situation with Zara as well as the man who had helped Fatima to escape, I had a plan that I thought could work. Seeing Fatima's distress over her friend's fate had only served to convince me even further of the necessity of my plan.

"We needed Malek to believe we had left, which we've done. Now, we can go back, but not as the princes of Lassaria and Silatria. As far as anyone knows, we are two foreign merchants. We change our clothes, arrive on a smaller ship, and no one will know the difference. It worked for Fatima to get out, and I think it will work just as well for us to get back in. The palace is so huge and spread out that the chances of anyone recognizing us out of context are small. We only need to get as far as the administration buildings, not into the emperor's home."

"What will you do in the administration buildings?" Fatima asked, following along just as eagerly as Arthur.

Arthur, though, had already figured it out. "Adil," he said slowly, before explaining further to Fatima. "Zara's father. He can get access to Zara."

"Right," I agreed. "Trying to get into the emperor's lodgings or the harem itself would be too difficult, but if we can get Adil to get Zara out, we might have a chance. He should also know where the prison is."

"The prison?" Fatima repeated curiously, her pretty hazel eyes filling with hope. "Where Khalid will be?"

Her revelation earlier that we had met each other before had taken me completely by surprise, but as soon as she said it, the memory surfaced from deep inside me, a memory I had completely forgotten I had.

As the crown prince, my brother, Cassian, had been the frequent target for other royal and noble families who were looking for a good match for their daughters. At first, I thought it funny how he kept getting paraded in front of these visiting delegations, but eventually, I grew jealous too. No one ever came specifically to offer their daughters to me. Sometimes, if they had two daughters, they would suggest one for me, as an afterthought, to sweeten the deal.

Fatima's family had been one in a long line of potential matches for Cass, and I probably wouldn't have remembered them at all if it weren't for Fatima herself. She had been just a child, as she said, but that meant she didn't yet have all the proper manners and reserve that most princesses did. While Cass stood there stiffly, enduring the meeting as best he could, clearly not happy about the prospect of being forced to marry this little girl, I did an impression of him, mostly to alleviate my own boredom, but also to see if I could get a reaction, and to my delight, the girl smiled, her big, hazel eyes dancing in amusement.

No one paid any attention to me besides her, so I grew bolder, imitating my father and hers as well, and her smile grew wider until she giggled aloud and her mother quickly silenced her. Even after that admonishment, her eyes kept returning to me, full of warmth and humour, and even though she was only a girl, no one had ever looked at me in quite that way before.

After they left, her name kept coming up in serious considerations for the position of Cass' wife due to her family's wealth and connections, and the idea that those eyes would one day be focused on him instead of me sat bitterly in my chest. But then, of course, Actilia had been plundered and her father killed, and I had forgotten about the whole thing, not making the connection between those brief moments of shared camaraderie in a throne room and the beautiful young woman I saw by the reflecting pool in a foreign palace, until she reminded me of it.

That must have been why I felt such an instant pull towards her. I had recognized her without realizing it, and just as I had on that long ago day, I wanted to help her. Only now, instead of providing distraction and amusement, we were playing with life and death: Khalid's, Zara's, and our own.

"We have a great deal of money and gold," I told Fatima. "I'm sure we can bribe the prison guards to help us get Khalid out."

On our tour through the palace, while Arthur and Zara were checking out the security arrangements, I had looked for different things. I noticed the way money exchanged hands in several different ways, quietly and inconspicuously, to let things pass through the checkpoints that shouldn't. The men close to the emperor might be loyal to him, but the other officials throughout the palace could be bought, I felt certain of it. Malek thought the palace secure, but my brother Cass had thought the same when it came to our own castle. What neither of them realized, and what I had learned from Westley Eastam, was that when men felt no personal connection to the man they served, they could be persuaded to act against him with remarkable ease, so long as the price was right.

"Do you speak the language?" Fatima asked us in her own accent. "How will you speak to the guards?"

I had a couple of options. "There are translators at the port that we could hire and bribe as well. Or, if you want to come with us, you could translate for us. I know you just got out and I know it's a risk. If you would rather not, we will completely understand."

Fatima didn't hesitate. "If I can help to save Khalid, I will go."

"Where are we getting another ship?" Arthur asked, and for that, I pointed to the waters around us where vessels were dotted along the coast.

"We pick one that will work and we buy it for the day. Simple as that. Our ship can remain close by so that we can make our getaway once we have everyone we want to leave with."

"You seem pretty sure of yourself," Arthur pointed out warily, but I could see the spark of excitement in his eyes too. The idea of sailing away without taking action had gone against every instinct he had. He would take any risk to help Zara, and we needed that attitude if we were going to succeed.

"I did learn a few things from Eastam," I told him. "He did things that shouldn't have been possible, that any sane person would have never attempted. His success often came down to his boldness and doing things no one expected him to do. But where he only ever cared about helping himself, we'll use those same techniques to gain freedom for our friends. Are you with me?"

I could have predicted his response almost word-for-word: "What are we waiting for?"

CHAPTER TWELVE

~Arthur~

It looked like I'd been wrong about Eric, and I couldn't be happier about it. The weeks I'd spent with him tracking Eastam down hadn't left me with the best impression, and though he'd been more serious on this journey, I still thought he was focused only on Fatima and himself, getting her out and getting his trade deal. However, as he pulled clothes out of his trunks that should help us pass as traders from a kingdom close to Actilia, I had to admit I'd underestimated him.

"I spent a lot of time feeling sorry for myself after getting duped by Eastam," he explained while we changed our clothes and covered our heads, making ourselves look as different from before as we possibly could. "I thought no one would ever see me as anything other than a disgrace. Someone special helped me to see how that attitude didn't do me any favours, and the more I thought about it, the more I realized that despite how Eastam used me, I'd learned things from him too. Even if you hate the man, which I know you do and I do too, you have to admit his achievements were impressive. He cheated death so many times. He got himself out of our prison and he poisoned my father. He never accepted that things were impossible, not so long as a person existed whose greed he could appeal to."

That kind of reasoning had never made much sense to me since I didn't understand the kind of self-interest that would drive someone to betray those he had sworn to protect, but if tapping into that would help Zara, I would happily give it a try.

I could think of nothing I wouldn't do for her, including leaving her behind that morning since she asked me to. Malek himself had come to wish us farewell, or at least he gave that excuse for coming to see us. I suspected he really came to make sure we actually left, especially when he offered to send some of his own men down to the harbour with us to ensure we got away with no 'unnecessary delays'.

Eric kept a hand on my shoulder through the whole exchange, as if he feared I would attack the crown prince right there in the middle of the palace, and the idea certainly tempted me. The only thing that held me back was knowing that Zara would be held accountable for my actions, and so I simply thanked him for his hospitality and walked away, each step torturous in the knowledge that Zara remained behind me, locked away in the harem at that man's mercy.

Without doubt, I had never had to do anything more difficult in all my life. Breaking back into the palace seemed positively simple in comparison.

The dress Fatima wore was dusty and torn, and she told us about how she'd traded Zara's dress for the beggar woman's dress to aid her escape. "Very clever, but they won't let you in the palace looking like that," Eric mused as he looked her over. "It would be better if you dress in my clothes instead. We'll secure your hair up under your hat, and you could pass for a very pretty boy."

Fatima's cheeks coloured as she took the clothes Eric offered. "I'll just be a moment," she promised, stepping out of the room to go get changed.

"Are you sure we should take her along?" I asked Eric once we were alone. "Endangering ourselves is one thing, but we did all of this to get her out in the first place. What if she's recognized?"

Eric had an answer ready for me. "Nobody recognized her on the way out. It will help us to have someone who speaks the language and knows the culture more than we do. She got out, so we know she can deal with the pressure. Most of all, she wants to help her friend."

"I understand all of that, but the risk..."

"She's coming, Arthur," he told me firmly. "Her whole life, everything has been decided for her. Now, she wants to take action and I'm not going to stand in her way. Sometimes, we need to make our own choices."

Put that way, I had to give in too.

We pulled up alongside a large fishing vessel, and after some negotiation, the men manning it agreed to sail us to the harbour in the capital city and wait for us there. Eric paid half the offered fee now with the other half promised to them once they returned us to our ship. The amount easily exceeded what they made in a month, so their incentive would be high, and we paid them out of the money Malek himself had given us as part of our trade deal. There was something immensely satisfying in using his own money to try to outsmart Malek at his own game.

When we arrived at the port we had left only a few hours earlier, officers boarded our ship just as they had on our initial arrival. Unlike that time, where we presented our royal seals, this time, Fatima told them that we were merchants from one of the kingdoms neighbouring Actilia, here to meet with the administration officials about a business deal. Her accent helped to convince them of the truth of our origin, and the money that Eric offered helped to smooth our way. Before long, we were released from the harbour with directions to the palace.

"That went well," I murmured to Eric as we walked back up the same hill we had descended earlier that day.

"Getting in will be the easy part," he told me, mirroring Malek's own words on the subject. "When we want to get out is when it will get difficult."

At the palace gate, Fatima's explanation and Eric's coins gained us entry to the first level. We had no weapons to surrender at the second gate, supporting our story that we were simply merchants, and I heard Fatima use Adil's name in her conversation with the guard there. When we'd been admitted after another small bribe from Eric, I asked Fatima what she'd said.

"They wanted to know who we were meeting with. I had to give a name and I didn't know any others. I hope that's okay."

"That was quick thinking," Eric assured her. "We do need to speak to him anyway, and it gives us some extra legitimacy. Well done."

Eric remembered the way back to Adil's office with no problem, and we found ourselves facing the same clerk who had taken us in to see Adil a few days earlier when we first arrived as royal visitors. If we were going to be recognized, this seemed a likely time, but when Fatima introduced us, making it clear that Eric and I didn't speak the language, the clerk only gave us a cursory glance before focusing on Fatima. They spoke for a few minutes before the man left us with instructions to wait where we were.

"He said he'll pass the message on but that it could be a significant wait," Fatima whispered to us once the clerk walked away. "Hopefully, my message will work."

"What did you say?" Eric asked curiously.

Fatima gave a sheepish shrug. "I told him we had heard about his daughter's return and wanted to discuss a new business opportunity for her, similar to the one the Actilian princess just took part in."

Her phrasing was both clever and accurate, and Eric and I both tried and failed to keep from smiling. Having Fatima along had definitely proven to be an asset so far, and hardly any time passed before we were being summoned to Adil's office.

This time, he sat on his own in the large office, and he greeted us politely in front of the clerk, introducing himself to us and shaking our hands, but as soon as the door had closed, Adil dropped any pretense of not knowing who we were.

"Why have you come back here? What is the meaning of this, Your Highness-es?"

"We came back for Zara," I told him. "And this time, we're not leaving without her."

"It's not possible…" he tried to protest, but Eric didn't give him a chance to continue.

"It's not only possible, it's happening. Everything is already in motion, and this is your chance to not only help your daughter, but to make up for what you did to Fatima as well."

When Eric indicated the woman next to him, who Adil must not have recognized before now, Zara's father's mouth fell open in surprise. Hesitantly, he walked over to her and bowed his head. "Your Highness. I am sorry for the part I played in your imprisonment here."

"I'm sorry for what my father and brother did," Fatima replied magnanimously. "It's in the past now, so let's leave it there. But Prince Eric is right: we need your help to save not only Zara, but my friend, Khalid, as well."

Adil looked between the three of us, his mind obviously racing, before clasping his hands in front of him. "Tell me exactly what you are thinking."

~**Zara**~

The mood in the harem that morning felt solemn. I heard whispers among the other women that Malek had called upon Sade last night in his frustration at not being able to have me, and that she had come back with bruises on her body. She was not at breakfast, and I understood that the women were only excused from appearing with explicit permission from Minsa herself.

Guilt tried to worm its way into my chest, but I pushed it away. Malek's behaviour was not my fault, and if I took everything he did personally, I would never know a moment's peace. I couldn't protect every single member of the harem without getting rid of Malek himself, and as tempting as that idea might be, I needed to consider my family as well, along with Arthur. More people were affected by my actions than just me, and killing the crown prince would definitely come with repercussions, no matter how tempting it might seem.

At lunch, I received a message from my father letting me know that Arthur and Eric had departed, and both relief and despair rushed through me. As glad as I felt that Arthur had gone where he would be safe, I hated it as well, and the idea that he still thought I meant it when I said I didn't love him made me feel slightly ill.

"May I return to my room, Your Highness?" I asked Minsa, bowing my head to her politely as I approached. "I'm not feeling well."

Obviously, she thought I meant because of my menstruation. Nothing remained a secret in the harem, it seemed. "You are not allowed to hide every month," she warned me. "But I will make an exception today while you adjust."

"Thank you, Your Highness."

As much as it grated on me, I would treat her politely until I had a firmer plan about how I could get out of there, and as soon as I reached my room, I sat down to begin to think of one, taking stock of the advantages and disadvantages I had.

My father and his connections and knowledge of the palace were a clear advantage, so long as I could convince him to use them on my behalf. The reluctance of the eunuchs to engage with me at all would be an obstacle I would need to overcome, as was Minsa's need to control my movements. Malek, of course, remained an obstacle too, but so long as I could avoid him until I had a chance to regroup with my father…

No sooner had the thought crossed my mind than my door burst open, taking me by surprise. There were no locks on the door, but I hadn't expected anyone to simply walk in, and when I turned to see who stood there, my stomach sank.

"Your Highness." I greeted Malek with all the deference I could muster as my mind raced, trying to figure out what he would have come. With Arthur gone, he should have nothing more to say to me. "May I help you?"

"You think you're very clever," he declared, his eyes narrowed as he closed the door behind him. His presence in my room surprised me for more reasons than one. Given my current 'unclean' state, he shouldn't be around me at all, and even excepting that, the ruler generally didn't visit women in the harem's bedrooms. All sexual activity took place in his rooms, away from the other women.

"In general, I believe I'm quite clever," I agreed mildly. "But I'm not sure what you're talking about in particular."

His lips curled unpleasantly. "This monthly bleeding seems awfully convenient."

My heart beat a little faster as I tried to keep a straight face. From the things I'd heard, he was forbidden to check for himself. The servants had that responsibility, and he would have to take their word for it. "I can assure you it's not convenient for me. No woman would ever say such a thing."

His smile grew bigger, and crueler. "I do like your smart mouth, Zara. I'll like it more when you beg me with it."

In an instant, he came to my side, grabbing hold of my arm with one hand and pulling me to my feet while the other hand slid expertly down the loose harem pants I wore. As I cried out in surprise, his fingers pushed roughly inside me. I shoved him back as hard as I could, glaring at him, but not in time. He raised his fingers in front of him and in front of my face too, in the space between us.

"Just as I thought," he said, his voice dangerously low as he looked between me and his clean fingers. "No blood."

"I must have dried up just looking at you." The words were out of me before I'd thought them through, and though Malek's eyes narrowed again, I caught a flash of excitement in them too. My insults were turning the sick bastard on. As someone who had people to cater to his every wish, he'd probably never had anyone stand up to him before.

Did that explain his interest in me in the first place? That long ago encounter where he'd given me an order and I refused it, did that seal my fate long before I understood a thing about it?

"I'll be the judge of that," he threatened. His hands went to his own pants, and as I followed his movements, I could see the growing erection there. Did he actually intend to force me? Had he forced himself on Sade the night before? He was even more disgusting than I thought, but if he wanted a fight, I would give him one.

However, before he could pull his pitiful cock out, someone else knocked on the door.

Growling in dissatisfaction, Malek yanked the door open again. "What?"

The eunuch who stood there froze in surprise at seeing the prince in my room. "Your... Your Highness, I'm so sorry. I didn't realize..."

He bowed, unable to put any further words together, and Malek made another impatient grunt. "What did you want? Spit it out."

"The... the minister. His daughter. He's here. To see her, he wants."

The words weren't in order, but I understood them well enough and so did Malek as he looked over at me suspiciously. "Why is your father here?"

I could give him a genuine shrug, as I had no idea. "I don't know, Your Highness. I haven't spoken to him yet."

Malek's lips tightened as he turned back to the eunuch. "Bring him here. Immediately!"

He shouted the last word when the man didn't move instantly, and the poor eunuch scrambled away, his head still down.

"I will stay to hear what he has to say," Malek informed me, reaching down to adjust himself. "Then, we can pick up where we left off."

With that threat echoing in my ears, I awaited my father's arrival, which didn't take long. His eyes were bright as he entered, but when he saw Malek there, his expression dimmed considerably and he bowed his head. "Your Highness. What are you doing here?"

"This is my harem, Adil," Malek responded coldly. "I can be here whenever I want."

"Yes. Of course." My father lowered his head even further, but Malek's presence had obviously thrown him and he glanced over at me from the corner of his eye almost helplessly. Clearly, whatever he had come to say, he didn't want to repeat in front of the prince.

"What are you here for?" the prince prompted impatiently. "I granted you permission to visit the harem on the understanding that it would be used only when necessary, not simply to chat."

No such stipulation had actually been made, but arguing that point didn't seem like the best use of our time or energy. "What is it, Baba?" I asked, more gently. "I have no secrets from Malek."

I hoped he would understand my words, that he should feel free to tell me whatever he had to say, and I would find a way to explain it to Malek afterwards, if necessary. I needed to know what had been so vital to tell me that he had come here on my first day in the harem.

"It is the prisoner, Khalid," my father explained, his eyes darting between me and Malek. "He has requested to speak to Zara. We think he may give up Fatima's location, but only to her."

Cold disbelief flooded my veins as I looked over at Malek. "Are you still looking for her? You promised me you would discontinue the search."

"I will give up when there's no chance of finding her," Malek reasoned. "But if the boy will give her up, I cannot let her go. It's a dangerous precedent to set."

Of course. He didn't want any of the other women thinking they could simply leave if they wanted to. His word to me obviously meant nothing, and if he found Fatima, he would find Arthur and Eric too. I couldn't let that happen.

Were my father's words true, though? Or was he trying to give me some kind of message?

"So, you will grant her leave to visit the prison, Your Highness?" my father asked. "I will accompany her, of course, and return her safely afterwards."

That made things a little clearer. It felt like he wanted to get me out of the harem, but for what purpose?

"She can go," Malek agreed, rather to my surprise, until he added a further condition. "But I will accompany her as well. I assume that's not a problem."

The challenge in his words couldn't be clearer, and my father couldn't refuse it as he bowed to his prince once more. "Of course not, Your Highness. Please, follow me, both of you."

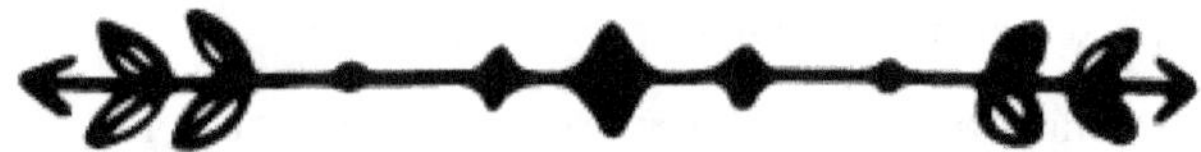

~Fatima~

Moving through the world as a man, even a small, unimpressive one, was a completely different experience from anything I had known before. Wearing Eric's clothes, everyone accepted me as male. There were no lustful stares and no derisive looks either. People listened to me and treated me just as they would any man, which was to say they treated me as if my words had importance. It gave me a fascinating insight into the gendered world we lived in, but it all paled in significance next to our conversation with Adil.

As soon as we were alone with him in his office, Eric laid out his plan, explaining how we wanted to rescue Khalid from the prison and take Zara out of the palace as well. Eric said he had enough money to make it happen, but we needed Adil's help to find the prison and to get Zara out. After they had gone back and forth a few times with questions, Adil nodded slowly.

"It's possible. They won't be expecting anything so quickly after your departure and on the heels of yesterday's escape. You'll have the element of surprise." Among his papers, Adil had a plan of the palace and he laid it on the table for us all to see. "The prison is here, with its own entrance and exit so prisoners don't have to be paraded through the palace unless it's deemed advisable to set an example."

"So, we could use this exit to get out?" Arthur asked, leaning close to look at the plans carefully.

"It would be best to," Adil agreed. "But you will need a lot of money, a lot of persuasion, and a lot of luck."

"We have the first two," Eric assured him. "And I believe I make my own luck."

He might be right about that. My luck had certainly changed ever since his arrival in the palace.

Adil said he had an employee he trusted who would take us down to the prison on the pretext of giving us a tour, while Adil himself went to the harem.

"How will you get Zara out?" Arthur asked.

"I will have to bring her to the prison," Adil suggested. "Then we can all leave together."

"We?" I didn't miss the word he used. "You're coming too?"

"Of course he is," Eric replied on Adil's behalf, not at all surprised. "They'll know he helped his daughter escape. This time, we're not leaving anyone behind. What about your family?"

Adil had a plan for that too. "We have an emergency procedure in place if we need to leave. I will stop at my home first to let them know it's time, and they will go to the harbour. There's room for all of us on your ship?"

"Yes," Eric and Arthur agreed in unison.

"You're welcome in Lassaria," Arthur promised. "All of you."

"In that case, I suppose we should get moving." Adil looked around his office almost wistfully before giving his head a shake. "Hopefully, this is the last big adventure of my life."

He called for his employee and explained the situation in only as much detail as necessary. The man would take us to the prison, do anything we asked of him, and turn a blind eye to anything we did. When Adil said goodbye to him, the younger man understood he would not be coming back, and they exchanged a warm embrace before Adil left us to return to his private quarters and the harem.

How strange it felt to think of how near we were to the harem, the place where I had spent so many years. The other women were all still there, their day going on just as every other day before it had, only with Zara there in my place. My children from Malek were also only a few minutes' walk away, but even if it were possible to take them with me, I had no idea what they looked like or even what their names were. They would know nothing of me either. They belonged to Munisia, and here, they would have to stay.

Leaving Adil's office, we followed his colleague through more parts of the palace I had never seen before, through back doors and narrow alleys and hidden passages until we arrived at the prison entrance. The man gave his credentials and explained that we were foreign visitors who had an interest in prison construction. We had Adil's approval, and that, along with the gold coins that Eric pressed into his hand, proved sufficient for the man guarding the door to let us through. We were each handed a lantern to light our way as there would be no natural light within the walls.

The prison had been built against the outer wall of the palace on the side of the hill and went down for three floors, according to the map Adil showed us. The pit where Khalid would be kept was down on the bottom floor, but we couldn't go straight there. We needed to keep up our act for a little while so we didn't raise any suspicions, but with each step, my heart beat a little faster. Hopefully, Malek hadn't been lying about the change in sentence. Hopefully, Khalid would actually be there, still alive. I peered into each cell we passed, holding my lantern up to check if any of the men looked familiar, but I didn't recognize anyone among the desperate, shadowed faces that looked back at me.

At last, we descended the final staircase where another guard stood outside an iron gate. When our guide explained we were there to learn about the prison, the guard welcomed the break from the monotony of his job and explained it to us himself, sending the first man away. "This is one of the innovations of the Munisian prison. People called it the pit of Limbo, because when you're inside, you can't be certain of anything. Is it day or night? Are you alive or dead? Does the world still exist? In the pit, nothing is clear. And even if the world does exist, it has forgotten all about you. Some of the men are even served only by a deaf and blind man who lowers their food to them daily. There's no one to speak to."

He said all of this as if it were something to be proud of rather than cruel and inhumane, and my heart ached at the thought of Khalid having to spend even a day here. Hopefully, it would only be a few minutes longer.

"How many pits are inside?" Eric asked, and I translated the question for him.

The man answered eagerly. "Four, though only three are occupied at the moment. We just filled one of them yesterday."

That must be Khalid, a fact which Eric recognized immediately too. "Can we see that one?"

For the first time, the guard hesitated. "No one is allowed in with the prisoners. Not even I can see them. I can take you to the empty one, if you like."

"We'd like to ask the prisoner some questions to be sure it's appropriate for our own use," Arthur tried. "No one would need to know you let us in, and we'll compensate you for your trouble, naturally."

When I had translated all of that, the guard grew even more wary. "Where did you say you were from?"

Eric didn't respond to that. Instead, he punched the man hard, knocking him out cold as I gasped in surprise.

"We can't waste any more time," Eric explained as he dragged the man's unconscious body over to the wall and removed his ring of keys from his pocket. "Looks like we've got a one in four chance. Let's move as quickly as we can."

It took a few tries before he found the right key for the main door, and once inside, we found ourselves in a narrow hall, presented with four more locked doors, each with their own unique lock.

"Khalid?" I called out, not sure how thick the walls were or how deep the pits inside were. Any chance to narrow down the search would make things quicker.

Unfortunately, we couldn't hear any response, so Eric got to work on the first lock. After finally getting inside, we stepped into a small, square room with what looked like a deep circular well in the middle. Around the hole, the floor was wide enough for one person to stand, with a little more room in each of the four corners. The width of the pit in the centre, on the other hand, couldn't even accommodate a person lying down inside it, and the stench coming from the hole overpowered us as soon as we walked in, a smell of sweat, urine and decay. I began to cough as I tried not to breathe in too deeply.

"Khalid?" Eric called down into the darkness, covering his nose with his hand.

Again, we couldn't hear any response, but the hole was so dark and deep that we couldn't tell if the silence meant the pit lay empty or if we simply couldn't hear the response.

"Let's try the next one," Arthur suggested. "We can come back if we have to."

Closing the door behind us again but leaving it unlocked, we moved to the next one. This time, the poor man inside did respond, begging us for help, but the voice didn't belong to Khalid.

"We can't help everyone," Arthur apologized to me, seeing the look of dismay on my face as Eric refastened the lock. "We don't know what that man's done."

"Is there any crime that deserves this punishment?" I wondered, and to his credit, Arthur didn't try to argue otherwise.

In the third room, the smell didn't hit us quite so hard, and when I called out for Khalid, a dismayed voice answered us from deep in the ground.

"Fatima? No! What are you doing here?"

"That's him!" I exclaimed to the others, though of course they must have already realized it when he said my name even if they didn't understand the rest of what he said. Together, we walked around the pit to the corner on the far side of the room where there would be the most room. "Now, how do we get him out?"

"That's not what you should be worried about right now."

A new voice spoke from the door, and my stomach sank to my feet as I realized who it belonged to. Swinging my lantern around, its light landed on the three people who stood in the entrance to the room: Adil, Zara, and Malek himself.

CHAPTER THIRTEEN

~Arthur~

Malek winced as the light from Fatima's lantern hit his eyes, and I immediately lowered my light, my heart beginning to pound furiously in my chest as I motioned to Eric to also lower his lantern, keeping it away from his face.

Malek showing up definitely wasn't part of the plan.

I couldn't begin to imagine how he came to be there, unless Adil had sold us out, but my gut told me otherwise. Whatever wrongs he'd committed in the past, Adil wouldn't endanger Zara in that way. Her happiness mattered to him, as it did to me; we understood that much about each other, man-to-man.

Adil also held a lantern, the only lantern between the three of them at the door, and he quickly followed my lead in lowering it, no doubt sizing up the situation as quickly as I had. Malek had only heard Fatima speak and he might not have recognized me and Eric in the darkness yet. Until we knew exactly what Malek's presence signified, it seemed prudent to try to keep our identities a secret.

"You made a big mistake in coming back here, Fatima," Malek threatened as he squinted into the darkness, trying to focus his eyes again after the bright flash of light.

"I'm not going to let you harm my friend." Though she must be terrified, her anger towards Malek outweighed her fear and her voice carried strongly through the small space, echoing down into the pit below us. "You've never cared for another person in your life, so you wouldn't understand how it feels. When you love someone, you put their needs first."

Malek's reply was cold and cruel. "You're right that I don't understand. I don't understand why you would risk your life for something so foolish, any of you. You and these men helping you will also be punished. My men are waiting just outside. There will be no escape this time."

Referring to me and Eric as 'these men' seemed to confirm my suspicion that he still didn't know exactly who we were, but the reference to men outside concerned me. Was he telling the truth? If so, how many men were there? *Where* were they? Even if we could find a way to get past Malek, we still needed to get out of the prison and we had no weapons with us.

Before I could decide what to do next, however, Zara took matters into her own hands. "Baba? May I borrow your knife?"

Her words were so polite and mild-mannered that it took all of us a second to realize her intention. That second proved one too many for Malek, since Adil immediately handed his weapon to his daughter, and as soon as the knife handle hit her palm, Zara had the prince up against the wall, the blade pressed to his neck. I could just make out their forms in the murky darkness across the chasm of the pit.

"He only has two men outside," she announced to the entire room as pride and admiration ran through me. She never failed to impress me. "Get Khalid out, quickly."

We didn't need to be told twice. Just before Malek arrived, Fatima had asked how we intended to rescue Khalid, and she didn't know our plan only because she hadn't changed her clothes with me and Eric. When we got dressed, he had handed me a length of strong rope from the ship to wrap around my body beneath my tunic and he had done the same. Now, we both unwrapped them before tying the two lengths together with a sturdy knot, placing our lanterns on the floor. Still keeping silent, Eric lowered one end of the rope into the dark hole.

Fatima called out something to Khalid in his own language, presumably asking him if he could feel the rope, and a moment later, we felt a tug from the other end.

Working in tandem with no words between us, Eric and I braced ourselves for his ascent. Eric secured the other end of the rope around his waist and leaned back against the wall in the corner of the room, wedging himself firmly against it as he held onto the rope tightly. Meanwhile, I faced him, pushing him back onto the wall and using all my weight to keep him steady. Hopefully, it would be enough.

When Khalid pulled on the rope with his full weight, Eric staggered forward but I pushed back, both of us using every ounce of our strength. This effort marked the difference between life or death, not just for Khalid but potentially for us too, and neither of us intended to go down without a fight.

"Even if he gets out, you're not getting away," Malek sneered, still making a nuisance of himself even with his neck exposed to Zara's blade. "You'll all pay for this, but especially you, Zara. While the others get a swift death, you'll get much worse. I would have made you my wife, but now I'll have my use of you, and when I'm done, I'll gift you to the palace guards. You can service them until it kills you. You think you had it bad in those foreign lands where you traded your body for money? You haven't seen anything yet."

"Arthur!" Eric's whispered hiss in my ear made me realize that my concentration had slipped, my mind focused on the conversation across the room instead of the task at hand, and my body being pulled towards Zara by an instinctive need to defend and protect her. With Eric's warning, I immediately pushed forward again, as hard as I could as Khalid continued to climb.

"You're very confident for someone with a knife at his throat," Zara observed, not sounding flustered in the least by what Malek had said. "Maybe I should threaten something you truly care about instead."

I couldn't see anything that might be happening as sweat trickled down the back of my neck from the exertion of holding Eric steady, but Zara's next words made her meaning clearer.

"You seem to like relieving other men of their manhoods. Perhaps I should take yours too."

A yelp sounded out in the small space, which I could only guess came from Malek. Exactly what Zara did to him to elicit that sound remained a mystery to me.

"Zara," Adil warned her softly. "You cannot injure him. It is the highest crime against the empire. The punishment would be worse than anything you can imagine.""Only if they catch me," she shot back while Eric and I continued to struggle to maintain our balance. My body had never felt so strained as I fought against the pull of Khalid's weight and the desire to help Zara with Malek. "Once I'm free, they'll never be able to find me."

"You'll never be free," Malek snarled, apparently not knowing when to quit. "You belong to me. You always have."

"You're a deluded, pathetic little man." For a moment, Zara almost sounded sorry for him. "But we agree on one thing: as long as you're alive, you'll be a threat. It's lucky for me, then, and for Fatima, and Sade, and all the other women who despise you, that you're clumsy enough to fall right onto my knife."

"Zara!" Adil cried right as Khalid emerged from the pit. As Fatima helped to pull him to safety, Eric and I collapsed on the floor, and I turned my head back just in time to see Zara twisting the blade of her knife into Malek's stomach, the scene illuminated only by the lantern's dim light.

She did it. She actually stabbed him.

He looked just as surprised as the rest of us. "You... you can't," he gasped.

"Except that I just did. You can't tell me what to do. You never could. Goodbye, Malek."

With that, she lowered him down against the wall, the blade still in his stomach, holding him there until he went still. Satisfied with her work, she stood up and turned to her father.

"When the guards find him here, they'll face death themselves for letting someone kill him. If they claim he fell accidentally instead, they might only lose their job. We'll leave the blade and they can come up with a story about..."

As she spoke, her back to Malek, I saw a movement behind her. Using what must have been his last of his strength as his life's blood seeped into the robes he wore, dripping onto the cold stone ground, Malek pulled the knife from his stomach and staggered to his feet, his eyes fixed on Zara in pure hatred.

"No!" I cried out, breaking my silence for the first time since they'd appeared.

It couldn't end this way, not after everything she'd been through. But laying on the ground, my body still shaking from the exertion of pulling Khalid from the pit, I could do nothing but shout to warn her as my heart leapt into my throat.

However, Adil had also noticed Malek's movement, and he echoed my cry as he shoved Zara to the wall and threw himself between his daughter and his prince, taking Malek by surprise. The prince stumbled back along the narrow ledge, trying to grab onto Adil for support, but the momentum proved to be too much for both of them.

In the next second, both men tumbled together over the edge into the deep, dark hole. The lantern Adil had been holding went with them, casting an eerie glow up the dark walls as it fell.

"Baba!" Zara screamed just before a sickening crunch of bone echoed through the room as the falling men hit the ground at the bottom of the pit.

For a long, breathless moment, no one spoke. In stunned silence, none of us quite able to believe what had just happened, I scrambled to my feet, rounding the hole to go to Zara and wrapping my arms around her as she stood there in shocked disbelief.

Finally, after what seemed an eternity, a quiet voice called from the depths. "He's dead. The prince is dead. For good."

Keeping Zara behind me, I got as close as I dared to the edge of the pit and peered down into it. The lantern was still glowing and the two bodies were tangled up together so much that, at first, I couldn't tell where one ended and the other began. Adil raised his hand, which helped to make a bit more sense of the jumble, and I caught sight of Malek's head at an unnatural angle to his body, his neck broken and his eyes lifeless.

His life had been ended twice, it seemed; once by Zara, and again by the fall. There weren't many people I would say deserved an end like that, but when it came to Malek, I couldn't bring myself to regret his death for even a second.

"Perfect," Eric called out, clearly also not feeling any pity over Malek's demise. "We'll send the rope down again and you can come up."

"No... no, I don't think so," was Adil's reply, and as I watched, he gestured down to his own side, where the knife had somehow lodged itself during the struggle and the fall. "There's no point. You've spent too much time here already. You need to go before they get suspicious and send more men down here."

My heart sank as Zara peered over my shoulder, taking in the whole scene. Instinctively, I knew Adil was right; even if he could climb out, it would slow us down, and in the end, he would lose too much blood. He might survive a day or two, at most, but sooner or later, it would claim him.

Zara tried to convince him otherwise anyway. "Baba, you have to try. Arthur has a doctor with him, we can get you to the ship and he'll treat you."

Her father gave her a sad smile as the light in the lantern began to flicker. "You never give up, Zara. It's one of my favourite things about you and the reason why I never fully accepted that you were dead. You will be a wonderful queen. I wish I could have seen it."

I hadn't made Zara that offer yet, but in the circumstances, I could hardly complain about Adil ruining the surprise.

"Baba, please." As Zara's voice broke, I wrapped my arms around her even tighter. "You have to try."

The fact that she simply repeated her request rather than making a new argument told me all I needed to know; she knew we had no choice. Deep in her heart, she knew how this had to end.

Adil addressed me instead of responding to her. "My wife and daughters will be waiting at the harbour by the fourth pier. Please, take them with you."

"Of course we will," I promised him as Zara let out a muffled whimper beside me, a defeated sound I had never heard from her before.

"I love you, Zara," Adil added. "Take Fatima and go. Be happy, all of you."

He gave us one more smile before the light from the lantern died entirely, plunging the pit back into darkness.

Zara's body trembled against me as I pressed a fierce kiss to her forehead. She would need time to grieve, but that time hadn't come yet. "We have to go. We're not in the clear yet."

Words seemed to fail her, but she nodded, letting me lead her from the room as Eric, Fatima and Khalid followed behind. We had broken into the prison, freed our prisoner, and caused the death of the crown prince.

Now, we needed to get out of Munisia before anyone realized exactly what we'd done.

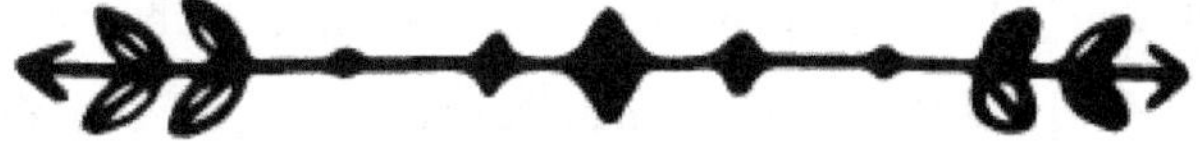

~Eric~

A somber, dark mood hung over our small group as we made our way out of the room with the pit. None of us wanted to leave Adil down there, but he made the choice and I respected it. We might have been able to pull him out even with his injury, but the more time we spent here, the greater the chance we would be discovered. In reality, we could consider it a miracle we hadn't been interrupted by anyone other than Malek yet.

It would also slow us down on the way to the harbour to have an injured man with us and could attract unwanted attention. The chances that he would survive were next to none. For the sake of his daughter and for all of us, he told us to go, and it made sense when I examined the situation objectively.

That didn't make it any easier for Zara, obviously, and Arthur had his arm around her in support as we left the room. "Where are the men who came with Malek?" he asked her gently.

"At the stop of the stairs," she replied, her voice missing its usual vivacity. "When he saw the guard knocked out down here, he should have gone back for them, but he didn't."

That had been Malek's fatal mistake, born of his belief in his own invincibility. Everything had revolved around him for his entire life, everyone catering to him at all times, and in the end, he died almost alone, in ignominy. It might be days before anyone retrieved his body, which seemed to be a rather fitting end for a man who had always been so convinced of his own importance.

Arthur looked over at me next. "Do we have room for the guards too?"

I knew exactly what he meant and I gave him a nod before turning to Fatima. "Will you translate for me?"

"Of course," she agreed. Khalid kept closer to her other side as we returned past the still-unconscious guard in the main room.

Adil's clerk who had accompanied us was still waiting for us there, having seen Adil, Zara and Malek go in, and Zara tearfully explained to him what had happened. He promised that once we were safely out, he would go back to try to help Adil, though I truly believed nothing could be done.

With that arranged, we headed up the stairs to the next level where Malek's guards had their swords out as soon as they saw us, shouting at us in their own language.

"Ask them if they have families of their own," I instructed Fatima, and though she gave me a curious look, she did as I said.

"They're unmarried, both of them," she told me after speaking with them for a second, and I nodded in relief. That would make things easier.

"Tell them Malek is dead. As his bodyguards, they will be blamed for his death if they try to turn us over. Even if we're punished, they will be too. Their only other choice is to come with us now and start a new life in Silatria. Life or death; that's what it comes down to."

Fatima told them all that and probably more besides, based on the length of the conversation as the men debated between themselves, their eyes wide with fear. Finally, they turned to me and nodded.

"They'll come," Fatima confirmed.

"Tell them to give me and Arthur their weapons."

Once we were armed, we both felt a little more secure, and our group crept further along towards the back door that Adil had shown us on the map. A guard stood sentry, of course, and he looked completely dumbfounded by the group that appeared before him.

I held up the new sword I had just acquired. "Tell him he can let us out for a fee, or we can kill him and go out anyway."

Fatima passed on the message, and, unsurprisingly, the man took the bribe. We said goodbye to Adil's clerk and found ourselves on a steep, narrow road on the side of the hill beside the palace.

"Now what?" Fatima asked, and Arthur and I exchanged glances, understanding each other perfectly once more. We had everyone we came for, except Adil, so we wouldn't delay a minute longer.

"Now, we run."

We must have made quite a sight racing through the streets of the Munisian capital: two pale men in merchant's clothes armed with swords, two of the prince's guards in the palace uniforms, a woman wearing the costume of the harem, Khalid in his prisoner's rags, and Fatima still dressed as a boy. We attracted a fair bit of attention, but I ignored all the stares and shouts. People could talk all they want, we simply needed to get away.

As the harbour approached, my heart pounded as I scanned the forest of ships, looking for the fishing vessel we had arrived on. Not until I saw the men hastily untying the moorings could I finally begin to relax.

Arthur and Zara separated from us to go and find Zara's family while I pressed a few more gold coins into the hands of the harbour officials to let us take priority in leaving. Soon, the pier of the harbour was behind us, the palace on the hill growing smaller as our motley band stood together on the deck of the ship, watching in silence as we tried to process everything that had just happened.

"Maybe they will get him out," I heard Arthur whisper to Zara. He stood behind her with his arms wrapped around her. "Maybe he can survive."

"Even if he does, I'll never see him again." Her voice sounded low and dull in reply. "All I wanted in coming here in the first place was to see him safe, and in the end, I killed him. All I brought is pain."

"Not to Fatima," I couldn't help interjecting, and Fatima quickly nodded to back me up. "You have given her back her life, and Khalid too. And think of this: how much worse would Malek have been when he became emperor? You have spared the whole country the pain of finding out. We are all sorry about Adil, but don't lose sight of the good you've done."

Arthur smiled at me gratefully before leading Zara away from the group to speak to her in private.

Malek's guards stayed huddled together as did Zara's family, speaking to each other softly as they watched their home disappear. I couldn't really imagine how they felt, but between Arthur and I, we would make sure they were all comfortable and cared for. Hopefully, they would find their new life even better than the old one.

Meanwhile, Fatima introduced me to Khalid officially, and I shook his hand warmly. He was clearly a man of principle and courage, and we could find a good position for him in the Silatrian court. He would need to learn the language first, but we had several weeks before we arrived. We'd need some way to pass the time and since I intended to spend as much time getting to know Fatima as I could, it seemed as good a project as any.

This trip had not turned out at all the way I thought it would when we set sail a month ago, but with Munisia behind us and Fatima beside me, the future seemed a lot brighter than it had for a very long time.

~Zara~

My whole body felt numb as I sat next to Arthur on the shipping vessel. The cool sea wind whipped against my body, making my loose harem clothes billow around me, but I hardly even noticed.

I hadn't even needed to say anything to my mother. Whether the fact that I came to get her instead of my father tipped her off, or whether she saw something in my face, she knew what had happened before I had a chance to say anything, and her own face crumpled in despair.

"Adil." She whimpered his name as my sisters all looked at her in dismay.

"Mama? What's wrong?" they asked in confusion.

"We have to go quickly," I told them simply and to her credit, my mother nodded, understanding that the time for grieving would come later. My father had risked, and ultimately lost, his life to help us be free; if we didn't at least manage that, his sacrifice would be in vain.

Once we were on the ship, my mother asked me only one question, coming over to where I stood with Arthur's arms still wrapped around me from behind. "Is he dead?"

I answered as truthfully as I could. "He was still alive when we left, but it seemed imminent. He told me to leave him there and go."

"Damn stubborn man," she muttered as her eyes filled with tears. No matter what disagreements my mother and I had, I knew she and my father loved each other with all their hearts. Theirs had been a happy union, and my heart ached for her as much as for myself.

"I'm sorry," I managed to say even as my own tears sprang to my eyes, but my mother shook her head at me.

"He often told me his only regret in life was losing you. You erased that pain by returning, and he wouldn't have made the choice for us all to leave if he didn't think it would be for the best. I have to trust that he knew what he was talking about. I hope that your man will keep his word."

She glanced at Arthur over my shoulder who, of course, didn't understand a word of what we were saying, but the warmth of his body conveyed his solid support anyway.

"He is a man of honour," I told her. "He will care for all of us just as Baba did."

Of that, at least, I could be certain.

After an hour's sail, we rendezvoused with Arthur's ship. Just one day earlier, I hadn't been sure I would ever see it again, but now, the sight had never been more welcome. Eric paid the fishermen the remainder of their fee for transporting us as the rest of us moved back to the larger ship in preparation for the long journey back to Lassaria.

"Will you help me to get your family settled?" Arthur asked, and I knew exactly why he asked. He wanted to distract me from my sorrow with practical matters, and I appreciated it. We had several more people now than we'd had on the outward journey, and Arthur gave up his own room for my mother and sisters to share.

Malek's two guards shared another room while Eric and Khalid were roomed together and Arthur's men were delegated to even tighter quarters. That left Fatima as the only person on the whole ship with a room to herself, but she couldn't reasonably share her room with anyone besides me, and Arthur didn't seem to be willing to let me out of his sight. He and I would share the smaller room next door to my family, the one that had technically been mine on our original journey as we tried to maintain the appearance that we were merely friends. It seemed that no longer concerned Arthur, and I couldn't bring myself to worry about it either, not after everything that had happened.

As soon as he had made sure that everyone had been taken care of, Arthur took some food from the galley and brought it to our room, closing the door behind him and leaving us in complete privacy for the first time in two days, since that evening in his room when he and I made love for the first time.

He held out some bread to me, but I didn't want food. I wanted answers instead. "Why did you come back? I told you to go. I told you I didn't love you."

His blue eyes were soft with compassion and affection. "Do you think I believed that? You are a good actress, Zara, but not that good. I begged your father to tell me the truth and he did, that very night."

He did? That only raised more questions in my mind. "Then why did you leave at all?"

Arthur smiled at my sudden change of direction. "Because you asked me to. I trusted you had a plan and I trusted you to carry it out, even though it killed me not to be able to help you."

"But then you came back anyway." I didn't understand and he hadn't made things any clearer.

"You can blame Eric for that. He came up with the plan to return in disguise. Very clever, actually. We almost pulled it off."

I loved him even more for the genuine sadness in his eyes and the respect he clearly had for my father. "That death was too good for Malek," I spat bitterly, my own sorrow mingling with anger at the man behind it all. "I wish I'd cut his cock off when I had the chance."

"I would have liked to have seen that," Arthur agreed, his expression hardening at the mention of the former crown prince. "Did he... touch you?"

He stumbled over the question, not wanting to know the answer but asking it anyway. Just the thought that Malek might have had his way with me made him look queasy.

At least I could reassure him on that point. "No. I managed to hold him off for one night. I'm not sure how much longer I could have done it, but he never got to 'make use' of me, as he so elegantly put it."

Relief flashed across Arthur's eyes as he took my hand and led me gently to the bed, sitting down next to me. "I suspect you would have found a way. I don't know if there's anything you can't do, Zara."

His belief in me and his trust warmed my heart, and I could hardly believe I was there with him, hearing him saying such sweet things. When I lay in my harem bed last night, it seemed almost impossible.

"What will happen to the other women in the harem now?" he wondered.

The answer made us both grimace. "The next eldest son of the emperor will take his place. He can decide if he wants to keep any of the women for his own harem, or if they will be 'retired'. Those he doesn't want will be moved out of the palace, out to the country where they will live out the rest of their lives alone. Those he chooses will have to go to him. They will have no choice in the matter at all."

"I wish we could help them all," my sweet prince sighed, and for the first time since we left my father in the pit, I almost smiled.

"You would change the whole world if you could. If all men were like you, the world would be a much better place."

He blushed at the compliment, shaking his head, but I wouldn't let him put me off. My words were true, and I wanted him to know it.

Placing my hand gently against his cheek, I turned his head to look at me. "I have seen half this world, Arthur, and you are the best thing I have ever found."

"Zara."

The weight of emotion in his voice as he said my name was more than I could take, and before I even knew I meant to do it, I kissed him with all the passion inside me. All the anger, the frustration, the sadness and the joy, the hope and the pain, everything I had felt since we were last together came pouring out of me, and Arthur simply took it, sharing the burden with me with all of his usual empathy and grace.

When I began to pull at his tunic, he drew back to look in my eyes. "Are you sure you want this right now? We can simply lie together and rest or talk. I don't want to rush you."

He put my needs above his own, as always, but right now, I wanted only him. "I need to know what we did it all for," I told him honestly. "I need to remember why we risked so much."

That answer seemed to satisfy him, and it didn't take long for him to remove my harem clothes. He tossed them on the ground, and if I had my way, I would toss them into the sea. I never wanted to see them again.

The first time we made love was rough and fevered. I pushed him down onto the bed and climbed on top of him, working off all the energy from my unsettled emotions through the motion of my hips against his. Faster and faster, I stroked his hard cock with my body, until my pain morphed into pleasure, and satisfaction at the pleasure I could bring him. After we both came, I collapsed against him, completely spent, and at last, I let myself cry.

Arthur held me gently, not making any effort to comfort me, understanding that I simply needed to let it all out. He lay me down next to him with his strong arms around me, wiping away my tears from time to time and placing gentle kisses on my forehead until my tears were finally spent. Even after my eyes were dry, we simply lay there silently, feeling the weight of the moment, until I raised my face and gently kissed him again.

When we made love a second time, it felt different. Whereas the first time had broken me open, now, with his kisses and gentle caresses, Arthur put me back together again. His hands were slow and steady, his lips firm and caring, and his cock, when he slid it inside me, felt not like an invasion but a completion.

Whether I believed in fate or destiny or karma, or not, somehow, I knew that the two of us together in this way were always meant to be. And when he looked down at me in wonder, his hands cradling my face as his hips thrust against mine, I knew he felt it too.

"Will you marry me, Zara?"

The question, in these circumstances, was so ridiculous that I had to laugh, and thankfully, he laughed too, understanding that the situation hardly made for an ideal proposal, especially for a prince.

And yet, he meant the question sincerely, and I knew he did. My father had said I would be a great queen, and Arthur said he had spoken to my father. It didn't take a genius to figure out that Arthur must have shared his intentions with him. He didn't ask it idly or in the heat of the moment.

When I looked back up into those sweet blue eyes, my answer was never in any doubt.

"I will, Arthur. I love you."

The joy in his eyes brought me to tears once again, but this time, they were tears of happiness. "It won't be easy," he warned me, his body still moving within me. "We will still have some challenges to face."

"I don't even know what easy is anymore," I countered, making him smile. "After all we have been through, I can't think of anything that could stop us."

"I love you," he whispered as my body began to tremble once more.

"I love you, Arthur." His name left me as a sigh as I came, and he shuddered against me again, each of us completing the other, as we were always meant to do.

Life might never be easy, but with him, it would always be worthwhile.

CHAPTER FOURTEEN

As the weeks passed, the others all grew restless from the long days at sea, but for me, they were full of excitement. We might be confined to the ship, but after being restricted to the harem rooms for so long, being stuck in one place felt normal to me. What made it so exciting was that for the first time in years, I had new people to talk to.

One person in particular I looked forward to seeing each morning, one man who made my heart beat a little faster every time he looked my way, which happened quite often, to my delight. Eric spent most of his time with me, helping me to teach Khalid his language as well as simply talking with me as we got to know each other.

"Cousins of yours took control of Actilia after the Munisian sack of the city," he explained to me one afternoon after we had finished with Khalid's language lessons for the day and my friend had gone to spend time with the other Munisian men. "But technically, the throne is rightfully yours. If you wanted, I could help you petition for it to be returned to you."

The fact that he thought me worthy to rule a kingdom flattered me, but I had no such designs on power. "It's been years since anyone in Actilia even thought of my name, and my cousins will have grown accustomed to their power. I would need a strong husband to even make the claim, and the truth is, it simply doesn't mean that much to me. After all the years in the palace with Malek, a simple life sounds far more appealing."

At first, I wondered if it made me cold that I stood there and watched the only man I had ever been intimate with and the father of my children tumble to his death and felt nothing inside, but when I tentatively voiced those thoughts to Eric earlier on in the voyage, he quickly dispelled that notion.

"You would have every right to celebrate his death and dance on his grave. As you pointed out to him so strongly, he never understood what love or loyalty were. You don't owe him even a moment's regret for the way his life ended."

His certainty of that fact helped to reassure me, and I didn't waste another moment's worry on it after that.

"So, what would you like to do with your new freedom instead?" Eric asked after I turned down his offer to help me reclaim my royal status.

"Honestly, just having something useful to do and a family of my own, with a man who is devoted to me and children I can raise and get to know, sounds like heaven to me. Actilia is now just as foreign to me as any other place, so all things considered, I would be happy to stay in Silatria, if it's okay with you."

In my reply, I left out some of my thoughts; namely, that the man I pictured in that scenario looked very much like the one sitting in front of me.

There were still traces of the playful boy I remembered from our childhood meeting, but life had added the weight of worry and responsibility to him, as it did to us all. When I told him the other day, after hearing the whole story of what had transpired during his time in Munisia, just how heroic his actions had been, he shook his head.

"I'm far from being a hero, Fatima. I've spent a long time being jealous and petty and selfish. My brother very nearly got hurt because of me, and my father *was* killed, perhaps not directly because of my actions, but they played a part. If you called me a hero in the Silatrian court, you wouldn't find many who agreed with you."

"I don't care what anyone else thinks," I assured him. "To me, you will always be the hero of this story."

The smile he gave me then looked very much like the one he gave me now as we discussed my future, a smile of tentative hope. "What kind of things do you consider useful for you to do?"

He asked some hard questions. "I'm not sure, but I'm willing to learn a skill or a trade. The only thing I really have any experience at is being a princess, and there is not a great need for those."

He chuckled, almost nervously, before changing the subject.

Later that night, after we had all eaten dinner together, Eric asked me to walk with him on the deck. The only place on the ship with any real room to move, the deck was often filled with people wanting a break from the confines of their rooms, but tonight, we were the only ones there besides the crew sailing the ship.

Eric's hands fiddled nervously with the edge of his doublet as he walked slowly next to me, cutting his strides short so we wouldn't run out of space too quickly. "Fatima, when we spoke earlier, you said you'd like to live in Silatria permanently."

I didn't know for sure where he was going with this, but his uneasiness made me nervous too. Had he brought me here to tell me that wouldn't be possible? What else would he be worried to tell me?

Anticipating a rejection, I tried to smooth the way to make it easier for him. "Yes, I did, but if it's inconvenient for you, I can explore other possibilities. Perhaps Zara would let me live in Lassaria..."

Zara and Arthur had shared the good news of their engagement with us all the day after we left Munisia, and I felt truly delighted for her. Arthur seemed like a kind and loving man, though not quite so handsome or brave as Eric, at least to my eyes.

However, my thought remained unfinished as Eric cut me off. "No. I mean, I'm sure she would be happy for you to live there, but it's not a problem for you to stay in Silatria if that's what you would like. That's not what I meant."

"Oh." In that case, I still had no clue what he wanted to tell me. "Then what is it?"

He grimaced as he muttered under his breath. "This didn't used to be so hard."

"What didn't?" I still felt completely lost.

Shaking his head, Eric began again. "I simply wanted to tell you that you would be very welcome at the Silatrian court. My brother, Cassian, and his wife, Cordelia, will be delighted to have you there. I could help you secure a position that you would find interesting."

All of that sounded wonderful, which only made his behaviour more confusing. There had to be a 'but' coming. "So, what's the catch?"

My question startled him as he looked over at me in surprise before breaking into a sheepish smile. "Well, when you put it like that, I suppose I am."

"What?" I kept saying that, but for the first time since we met, it felt like he was truly speaking a foreign language.

Eric took a breath before coming to a full stop and turning to face me. "I've only done this once before and it didn't turn out very well, so if you're not interested, please, just say so plainly and we'll move on."

"Interested in what?" He still hadn't told me what on earth he was talking about.

Finally, he did. "In me. From the moment I saw you by that pool in the palace, I've known, more clearly than I've known anything in my life, that we were meant to meet. Finding out that we had already met before only made that feeling grow stronger. Over the past weeks as we've gotten to know each other, I'm awed every day by your intelligence and strength and resilience. I have a reputation at home, I need to be honest about that, and if you agree, you will have to put up with rumours and speculation and whispers in the court, but eventually, the novelty will pass and they'll lose interest."

I followed along right up until the end, but he lost me once more with his talk of agreement. "What am I agreeing to?"

He swallowed nervously before nodding to himself, as if spurring himself on. "To be my wife."

His *wife*? Could he be serious? My lips parted in disbelief as I stared up at his handsome face, with his pale skin and dark eyes that watched me nervously, waiting for my response.

"But... but you are a prince."

"And you are a princess," he pointed out, correctly.

"A princess who has been enslaved. A princess who is far from pure."

Eric's lips twitched in amusement. "If you're expecting to find me a virgin, I'm afraid that ship has sailed too. I would never judge a woman for her experience, and in your case, the choice wasn't yours anyway."

"But..."

"Fatima." He cut me off gently, his hand resting softly on my cheek, touching me for the first time in the way a man might touch a woman he cared for, at least from the things I had heard. Malek had never touched me in such a way. "Forget what the rest of the world thinks. Tell me what's in your heart. Do you feel something for me too?"

I didn't know how he could doubt it. "You are my hero," I reminded him, his tender touch bringing tears to my eyes. "And the boy who made me laugh. Of course I have feelings for you."

For a moment he simply stared at me, as though he couldn't quite believe the words I'd said, and then, slowly, a smile spread across his face. "So, you will marry me?"

"If you are certain that's what you want, then yes. Of course I will."

With his hand still on my cheek, Eric bent down and kissed me, softly and sweetly, and as the boat rocked gently beneath us, for the first time in many years, I felt truly alive.

~Eric~

Home never meant that much to me before. After my mother died, the Silatrian castle became just a building, a place to sleep and eat and make plans, and the people in it were simply supporting players in the story of my life where I had the undisputed starring role.

Now, as I saw the castle's familiar silhouette rising in the distance, it meant something new to me. There, I would start the next chapter of my life, the one that Fatima and I would build together. I brought my brother, the king, a trade agreement, as I promised, to replace some of the kingdom's wealth that had been lost through Westley Eastam's scheming, but more than that, I returned with a new sense of purpose and understanding of my place in the world. I would never be king, but I didn't want to be. I didn't need power or prestige or acclaim. In Fatima's eyes, I was a hero, and I needed nothing more.

At last, I'd found my home.

When I told Arthur back on the ship that I intended to propose to Fatima, he couldn't have looked more shocked. "You haven't even slept with her, have you?"

I hadn't realized he monitored my movements that closely, but he had it right. "No. We haven't even kissed."

"And you want to marry her? What if you're not compatible? It's one thing to sleep around when you're unmarried, but to cheat on your wife…"

I cut him off before he could say it. "I'm not planning to cheat on anyone. I have slept with enough women to know what's out there and to know what I never found in all the women I've been with. Fatima gives me exactly what I need, and it's not unusual for a royal wedding that we haven't been intimate at all. I hadn't kissed your sister either and I still would have married her."

Arthur's lips pursed in disapproval. "Just when I'm starting to like you, you have to bring that up and ruin it."

"Don't worry, it'll go back and forth a few more times, I'm sure."

Arthur might only be my sister-in-law's brother, but after all we had been through together, first with tracking Eastam and then with the trip to Munisia, our relationship felt closer to actual brothers, supporting each other but also comfortable enough to give each other a hard time too. And when I told him that Fatima had accepted my offer, he seemed genuinely pleased for me, just as I was for him and Zara.

When we set out from the Silatrian castle nearly three months earlier to track Eastam down, we could never have imagined what the journey would bring.

Our ship landed first thing that morning at the Silatrian port, and after getting our bearings back on land, we left Zara's family at an inn in the port town while Zara and Arthur accompanied Fatima, Khalid, the two Munisian guards and me back to my brother's castle. Khalid and the two guards would receive positions at the court as I'd promised, Fatima would marry me, of course, and Zara and Arthur simply wanted to pay their respects to Cass and Cordelia before they carried on to Lassaria.

"It's just as I remembered it," Fatima told me, her eyes shining with happiness as she took in the castle ahead of us. "I can't believe after all this time, I will be married here after all. Life is strange sometimes, isn't it?"

It certainly could be. Strange and cruel and confusing and a lot more besides, but sometimes, it could be wonderful. Those were the times that made life worth living.

News of our arrival spread quickly and by the time we all dismounted and made our way into the great hall, my brother and his wife were waiting for us, sitting on their thrones beneath the satin canopy.

"Eric." Cass got up from his throne to offer me an embrace. "It's good to see you."

"And you, Your Majesty." I hadn't seen him yet since his coronation and I had to admit, the position suited him. He looked at ease and happy, although perhaps that had more to do with the woman next to him than with his position. Cordelia also stood to greet me, and I bowed to her politely before lowering my voice. "Congratulations on your pregnancy, Your Majesty."

Cass and Cordelia exchanged startled looks. "How do you know about that?" Cass asked, keeping his voice low as well. "We haven't announced it yet."

"Lady Elodie has loosened the dress around Cordelia's waist. She's not showing yet but I would guess Elodie wanted to give the baby some breathing room."

Cordelia arched her eyebrow at me with a look somewhere between respect and annoyance. "You pay that much attention to my body?"

"I'm trying to be more observant in general," I explained. "And I am honestly delighted for you. It's reason to celebrate, and I have good news of my own to share."

I took a step back to allow Fatima to come forward. We had made a stop on the journey home to pick up some new clothes for her and Zara, but when Fatima came out of her room on the ship that morning, she admitted she feared she would be underdressed for the court. I couldn't see it; she looked perfect to me.

"This is Princess Fatima of Actilia. Fatima, my brother, King Cassian, and his wife, Queen Cordelia."

"Actilia?" Cass repeated in surprise as he gave Fatima a welcoming nod. "I remember you, Your Highness, from your visit here many years ago. Forgive me, but I thought your entire family had been killed in the attack on your city."

"They were all killed except for me," Fatima explained. "The Munisian attackers took me back to their emperor, and Prince Eric helped to negotiate my release."

That was a very idealized version of what happened, but the summary made me smile as Cass gave me an almost impressed look. "How very chivalrous of you."

"Don't give me too much credit yet. I haven't told you the rest."

His expression immediately turned wary. "What's the rest of it?"

"I'll tell you the whole story later, but the important part for now is that Fatima has agreed to be my wife. If we have your blessing, of course."

Again, Cass and Cordelia looked at each other in surprise. They seemed to have an entire conversation with their eyes before my brother turned back to me. "If that's what you want, then yes, of course, you have my blessing. It seems like we have a lot to catch up on."

They said hello to Arthur and Zara, offering their congratulations on their engagement as well, and we were all invited to dine with them later once Cass had finished his duties for the day. I made sure Fatima had a comfortable room not far from mine before I took Khalid on a brief tour.

"You'll need to know the castle inside out if you're going to be Fatima's private bodyguard," I explained as we went through another of the secret passages. I'd chosen that role for him since I could think of no one better suited. I already knew he would protect her with his life.

"I learn very speedy." Khalid was still learning the language, but he had made incredible progress in the last few weeks. He understood almost all of what I said to him but his responses were more stilted. Fatima had tried to teach me some of her native language at the same time and my progress seemed pitiful compared to his. "What is here?"

He pointed down one of the hallways not far from the Queen's rooms where shrieks of laughter could be heard from one of the rooms. My brow furrowed as I tried to guess what might be going on. "I don't know."

Together, we headed towards the sound and found a blonde woman surrounded by a sea of feathers from a pillow which had burst. She giggled in amusement as she ran her bare feet over the feathers, while Arabella Eastam watched her with disdain. Arabella's presence helped me to recognize the blonde woman as Cordelia's sister, Charlotte.

Her laughter died off as she caught sight of us at the door and her eyes widened in surprise at Khalid's unusual appearance. His dark skin would be a novelty for many people in the castle and Charlotte had an unusual way of looking at things anyway, which she quickly demonstrated. She marched right up to Khalid and took hold of his arm, holding it up to look at it better.

"My lady, this isn't appropriate," I chided her, gesturing to Arabella to come and get her ward, but Khalid shook his head at me.

"She is good." With the same kind of curiosity, he reached out to touch her loose, blonde hair, a colour he had probably never seen before since all the women of Munisia had dark hair, and soon they were pointing at parts of each other and laughing together while I watched in befuddlement.

I mentioned it to Fatima later and told her what I knew of Charlotte, ending with a blunt summary of her mental state: "She's not all there."

The next day, while we were walking together, we saw Khalid and Charlotte together again, talking and gesturing and laughing, and I asked Fatima if she had told Khalid what I said.

She smiled in amusement as she watched her friend enjoying himself with the damaged princess. "I told him. He replied that, thanks to his castration, he's not all there either, so they should get along fine."

Well, when he put it that way, who was I to judge?

Arthur and Zara left the next afternoon, intending to return to the inn where Zara's family waited and then carry on to Lassaria. They invited us all to attend their wedding which they hoped would take place very soon.

"Zara may already be with child," Arthur admitted to me sheepishly. "We shouldn't delay for long."

My answer was completely sincere and heartfelt. "I wouldn't miss it."

When we had waved them off and I turned to go back into the castle, I noticed someone I hadn't had a chance to speak with yet and asked Fatima to excuse me for a moment. The woman turned and went back into the castle before I caught up with her, jogging down the hall in an attempt to keep up. "Lady Elodie. Please, wait."

At the sound of my voice, she stopped and turned back, curtseying to me formally. "Your Highness. Welcome home."

"Have you been avoiding me?" I had seen her husband, Bran, a few times already since we returned, but not her.

"Not exactly," she said, which sounded like less than a full denial. "I didn't want to get in the way. Congratulations on your engagement. I'm so pleased for you."

She meant that sincerely, I had no doubt, and I offered her my gratitude with equal earnestness. "Thank you. And thank you for helping me find my way. It disappointed me when you turned me down, but you gave me a lot to think about. You made me want to be a better man, the kind of man that a woman like you would love, and although I don't flatter myself that I've done it already, I think I'm on my way. The man I was when you met me would not have won Fatima's trust and affection."

Elodie gave me a soft smile. "You were always that man, Your Highness. You just hid that part of you away for a little while. I'm so glad you've decided to let him shine through again."

"It seems we've all found a place for ourselves," I agreed. "And congratulations on your upcoming child. You and Bran must be very happy."

Her eyes widened in dismay. "How do you... I haven't even told Dee yet!"

"The female body was once my subject of expertise," I reminded her. She shook her head at the reminder, but she knew I meant it as a joke. "Now, there is only one woman I want to be an expert in."

"Then she is a lucky woman indeed. Congratulations again, Your Highness."

"And to you."

It seemed the changes would keep on coming for all of us. Life never stood still, but that made it exciting, and right now, mine couldn't get much better.

~Fatima~

Life in the Silatrian court was about as far away from being in the Munisian harem as I could imagine. No one questioned any of my movements, for a start. I could go where I pleased, speak to whomever I wanted, and rather than waiting on anyone else, I had a trio of maids assigned to me who must have thought it strange that I did so many things myself rather than asking for their help.

The women were different too. Aside from Sade, who had been more of an employer than a confidant, I had no friends in the harem to speak of. Khalid had been my only companion but he wasn't a woman. I had begun to wonder if perhaps other women were simply not like me, but after spending time with Zara on the journey home and then, especially, meeting Cordelia and Elodie in Silatria, I came to realize there *were* other women I could relate to and enjoy myself with.

Lady Elodie reminded me of Sade in some ways: reserved and proper, but she also had a vivid imagination and guileless curiosity. She wanted to hear all about my experiences, asking me questions about each detail, while Cordelia, or Dee, as she insisted I call her, watched us both with amusement.

"She's going to work you into her own stories," Dee warned me. "You'll have all kinds of adventures you never imagined in Lodee's imagination."

That sounded just fine to me. For so long, I'd given up on having any kind of adventures at all; now, I felt overdue for some new ones.

Dee and Elodie were equally fascinated and horrified by the concept of the harem in general and my experiences in particular. When I explained how I had borne children only to have them taken from me, their hands went instinctively to their own stomachs.

"That would be the cruelest part of all," Dee declared. "A lot of women, especially royal and noblewomen, have to sleep with men they would rather not, but at least they have their children as comfort. He took even that from you."

They told me about their own husbands, and through the comments they made, I began to suspect that their experiences in the bedroom were vastly differ-ent from my own. "So, you actually enjoy being physically intimate with them?"

I asked tentatively. "Some of the women in the harem claimed they liked it, but I couldn't be sure if they were lying."

Both women gave me sympathetic looks as Elodie took my hand. "I didn't think I would enjoy it," she whispered to me conspiratorially. "I thought it would be a necessary evil on the way to having children, but it's actually quite pleasant."

Dee snorted in a very un-queen-like fashion. "It's a lot better than pleasant when your partner loves you and cares about satisfying you. Eric has had his share of women in the past, as he told you, and though I don't necessarily approve, I have to say that I never heard any complaints. Now that he actually has a woman that he has feelings for, I'm sure he will make it enjoyable for you."

That idea both excited and rather terrified me. What if I still didn't like it? What if there was just something wrong with me, or what if Malek had ruined the whole experience for me forever?

I had little time to brood over it though, not when Eric wanted to get married as soon as possible. "I know it's a little ironic since neither of us are untouched, but I'd like to wait until we're married to share a bed with you. After the way Malek treated you, I want you to have no doubt that I want *all* of you and not just your body."

His sweet words made me blush and set my blood racing. Not only did my heart beat faster but my whole body seemed to pulse in a way it never had before. "If you would like to wait, it's fine with me."

He couldn't fully suppress his groan of frustration. "It's what I'd like, but not what I'd *like*. I won't be able to last forever, Fatima, so I think we should get married this weekend."

"This weekend?" I repeated in disbelief. "Can a royal wedding really happen that quickly?"

"Cass and Cordelia were married just a few months ago and they had all the pomp and ceremony then. We can have a much quieter occasion. I'm the second son; no one cares about me."

He put himself down like that far too often. "I care," I assured him. "And I like having you all to myself anyway."

That put a smile on his face and when he kissed me, I could feel the extra urgency for both of us. We really should have our wedding as soon as possible.

In the end, it all came together easily. Though the wedding wasn't a full royal occasion, I wouldn't have called it quiet either. Several hundred of the kingdom's top courtiers and noble families were in attendance, but when I entered the church, I could only see the man waiting for me at the end of the aisle. In my mind, the boy from my childhood memory merged with the man who came to rescue me on the pier, both of them wrapped up in the handsome man in his uniform who took my hand gently as we made our vows to each other.

The king and queen threw us an elaborate feast afterwards. Dee explained the tradition to me ahead of time, how I would be taken to my room first by the other women but the men expected Eric to remain as long as he could to prove his self-control.

"I give him five minutes," Dee laughed as we headed upstairs. "At least you won't have any witnesses to your consummation though."

"Witnesses?" I repeated in alarm, making her laugh again.

"Don't worry, that honour is reserved for the crown prince. I'll tell you all about it later. For now, let's get you ready."

Dee and Elodie helped my own ladies as they got me out of my wedding dress and into a simple shift that would be much easier to remove. They brushed out my hair and crushed flower petals against my skin, and they had only just finished when Eric appeared in the doorway, dismay on his face as he took in all the women in my room.

"How much longer will you be?"

The question made all the women laugh at his eagerness, and Dee patted him on the shoulder on the way out. "Be good to her, Eric."

He never took his eyes off me. "That's all I want to do."

The women closed the door behind them, leaving me alone with my new husband as nerves and excitement chased each other around my body. He had also changed his clothes, the formal uniform he wore for the ceremony replaced by a simple white tunic and loose breeches.

"I mean it," he said, taking a step closer to me with a mixture of confidence and hesitation. "I want to make this good for you. If there's anything you don't like, anything that reminds you of him, just tell me and I'll stop immediately."

"I don't think I'll want you to stop," I told him honestly.

A quick smile flashed across his face. "Well, I might not *stop*, but I can try something different, at least."

He closed the remaining distance between us before taking my face gently in his hands and kissing me softly, just as softly as he had that night on the ship when he proposed.

"I want to erase every night you spent with him from your memory. I never want you to feel like anything is out of your control again."

His sweet yet possessive words, combined with the touch of his skin against mine, produced a reaction in my body unlike anything I'd ever known. A hunger began to grow inside me, an aching that I'd never felt. Any lingering fear I had about whether I might enjoy this faded away as Eric's hands moved down my body, his touch leaving a trail of fire in its wake.

"May I look at you?"

Malek had never asked permission for anything. My first night with him, when I was only 14, he ordered me to remove the silky robe the women had dressed me in while he watched, and he smiled in perverse pleasure as my hands and knees trembled.

Now, he was dead and cold, rotting in the bottom of that pit or buried in his family's crypt if someone had pulled him out, while I trembled for a completely different reason.

As soon as I nodded, Eric pulled my dress up over my head, gently and slowly, giving me plenty of opportunity to change my mind. I didn't want to, though, and when his hands connected again with my bare skin, I let out a whimper that made my cheeks flush.

"Don't hold back," he encouraged me, his dark eyes heated as he pulled me closer to him, his body pressing against mine. "I want to know what you like, and those noises are the best way for me to tell."

Everything felt entirely new as his hands continued to explore me. Malek had never touched me for my own pleasure. He would grab my breasts and squeeze or pull on them, seeming to enjoy the discomfort it caused me while he took his own pleasure, but he had never once cupped them as Eric did, and though he had occasionally bitten them, he never sucked them in a way that made my thighs clench. My hands formed fists as I tried to drive the old memories from my mind and focus entirely on what was happening right now.

"You're thinking about him, aren't you?" Eric's tone sounded gentle but chiding as he looked up at me.

I told him the truth. "I can't help it. It's the only point of comparison I have, but if it makes you feel better, the comparison is very much in your favour so far."

That made him smile, though I could tell it didn't fully satisfy him. He helped me over to the bed before continuing his exploration of my body, still fully clothed, still paying no attention to his own needs. My legs rubbed together as I tried to ease the growing ache there, and when Eric's hands moved to the same spot, I gasped in surprise. Why did that feel so good?

"Have you ever had an orgasm, Fatima?" He looked up at me again, his face not far from where his hands were.

I answered honestly again. "I'm not sure."

Eric's lips pressed tightly together in disapproval, though not directed at me. "If you have to wonder, then the answer is no. We're going to fix that, right now."

Lowering his head, his lips found the same spot his hand had just been, and my back arched from the bed in surprise. "Oh!"

That was only the beginning. He kept kissing me there, licking and sucking as his hands continued to touch me, the ache inside me building to a point where I didn't think I could hold on any longer.

And then, I couldn't. All the pressure inside me burst like a dam breaching, pleasure flooding my entire body in a wave, and when my body stopped shuddering, Eric looked up at me with a satisfied smile. "That's better."

I almost thought that meant we were finished, and if we were, I couldn't complain, but he stood up to remove his own clothing then and I realized that he still hadn't taken any pleasure of his own. So far, everything had been about me.

"I don't care that you have been with another man, Fatima, but I don't want there to ever be another here again besides me," he groaned as he slid his hard cock into me. To my surprise, I felt no pain or discomfort. He slid inside easily despite being larger than Malek had been. It had never felt like that before. "I won't lock you up to keep other men away from you, but you are mine anyway, and I am yours."

At this moment, I couldn't imagine wanting anything more in life than that. "Yes, Eric. I'm yours, and you're mine."

If I thought for even a moment that the reaction he caused in my body had been a one-time thing, he quickly proved me wrong. Another wave crashed over me as he thrust into me, whispering his devotion and his satisfaction, and when he trembled above me too, Malek never even crossed my mind.

CHAPTER FIFTEEN

I wouldn't have thought it possible, but over the return journey from Munisia, Zara and I somehow grew even closer. In the privacy of our small room, we spent hours in each other's arms, during which she shared everything that had happened in the harem with me and all the sorrow and guilt she felt over her father. She opened herself up to me in a way I knew for certain she'd never done with anyone before and with each passing day, my decision to propose to her was validated time and time again.

She was the most incredible, resilient, strong woman I had ever known, and nothing on earth would stop me from making her my wife. Not even my mother.

Zara also told me the things my mother had said to her before we left Lassaria in the first place, making my blood boil in indignation. As someone whose life had been scripted out far in advance and never ventured too far from that plan, my mother couldn't begin to imagine the things Zara had been through. What right did she have to deem her unworthy of the throne? Hopefully, when she learned that Zara was, in fact, a princess, she would change her tune, but I prepared myself to deal with it in case she didn't.

No one would ever put Zara down again, not as long as I had any breath left in me to defend her with.

Taking the side trip to Silatria had been Zara's idea, and it worked out perfectly. My sister's delight at seeing Zara again made us both smile, and she shrieked so loudly when I told her I'd proposed that her guard came running to make sure she hadn't been injured. "Sometimes, our path takes us on an unexpected journey to the place we were heading anyway," she mused after reassuring her guard. "And sometimes, it takes off in a different direction entirely. Either way, I think we've both been very lucky."

I couldn't agree more.

The visit meant I could pass on news of Dee to my family, including the news of her pregnancy, which should put my mother in a good mood. Perhaps it would help to soften the blow of the news I had for her. Seeing Eric and Fatima so happy together warmed my heart too. When he said he would come to Lassaria for my wedding, it seemed appropriate; he would always be a part of mine and Zara's story, so it felt fitting he should be there.

Zara and I returned to the port town where her family had stayed, and we all got back on the ship one last time for the short sail to Lassaria. As we disembarked, the appearance of Zara and her whole family drew a great deal of attention. Seeing one person with darker skin was unusual enough in our small kingdom; seeing a whole family threw people completely off. Zara held her head high, as always, but her mother and sisters seemed more affected by it.

Zara helped them all into the carriage I commandeered for our journey before she came to join me on horseback at the front of the travelling party.

"Are they feeling alright?" I asked.

"They're not used to *anyone* looking at them," she reminded me. "They've been so sheltered in the palace that it's strange enough to be out in public even without the staring. It will take them a while to adjust, but I'm sure they will. The women of my family are strong."

"If they share your blood, they must be."

With the slower pace set by the carriage, evening was approaching by the time we arrived at the castle, and the castle guard came out to greet us before sending word to my parents that I had returned. By the time we reached the great hall, it seemed half the court were waiting to greet us, and whispers swept the room as I walked in with the family of exotic women.

"Welcome home, Arthur." My father embraced me warmly as I passed on greetings from Dee and King Cassian and gave him the news of the goods I'd brought back with me and the trade deal that had been concluded. With business out of the way, my father turned to Zara and her family with a smile. "I see you have brought your friend back with you and a few more besides."

"I have." I took Zara's hand, ignoring my mother's look of disapproval. "While we were in Munisia, we found out that Zara's grandmother was the emperor's sister. Her father, Adil, is the current emperor's cousin. She is therefore of royal blood, as are her sisters, so I would like to reintroduce you, Your Majesty, to Princess Zara of Munisia."

The king appeared genuinely pleased as he took Zara's hand and kissed it. "A pleasure to meet you properly, Your Highness."

"And you, Your Majesty." Zara curtseyed gracefully but I could see the tension in her shoulders as she waited for my mother's reaction.

She didn't have to wait for long. "What proof do we have that this is true?" My mother's suspicious and haughty tone was, unfortunately, completely what I expected.

Zara tensed even further, preparing for a fight, but I had no intention of letting her fight this one. Ignoring my mother, I addressed my father again. "We have had a very long journey and my guests are eager to be shown to their rooms."

"Of course," he quickly agreed, giving his steward instructions to settle them all comfortably. I squeezed Zara's hand and gave her a nod, promising to come to see her soon, and when she and the others had gone, my father addressed both me and my mother. "Come, let's catch up in private."

We exited the great hall through the back door, into my father's receiving room, and as soon as the door had closed, the words exploded out of my mother as if she couldn't hold them in a second longer. "You're far too trusting, Arthur. Whatever she's done to convince you that she's a princess, it isn't true."

That objection was easy enough to overcome. "The crown prince of Munisia told me about Zara's heritage in the presence of the emperor himself. There are other witnesses too, including Prince Eric of Silatria. It would be easy for you to confirm. She *is* a princess, Mother, no matter how much you would prefer her not to be."

"It doesn't make any difference even if she is," she claimed stubbornly. "While you've been away, I've begun negotiations with the Bramley family about their daughter, Cecilia..."

"What?" My father sounded just as surprised as I felt. "Why would you do that?"

"Arthur needs a wife," my mother insisted. "He's at the age now when he should be settling down and having children."

"But we agreed he should have some choice..."

"He's taking too long to make up his mind," my mother interjected, sticking to her own narrative.

I didn't intend to listen to another word. "If that's how you feel, it's a good thing I already have a fiancée, then."

My mother's face went deathly pale. "You can't mean..."

"Of course I do." I saw no reason to mince words. "I love Zara. I suspect you already knew that when you threatened her before we left."

"You did what?" My father looked less impressed with each word out of my mother's mouth.

"Threatened is a strong word," my mother protested. "I simply told her she should remember her place and Arthur's reputation."

She couldn't have set me up better. "Well, since she is a princess, her place is married to a prince, and since I suspect she is already carrying my child, if you're so concerned about my reputation, we should arrange the wedding quickly."

My father tried not to smile as my mother looked like she might be about to faint. "You... you can't have children with her! They will look like... that."

She gestured vaguely in the direction of the throne room, and all traces of humour left my father's face. "You will not spout that nonsense again, Mathilde. People will look to us for an example. If we embrace Zara and her family willingly, so will they."

"I can't do that," she insisted, intransigent as always. "Either she leaves, or I do."

That was a bold stance and my father and I exchanged looks of surprise. Faced with that ultimatum, I couldn't guess how he would respond, but rather than answering her, he addressed me first. "Arthur, is there any doubt in your mind?"

"None," I assured him. "I love her and she loves me. No one would ever make me as happy."

He nodded almost sadly. "You are very lucky then, my boy. I can only imagine what that's like. I let myself be bullied into Dee's marriage arrangements, and thankfully it worked out for the best, but I won't risk your happiness as well."

My mother's mouth dropped open in shock, though whether she took offense to my father's support for me or the implied insult to herself, I couldn't say. "Didn't you hear me? I said..."

"I heard you perfectly fine," my father snapped. "And if that's your choice, then you know where the gate is to leave."

I had never heard my father stand up to my mother quite so firmly, and clearly, neither had she. Her mouth flapped open and shut a few times as she tried to decide on a reply, but apparently, nothing came to mind, and finally, she turned on her heel and stormed from the room.

"Do you think she's actually leaving?" I wondered, and my father gave a humourless laugh.

"I should be so lucky. I can't promise she'll be pleasant to your bride, Arthur, but you have my support. I'll have the staff start preparations immediately. This will be a wedding no one in Lassaria will ever forget."

"I know I never will." We embraced once more before I left him to go and tell Zara the good news. The wedding was on, whether my mother liked it or not.

~Zara~

Now that we were back in public, Arthur and I once more had to maintain the appearance of being betrothed with no carnal knowledge of each other, meaning he had to go to his own room at night and me to mine. However, just as he had on the ship, Arthur made use of the hidden passages within the castle, meant to be used by servants to attend to the rooms, and visited me at night while everyone else slept.

The king and queen weren't fooled, since Arthur admitted to me that he'd already told them I might be expecting, but they said nothing about it to us either. We couldn't be certain yet that I was with child, but since my fake monthly course to fool Malek, I had not had a real one, and nearly six weeks had passed. It certainly seemed possible that I might be pregnant. Perhaps it even occurred on that night back in the Munisian palace, the very first time we were intimate together. How ironic it would be if a new life came out of our brief time there, the heir to the Lassarian throne conceived against a wall in the emperor of Munisia's palace.

Arthur told me all about the conversation he had with his parents, holding nothing back from me. HIs mother's words stung, naturally, but what stuck out to me most in his tale had been the way Arthur had defended me and how his father had stood up for both him and me too. There would always be people like the queen in the world, people who felt they could judge the worth of a person simply by looking at them, but her actual power was limited. Since Arthur had the king's blessing, she couldn't do anything to stop the wedding besides making snide comments at every turn. In terms of denting my happiness, she could do nothing at all.

Though my own mother still had some way to go to learn the language, she understood the queen's body language well enough in that innate way that women often have, and after one particularly rude put-down from Arthur's mother as the seamstress arrived with the dress for my wedding, she turned to me in indignation. "I feel sorry for this king. He only gets one wife, and he's stuck with her!"

I couldn't help laughing. "Yes, in this case, it might have been better for the king to have a choice. I won't let her bother me though, Mama, not when Arthur loves me."

My mother and sisters grew more fond of my fiancé every day, especially as he made an effort to speak to them in their own language too. Their conversations were an odd mix of words in two languages and gestures, but they appreciated that he tried. My sisters were also fascinated by the other handsome, pale-skinned men of the court, so much so that my mother insisted on a guard outside their door at night, not so much to keep the men out as to keep my sisters in.

The night before the wedding, the royal family threw a great feast to welcome all the visiting dignitaries. Kings and queens of six other kingdoms were in attendance, including Arthur's sister, Dee, and her husband, King Cassian. Prince Eric and Princess Fatima were also there, having already been married themselves. To my great surprise, Khalid came too, in the company of Princess Charlotte. Arthur's whole family had never been together like this before, and with Dee's pregnancy now evident, the mood felt festive even without the added excitement of the wedding the next day.

Arthur promised me our wedding feast the following night would be even more grand, but I could hardly imagine how. Looking around the room at all the smiling, happy faces, the only thing in the world that could have made it better would have been having my father there too. None of it would have been possible without him and his absence marked the only small stain on an otherwise perfect occasion.

The morning of my wedding was a crisp, Lassarian morning, but the cold no longer bothered me as much as it once did. The bright, blue sky greeted me when I looked outside, and a crowd had already gathered in the courtyard below us as Dee and Fatima joined my mother and sisters along with my own ladies-in-waiting to help me get ready.

"Let's see the dress!" Fatima demanded eagerly.

"I bet it will make Arthur cry," Dee teased, but she had a point. My sweet prince had never been good at hiding his emotions. If either of us ended up crying during the ceremony, the odds were on him.

"Here it is, Your Highness." My ladies carried the garment like a treasure. Arthur had let me choose my own ladies to serve me from the daughters of Lassaria's noble families, and I had quickly rooted out those who looked down on me. The ones I chose were young and sweet, and over the moon to be assisting in a royal wedding.

The dress was still wrapped in the heavy cloth the seamstress had left it in yesterday to keep it protected, but as my ladies began to unwrap it, gasps of dismay and disbelief sounded throughout the room.

The dress had been ruined. It looked as though someone had taken a sword to it, slashing through the heavy fabric, and parts of it were singed as though they'd been burned. This couldn't possibly be an accident; someone had done it on purpose.

"Who had access to the dress?" Dee demanded as my ladies all whispered amongst themselves in distress.

"No one, Your Majesty," one of them whimpered. "We kept it in our own room. I don't know how this could have happened."

I had a very good idea how it had happened, or at least who was behind it. No one had a reason to want to embarrass me on my wedding day quite as much as my soon-to-be mother-in-law.

My mother's thoughts were clearly on the same line. "Evil woman," she spat as my sister's all wrung their hands in despair. My mother, however, had an idea. "If she is worried that you will stand out too much, perhaps we need to draw even more attention to your differences."

At this point, I would marry Arthur wearing his own clothes if I had to, but she had me intrigued. "What do you mean, Mama?"

"I need fabric in many colours, as many as possible."

I passed that on to Dee and my ladies, who hurried to their own rooms and returned with garments of every colour imaginable.

"Outside of the noble classes, Munisian tradition is to wrap layers around the bride," my mother explained as she picked up a thin blue shift and began to wind it around my body. "It is something for the groom to unwrap at the end of the night."

I could almost see the way Arthur's eyes would light up when I told him that. "Make me present, then, as vibrant as possible," I instructed the room, and they all dove in, choosing the colours and patterns that went best together.

The end product was about as far away from my original dress as it could get, but I loved it just as much. My own skin colour was just one of dozens in the overall image, each of them enhancing the others and creating a beautiful whole.

I was prepared for the gasp that echoed through the church, rising up to the arches that help up the stone ceiling, and I held my head high through the whispers that followed my procession down the aisle. The queen's face burned bright red in fury as I approached the altar, but my eyes were fixed on the handsome man waiting for me in his finest uniform, his blue eyes shining in delight and love.

Tears filled his eyes as he made his vows, to no one's surprise who knew him, but my tears were less expected. Arthur wiped each one away gently, just as he had when I cried in sorrow over my father.

As he promised, the feast that evening was even more spectacular than the night before, with more food than could possibly be eaten in one night. When I expressed dismay over that fact, Arthur promised me that everything left over would be distributed to the people the next morning in a Lassarian tradition, just one of many I had yet to learn.

I danced with my new husband, with King Cassian, with Prince Eric, and with the King of Lassaria himself, all while his wife stewed in her throne, refusing to move or smile. "Don't pay her any attention," the king told me, his jaw tightening as he looked over at the queen. "She will be taking a trip to our seaside property soon."

Arthur had pointed the castle out to me as we sailed by it upon our return, but I didn't know the family spent much time there. "How long will you be going for?"

"I'm not going anywhere," the king explained. "But she will go until she can behave civilly. I gave her every chance to adjust her attitude, but Dee explained to me what happened with the dress today. It's too much. You have handled it very gracefully."

"In the end, it's just a dress. I don't need any material comforts to be happy, Your Majesty. I only need Arthur."

"And he needs you." The king kissed my hand as the dance finished. "Welcome to our family, Your Highness."

Just as we were preparing to say goodbye for the night, a messenger strode into the hall and straight up to Arthur. "Your Highness, we have an urgent message for you from the Munisian emperor."

Arthur looked at me in surprise as Dee, Cassian, Eric and Fatima all came nearer, having heard the pronouncement.

"What does it say?" Eric wondered as Arthur took the sealed document from the messenger.

Breaking the seal, Arthur read the letter aloud. "Your Highness, we hope this letter finds you in good health and, perhaps, already happily married. Adil told us of your intentions towards his daughter just before his death."

He paused to look up at me in surprise and I felt equally stunned. When had my father talked to the emperor about that?

Arthur continued reading. "He also explained the circumstances of Zara's departure. Of course, we grieve the loss of our cousin and great friend. His wounds were too severe to survive, but we were able to speak of many things upon his return from the prison."

My heart and my throat swelled with each word. My father had been pulled out of the pit after all. He had survived long enough to speak to the emperor. The thought both cheered and saddened me. I was so glad to know he hadn't died alone with only Malek's body for company, but the confirmation that he had, in fact, died was still difficult to hear, no matter how much I thought I had accepted it.

Along with all my other emotions, fear also crept in. What exactly had my father told the emperor, especially when it came to Malek?

The letter went on to give us some vague clues. "We are also saddened at the loss of our heir and prince. His brother, Otto, shall succeed him as my heir, and in deference to his brother's work, will honour the trade agreement you had so recently concluded." Arthur's face shone with wonder as he looked up at me. "He knows. He knows what we did and he doesn't intend to punish us for it."

It certainly sounded that way. My father must have worked his magic one last time, but what he would have told the emperor, I couldn't begin to guess. "Maybe Malek's father didn't like him either?" I suggested. "Maybe in the end, we did him a favour."

I supposed we would never know. The emperor concluded by repeating his good wishes for Arthur's marriage, sending his condolences to my mother and all our family, and sending greetings to the king as well.

With any last remaining threat of repercussions of our escape removed, the party continued while Arthur and I bid everyone goodnight and retired to our room, finally able to go to bed together with no one able to object. My ladies tried to accompany me to help me undress but Arthur shooed them away.

"I can handle this," he said, his eyes glinting in anticipation, and when I told him how he could unwrap me, he looked every bit as excited as I'd hoped he would be.

As we made love in his bed, finally husband and wife, Arthur whispered to me as sweetly as ever: "We are never spending another night apart, Zara. Where you go, I go. Always."

"Always," I repeated, sighing as he brought me to ecstasy for the first time that night, but not the last.

It had taken a very long time, and the final destination was not at all where I expected to be, but after all my years of searching, I had finally found my way home.

EPILOGUE

~Cordelia~

Four years later

The little boy's eyes widened as he took in the throngs of people lining the street. The Lassarian castle stood at the top of the hill but the crowd stretched far down the street that led to it, everyone eager for a glimpse of the visiting nobility.

"Wave to them, Sean," I encouraged my son who sat across from me, next to his father, in the open-topped carriage. His sister, Adelaide, was fast asleep on my lap, not at all bothered to be missing the whole thing. There were some benefits to being eight months old. "They're here to see you."

He obediently gave a small wave and the crowd cheered in appreciation, making him duck down on the seat so no one could see him anymore.

Cass laughed as he gave Sean an encouraging pat on the shoulder. "It can seem scary when there's so many of them, but they just want to see you. Look, there are some children your age."

Sean peered over the top of the carriage again to where his father pointed, where a group of younger children waved strips of fabric in excitement. With a tentative smile, Sean waved back, and that time, the cheer startled him a little less.

Our trip marked Sean's first official foreign visit and it would be overwhelming for any three-year-old, but especially for our sweet little boy. More than once, Cass shook his head after we said goodnight to him. "I don't know where this sensitive side of his comes from. He definitely doesn't get it from you."

I punched him in the arm, making him wince. "Are you saying I'm not delicate and ladylike?"

"That's exactly what I'm saying." His eyes glinted mischievously as he pulled me into his arms. "But I would much rather have you than a 'proper' lady any day."

That day, we were visiting Lassaria for the wedding of my youngest brother, Henry. The last of our family to be married, he had shocked absolutely no one by proposing to one of Zara's younger sisters. They had been almost inseparable in the years since Zara arrived, and this time, my mother made no objection. After six months spent at the seaside castle after Zara and Arthur's wedding, waiting for an apology, she finally had to accept that none would be coming. If she wanted to return to court, she would need to swallow her pride, and eventually, she did.

She and Zara were still not particularly friendly, but they tolerated each other, much as my mother and I had done while I was growing up. At least there were no repeats of the wedding dress incident, and things thawed even further with the birth of Arthur's children. Apparently, my mother found it harder to dislike an innocent child for the colour of their skin than a grown woman.

The new Munisian emperor, Otto, sent a substantial dowry for the bride in her father's absence, which Eric wryly observed was probably partly in thanks to everyone at the court who had been involved in removing Malek and placing Otto on the throne in the first place. Though years had passed since Arthur, Eric, Zara and Fatima's adventure escaping the Munisian palace, none of us ever tired of hearing about it. Whenever we were all together, everyone begged Elodie to tell the entire tale. Although she hadn't been there herself, she told it better than anyone.

Eric and Fatima and their son, Frederick, rode in the next carriage behind us. Fred was only six months younger than Sean, having been conceived shortly after their marriage, and Fatima doted on him in the most heartwarming way. All mothers loved and appreciated their children, but having had so many of hers taken from her, Fatima never took a moment of their time together for granted. She was also pregnant again and glowing with happiness as she waved to the onlookers.

In the final carriage in our procession were Charlotte and Khalid, along with Elodie and Bran and their two boys. Charlotte didn't fully understand why we were taking this trip, but Khalid pointed out all the colours and cheering people, and she smiled and laughed, enjoying herself as she always seemed to do with him.

I asked Khalid once about his relationship with Charlotte, and he answered me completely honestly. "I never thought that love would be an option for me. In the harem, I would have never been allowed, and even afterwards, I thought that no woman would want to tie herself to a man who wasn't fully a man. But Charlotte doesn't care about that. She doesn't even know there is anything different about me at all, at least in that way. She is innocent and joyful and sees the world in such a positive way. Being with her makes me happy, and in the end, isn't that what everyone wants?"

Truer words were never spoken, and I couldn't be happier that those two souls had found each other, as unlikely as it seemed considering where their lives had begun.

Meanwhile, Elodie had blushed bright pink when I suggested they ride in the carriage alongside Charlotte and Khalid. "We aren't important enough, Dee," she protested. "No one will know who we are."

"They'll assume you're important because of the carriage," I argued back. "And think of how much fun Logan will have."

Elodie's eldest son, born only two weeks after Sean, was Sean's opposite in every way. As outgoing and confident as Sean was shy and reserved, the two boys made almost perfect foils for their fathers. Bran had always been the one keeping Cass in line, but I suspected that when it came to their sons, it would be the other way around. And sure enough, when I glanced behind us at the last carriage, I could see Logan standing on the seat to wave and bow to the crowd as Elodie tried in dismay to get him to sit down and behave properly.

Finally, we reached the top of the hill and the carriages entered the courtyard of my family's castle with no time to waste. We were ushered straight to the church where the rest of the congregants were already waiting. We only had time to wave across the aisle at my parents, Arthur and Zara and their children, and my brother Edward and his wife, Joanna, who was also pregnant. By the next time we all got together, we were going to be completely outnumbered by children.

The wedding was beautiful and mercifully short as the children began to grow restless, and as soon as the ceremony had ended, we headed up to our guest quarters. One of my ladies took Adelaide for the evening, but Sean would attend the wedding feast with us, at least for a little while. His valet dressed him in a miniature version of Cass' uniform and my heart melted at the sight.

"You look very handsome, Prince Cassian," I told him, kneeling down in my dress so I could look him in the eye as I straightened his tunic. Officially, he shared his father's name, but we always called him Sean.

He tugged uncomfortably at his doublet. "Fred says I have to get married too, Mama. I don't want to."

Fred was a bit of a troublemaker, like his father. He had no reason to bring that up just yet. "You will someday, Sean, but only when you want to. It won't be for many, many years."

"What if I never want to?" he asked, his eyes still full of concern.

"We'll see how you feel when you're older. But one thing your father and I agree on is that you will always be free to choose your own wife. You'll never be expected to marry someone you haven't met."

I didn't know if that made it better or not, but he seemed a little mollified as he took my hand to head down the stairs where Cass waited for us at the bottom. Cass whispered a few words of encouragement to him and, like the little prince he was, Sean raised his head even though his hands trembled as he walked ahead of us into the great hall.

"Sean!" His cousin, Samira, came barrelling towards him so fast, she nearly knocked him off his feet. Two months younger than Sean, she was as bold as her mother and just as beautiful, her skin a warm brown mix between Arthur's paleness and Zara's darker tones. "Come play."

"Can I?" Sean asked, his eyes flitting hopefully between me and Cass, and his father nodded.

"Just don't get into any trouble."

The warning seemed to fall on deaf ears as they headed off to join Fred and Logan, all three boys deferring to Samira's natural authority as they scouted out the table with all the sweets on it.

"They're going to give us headaches, aren't they?" Arthur asked as he and Zara came to stand next to us, his eyes also on the small group of children. Eric and Fatima were close behind them, and from my other side, Elodie hooked her arm through mine, Bran beside her.

"Without question," Cass agreed wryly. "And so they should. Life's hard enough when you're grown up. They should have some fun while they can."

Life could be hard, certainly, but looking around at all the people dearest to me in the world, I had to admit it could also be very, very good. Though the road to get here may not have been entirely smooth for any of us, in the end, we were all exactly where we were meant to be.

~~THE END~~

MORE FROM THE AUTHOR

<u>Contemporary Romance – New Adult/Clean</u>

It Figures duet
It Figures
Figuring It Out

<u>Historical Romance – 18+</u>

Lady in Waiting Series
Lady in Waiting
King in Training
Princess in Hiding

<u>Paranormal Romance – 18+</u>

Cold Lake Pack Series
The Curse and the Prophecy
The Spell and the Legacy
The Dream and the Destiny

Mismatched Mates Series
Mismatched Mates
Misguided Motives
Mistaken Meanings

Serena's Story
The Alpha's Second Chance
The Returned Mate
The Vampire's Consort

Sacrifice Series
Blood Donor
Life Giver

<u>Paranormal Romance – New Adult/Clean</u>

The Alpha's Prey

KEEP IN TOUCH

My Patreon account has daily updates from my works-in-progress, bonus chapters and more – join me there to comment and read along as my next books are being written: www.patreon.com/melodytyden

You can find and follow me on Facebook at: facebook.com/melodytyden

Join the Facebook group Melody's Romance Corner for fun games, interaction with the author and exclusive news and excerpts.

You can also sign up to my newsletter at www.melodytyden.com for all the latest news.